It's all true.

It's all possible.

It's not a nightmare.

Something is out there,
getting closer,
moving in the darkness,
gathering . . .

DARK◉MATTER™

In Hollow Houses

Explosions rip through a secret vault deep under the National Archives. Homeless people in Washington D.C. are brutally murdered by something that can't be human. A little girl has no idea her new friends have come from farther away than she can possibly imagine.

DARK•MATTER™

DARK•MATTER™

IN HOLLOW HOUSES

GARY A. BRAUNBECK

IN HOLLOW HOUSES
Dark•Matter™
©2000 Wizards of the Coast, Inc.
All Rights Reserved.

Cover art by Ashley Wood
First Printing: August 2000
Library of Congress Catalog Card Number: 99-69292

9 8 7 6 5 4 3 2 1

ISBN: 0-7869-1636-2
620-T21636

U.S., CANADA,
ASIA, PACIFIC, & LATIN AMERICA
Wizards of the Coast, Inc.
P.O. Box 707
Renton, WA 98057-0707
+1-800-324-6496

EUROPEAN HEADQUARTERS
Wizards of the Coast, Belgium
P.B. 2031
2600 Berchem
Belgium
+32-70-233277

Visit our web site at **www.wizards.com**

no one came

The buildings in this area of D.C. were as grey as the city street upon which they stood. Many of the corniced brick warehouses and storefronts had faded under the constant assault from city dust and traffic exhaust fumes that had settled on them like a curse from heaven. Bypassed by developers in favor of more desirable real estate, this was now a place of cold alleys and soup kitchens, makeshift narcotics labs, the homeless and transients, drug addicts, alcoholics, thieves, street-corner racists spouting their doctrine of hate to all who passed by, young runaways, and those only too happy to exploit them.

The buildings squatted like diseased animals waiting for someone to come along and blast them out of their misery. What few stores remained in the area sold mostly liquor and cigarettes and kept bars on their doors and windows. The clerks who worked these places were armed well beyond even the most

1

lenient definition of "legally." It was a cancer growth, this area, a breeding ground for violence, anger, and despair where the inhabitants accepted degradation as a way of life, where brutality was second nature, and where rape, murder, and robbery were looked upon the same way most people looked upon rush hour traffic: You put up with it and try to get away in one piece.

It was a place where the spirit would have to rally in order to reach hopeless, where the odd and the damaged, the despondent and the discarded, the lost and the shabby came when they reached the end of their rope and life offered no alternative but to crawl into the shadows of poverty and just give up.

Still, even in the most dismal of places, there can be moments of wonder.

No one knew who spray painted the words on the alley-side of the building, only that no one had been able to bring themselves to erase them. On some nights when the lost ones gathered under these words—the drunks, the addicts, the prostitutes—they talked about the words, about who might have put them there and why. Then, for some reason, they'd find themselves talking about their better days, days of childhood, days of marvel, of little sisters and mothers and girlfriends whose names escaped them, and for a little while none of them seemed as ruined or as tainted as the world had made them feel. The masks slipped away, revealing the souls underneath.

Tonight the buildings glistened from the drizzling rain, appearing to almost glow under the diffuse light of the sodium-vapor lamps that stood on the corners, torch-bearing zombies guarding the entrance to the world of the dead.

Mist rose from manhole covers like departing souls, creating a thin layer of stinking fog that rolled across the sidewalks, swallowing the scattered pages of rotted newspapers, reflecting the street lamps' light, and covering the concrete and cobblestones in waves of phosphorescent gloom.

For a little while on this night, in this place, toward the back of this alley, nothing moved.

Then a breeze like a whispered warning wafted down the alleyway, moist and weak, carrying with it the stench of the fish market a few blocks away, where Parcel Street dead-ended into Riverside Avenue. A window shutter on one of the abandoned upper floors creaked, groaned, then cracked against the brick. A paper cup tumbled along, end over end, until it skittered over a sewer grate and was impaled by a ragged piece of weather-sheared metal. A haunted voice coughed hoarsely. The echo of something that might be a car alarm or a last, agonized scream broke the quiet, then was quickly silenced.

The window shutter above creaked once more, then snapped away and clattered down, startling a stray cat that had been sleeping between the metal trash cans where the shutter hit. The cat screeched and darted from the alley in hissing, skitter-claw panic.

Above the alley, behind the jagged remains of a third floor window, a pair of cold bright eyes suddenly appeared in the shadows inside the abandoned warehouse. Unblinking and cold, they were eyes of purest silver. At first mere pinpoints, they slowly grew larger as they moved closer to the window, until each was the size of a baseball. Despite their brightness they were ancient things, filled with a longing for home. They had looked upon things no human being has ever seen. In the center of each glowed a fiery red pupil.

The sound of slow, staggering footsteps splashing through puddles neared the alley.

The silver eyes pulled back. Their owner drew in a thick, wet, pained breath.

The Lost Ones would begin to assemble now. Soon this alley would be filled them.

Soon.

The silver eyes retreated into the darkness, once again becoming mere pinpoints that eventually could not be seen at all.

The fog whispered its way down the alley.
Then silence.
Waiting.

During his four years as a staff reporter for the *Weekly Informant*, the nation's third most popular tabloid (Motto: "When You're Tired of All the Lies, Turn To Us"), Dan Kirkwood had been handed some plum assignments. This was most definitely not one of them, but since editor Martha Fowler had held him in less-than-glowing esteem since the lawsuit over that story he'd written about a certain movie star buying crack from a school boy, he knew he should be happy for *any* assignment. Still, heading into a dark alley in one of D.C.'s worst areas after sunset while fighting off a migraine was a punishment that seemed, in even the most charitable view, dangerously extreme.

At least she'd sent Ray Nolan with him. Any port in a storm.

Ray Nolan, the *Informant*'s best photographer, stood well over six feet in height. Big as life and three times as ugly, Nolan, a part-time body builder, looked like someone who'd just as soon snap you in half as look at you. The truth was, he'd never once had to call on his size and strength to defend himself—or anyone else for that matter, thought Kirkwood anxiously. The man simply hoped that people would get one look at his mass and back off.

Which is why Fowler had sent him along with Kirkwood on this assignment. "Ray'll scare the hell out of anyone who tries to start anything," she'd said.

"But what if he doesn't?" Kirkwood asked.

Martha Fowler smiled. "Then we won't have to worry about your being named in any more lawsuits, will we?"

Kirkwood tripped over a small pile of broken liquor bottles and stumbled into Nolan.

"Watch it, will ya?" Nolan snapped.

"Sorry, Ray."

They were stopped now. Kirkwood readied his micro-cassette recorder and flipped to a blank page in his notebook. Nolan checked both his own camera and the video camera that Fowler had insisted they bring along. Since the *Informant*'s Internet site had debuted, its webmaster had discovered the questionable art of streaming video, and Fowler insisted that there be at least three new taped interviews on the site each month. If during the course of taping these interviews, some-one happened to flip out or get into a scuffle with the police or take a hostage or two, Fowler's mood brightened considerably.

Kirkwood looked toward the transient camp and wished he had more protection than the canister of pepper spray and stun gun that the *Informant* furnished all of its field reporters.

"Ray?"

"What now?"

"Did you happen to bring your gun along? Please tell me that you brought it with you. Nothing would make me happier than to hear you say this."

Nolan lifted a corner of his jacket, and the pearl handle of his 9mm shone under the light.

Kirkwood's shoulders slumped in relief. "Have I mentioned lately that you're one of my favorite people in the whole wide world?"

"Then why'd you forget my birthday last month?"

"Your status was only recently upgraded."

"I'm so touched." Nolan dropped the corner of his jacket back into place, picked up the video camera, and said, "So where's your snitch?"

"Don't use that word around him, all right? He prefers 'information broker.' "

"You're kidding, right?"

"Yes, I'm famous with attorneys all over this country for my whimsical wit—what the hell do you think?"

"Fine. Where's your 'information broker'?"

Kirkwood checked his watch and said, "Should be here any minute now." He pinched the bridge of his nose.

"You getting another one of your headaches?" asked Nolan.

"Yeah, but I'm not going to take anything for it till we're back at the hotel."

"You sure? I've seen what you get like when one of those things hits."

"I'm sure."

They waited only three minutes more before a short, unshaven man in a fedora and tattered trench coat—looking like something that stepped out of a 1940s detective movie—came around one of the corners near the back of the alley. Paying no attention to the transients assembled around the various trash can fires, he made a beeline for Kirkwood and Nolan.

"Were you followed?" asked the man.

Kirkwood blinked. "Yes, a battalion of Khmer Rouge rebels have been chasing us since a disastrous poetry slam in Phnom Penh. Time is of the essence."

The man huffed impatiently. "You bring the money?" he said in a voice that sounded like he gargled with Wild Turkey five times a day.

"Good to see you, too, Chaney" replied Kirkwood, slipping a fifty into the guy's hand.

Chaney unfolded the bill, held it up to the dim light, then slipped it in his pocket. "Who's the gorilla?" he asked, jerking a thumb at Nolan.

"Horatio Hornblower, massage therapist and psychic advisor."

"Looks to me like he couldn't find his own butt with both hands," snarled Chaney.

"Charming circles you move in," muttered Nolan.

"Two things," said Kirkwood to Chaney. "One—please stop talking in *film noir* clichés before you give me a brain hemorrhage, and two, where's the woman you told me about?"

"Back there."

Chaney started to leave, but Nolan grabbed the back of his coat. "Hang on there, Deep Throat."

"You'll need to make the introduction," said Kirkwood.

"No way, you hear me? *No way.* That bitch gives me the willies. She gives *everybody* the willies lately."

"Be that as it may," replied Kirkwood, "you will point her out to us or I'll have Horatio here tie knots in your spine."

Chaney jerked himself loose and said, "Fine. Come on."

The three of them headed toward the back of the alley. As they approached the transients' camp, Kirkwood noted that there were three places along the way where this alley emptied into others, forming what he suspected was a maze that stretched all along the back of the buildings in this area. It would be easy to get lost back there and never be found. That thought, combined with the cold drizzle that was starting again, made him shudder and turn up the collar of his coat. He was starting to see the beginnings of flashing lights. The migraine would be hitting home soon.

Back here was another world, one composed of tarpaulin-sheet roofs and plywood lean-tos and cardboard-box castles where heaps of rags hiding human beings lay on moldy blankets or slept in the remains of chairs dragged from the city dump. Three large metal trash cans had been moved to form a triangle, and most of the homeless who were back here stood somewhere inside this triangle, warming their hands over the fires in the cans. The flames hissed, crackled, and snapped up into the air, throwing sparks. The sparks danced in twisting patterns for a moment, then were caught on the breeze and spiraled upward. Those who stood around the fires glanced up at the approaching trio. Against the glow from the fires, they looked as if their eyes might collapse back into their skulls at any second.

Kirkwood, Nolan, and Chaney stopped a few feet outside the triangle. Nolan started snapping photographs. The people gathered around the fires blinked at the sudden flashes of light but said nothing.

"That's her," said Chaney, pointing. "You sure you wanna do this? I'm telling you, she's Bad Hurt on two legs."

Standing beyond the fires of the triangle ten feet away from them was a thin, wasted-looking woman dressed in the ruined remains of a wedding dress. Kirkwood thought she looked like some character out of Dickens. If it weren't for the bruises on her face and the haunted look in her eyes, she could have been nobly waiting for Ronald Coleman to take her hand while the two of them were marched toward the guillotine. The dark circles under her eyes were made all the more hideous by the thick mane of startlingly bright red hair that flowed almost down to her waist.

"She's called Long Red," said Chaney.

"You could have just told us that," snapped Kirkwood. "I think we might have been able to figure out which one she was."

"She doesn't look so dangerous to me," whispered Nolan.

"Tell that to these folks. The last couple of people who hooked up with her have just—" Chaney snapped his fingers. "—disappeared."

The other homeless denizens seemed to make it a point to not make eye contact with her or acknowledge her presence in any way.

It wasn't just that they were nervous about her, they were scared of her, of doing or saying anything that might draw her attention to them.

Forget scared—these people were *terrified* of her. Kirkwood could feel it. Glancing at Nolan, he could tell that the photographer sensed it as well.

Kirkwood looked at Chaney and asked, "You told her we were coming, right?"

"Yeah, she knows. Did you, uh . . . did you remember to . . . ?"

Kirkwood reached into his pocket and flashed the small plastic bag. Inside it were six small rocks of crank. It made him sick to his stomach to have to do this, but Fowler wanted this story no matter how he got the information. She had given him the address of a local crank lab and five hundred in cash. "Any more comes out of your pocket, Hemingway," she'd said to him as he left the office. He'd half expected her to turn his ass in once he made the connection, but when he and Nolan had left the lab, the street had been mercifully free of the fuzz. Bigger circulation numbers were evidently more important than revenge to their esteemed editor.

"Okay, I'm gone," said Chaney. "Don't you come after me later and try to say I didn't warn you." He placed a finger against the rim of his hat and quickly snaked off into one of the passages.

Unseen by anyone within the triangle or without, a set of silver eyes looked down from the darkness of the warehouse.

Kirkwood asked Nolan, "Were you taping that?"

"I've got two hours of nothing but snow on here, otherwise."

"You ready for this?"

"Would it matter?"

That cryptic response did little to calm Kirkwood's already frazzled nerves.

As they made their way around the outer edge of the triangle, Kirkwood leaned into Nolan and whispered, "About your gun. . . ."

"Full clip, a round in the chamber, and the safety's off. Just don't bump into me again. You cause me to accidentally shoot off the Envy of All Mankind and I'm liable to get unpleasant." When Kirkwood said nothing in response, Nolan jostled his elbow. "You nervous?"

"Well, let's see. I'm in a crap-stinking alley at one o'clock in the morning, surrounded by people who look like they're touring in the road company production of *Deliverance*, and my only backup in case of an emergency is a pituitary case who calls his pecker the 'Envy of All Mankind.' Why would I be nervous?"

"A simple 'yes' would have been sufficient."

"So sue me. Everyone else is."

"You're getting that headache, aren't you?"

"How can you tell?"

"You only start babbling on like that when you're getting a migraine."

They came up to Long Red, and Kirkwood offered his hand in greeting. "Hello, miss, I'm Dan Kirkwood from the *National Informant.* Chaney said that he told you we were—"

"Not here," she said with a violent shudder, then pointed farther down the adjacent passage. "I need you guys to . . . to see what it wrote on the wall."

"*It*?" said Kirkwood.

Long Red glared at him with eyes devoid of fight or hope. "Didn't Chaney t-t-tell you?"

Kirkwood exchanged a quick glance with Nolan before responding. "We were told that you've had contact with some sort of creature that's been living in these alleyways."

She shook her head and gave an unpleasant laugh. "Huh-uh, not a creature, not any kind of monster." She leaned forward and gripped Kirkwood's forearm. "A *god.*"

"How do you know this?"

" 'Cause it looks different to everyone who sees it."

"I don't understand."

Long Red shrugged. "You can't unless you see it for yourself. It becomes your secret bliss."

"And what's your 'secret bliss'?"

Long Red stared at her feet for a moment. "I can't remember any more," she said sadly, "but I think it will tell me, if it finds me worthy."

She let go of Kirkwood's arm and started down the alleyway to the right, leading them to a spot where three alleys intersected and dead-ended. She gestured to the wall at the back. Nolan turned on the light attached to the video camera and shone it where she pointed.

Two words, written in letters that were, even to the most untrained eye, geometrically perfect:

SOMEONE COME

"And you say that this . . . this *god* wrote these words?"

"Yeah." Long Red hugged herself and shivered. "Did you, uh . . . you bring it?"

Feeling sick to his stomach—and more than a little ashamed of himself—Kirkwood produced the plastic bag and removed two crank rocks. Long Red took them out of his hand and slipped them into a pocket of her dress. Kirkwood wondered if the dress had come with pockets or if she'd added them during her years on the street. It seemed a silly thing to focus on, but at least it managed to distract him from the bad taste in his mouth and the pity he felt rising in him for Long Red. Somewhere there was a mother and father who never knew what became of their daughter. Kirkwood wondered if Long Red ever missed her family, ever dreamed of a loving home where her system was clean and her clothes new and moments like this—seamy, back-alley moments of sad degradation—were only dim memories of someone else's nightmare that vanished from her life when sunlight filtered in through her bedroom window.

Pulling himself from this sudden, surprising reverie, Kirkwood cleared his throat and asked, "Would you tell us exactly what kind of contact you've had with this . . . this *god*?"

"He takes me apart," replied Long Red.

"Excuse me?"

"He takes me apart. He cuts me open and takes out my parts and does stuff to 'em, then he puts me back together."

It took a moment for Kirkwood to recognize the expression on her face. Maybe part of it was because he didn't want to recognize it, maybe part of it stemmed from his having long ago buried what little remained of his compassion, but whatever the reason, those defenses were now down and he recognized the look on her face for what it was. She was looking at him like a lost child might look for help from a stranger with a kind face.

Kirkwood quickly dropped his gaze to his notebook and asked, "Could you maybe explain that in a little more detail?"

11

Long Red opened the front of her dress where it had been ripped open, then stapled back together. Running down the middle of her torso, from the center of her clavicle to the top of her navel, was a pinkish-white scar so perfectly straight that even the most skilled surgeon would be humbled by its precision. "Like I said," she mumbled, "he opens me up."

She stepped up and ran her index finger down the middle of Kirkwood's chest, chilling him worse than even the wind and drizzle.

"It hurts like hell," said Long Red. "All he does is touch me with his finger and it's like somebody's sticking a blade in me. He runs his finger down and peels me open. I don't bleed much 'cause he does something that burns me real bad, you know?"

"Cauterization?" asked Kirkwood. Beside him, Nolan was taping away.

Long Red shrugged. "Yeah, I guess that's it. Makes me stink like burned meat when he does it."

"Why don't you scream or run away?"

"Oh, I scream, all right. But no one ever comes to help. I can't run away, though. When he sees you, his eyes, they do something to your body, right? Turn your muscles to ice and you can't move—just have stand there and let him do whatever he wants. And if I run away, how will I ever remember my bliss when he chooses to show it to me?"

Kirkwood and Nolan exchanged glances. *Looney-Tunes, this one. Big Time.*

"What does he do once he's taken you apart?"

"He fixes me."

"Fixes you how?"

"At first it was my stomach, right? I'd been pukin' blood for a couple of days before I seen him the first time. I was back here, tryin' to find a place to lay down and wait for the pain to go away, and all over a sudden it—he—was just there, you know? Just standin' over me. He reached down and cut me open then he just pulled my stomach out. I was layin' there thinkin' that I was gonna die but I wasn't bleeding very much. And it . . . he held my stomach up to his face and looked at it. I could see where the hole was, I could see the blood dripping out of it and pieces of food and stuff.

"He just held his hand over the hole for a second and everything sorta glowed, right? Then he pulls his hand away and my stomach's good as new."

"That was the first time?"

"Uh-huh. After that, it was like I *needed* for him to open me up. After a while, he was takin' everything from inside me. He would fix, like, my lungs and other parts, only instead of putting everything back inside me right away, he'd lay my parts on the ground and stare at them, like he was trying to memorize the way everything was laid out inside of me."

"Did you ever . . . did you ever bring anyone else to meet this god? People who maybe needed to be fixed?"

"Yeah. There was Mousey. He was the last person I brung to him. He had some problem with his heart. He took out Mousey's heart and fixed it, then put it back inside and left. But Mousey, he turns to me and says, 'I ain't never gonna go through that again! I can't stand the pain!' But he was back here just like clockwork the next night, said he needed to be fixed again. But I could see in his eyes that he didn't *want* to be here, didn't want to need it.

"He don't fix everybody, though. Some people, he just kills. Like Jimmy. Jimmy was drunk when I brung him to him, and he laughed in his face then spit on him."

"What did it do?"

"It . . . he just reached inside and pulled all of Jimmy's guts out. Jimmy had just enough time to look down at all his insides slopped over the ground and scream, then he dropped dead."

"What happened to his body?"

"The thing sopped it up like a sponge. He does that sometimes, when he runs into someone he don't like or thinks ain't deserving of his help. He just opens them up, lets their insides drop out, then soaks up the mess."

"Is that what happened with Mousey the second time?"

"No. He fixed up Mousey's eyes that night." She shuddered. "I never heard nobody scream the way Mousey did. But no one came to help. After he left us alone that night, Mousey, he found himself a bottle of drain cleaner and drank it down. All his guts bubbled up through his mouth, and he died. I think he'd rather have died than face that thing again. And Mousey, he wasn't the first person who did that. I brung maybe three, four people to him, and all of them ended up killing themselves. It's horrible. It feels horrible and it hurts and you're so damn *scared* the whole time . . ." Her voice cracked and tears welled in her eyes.

"Why haven't you tried to kill yourself?" Kirkwood asked as gently as he could.

"I have," she replied. "I tried everything I could think of, but nothing works." She pulled back the sleeves of her dress to expose not only the old track marks but the deep, vertical scars. "I wish I could die," she said. "I don't wanna need to be opened up like this anymore."

"Why do you think you don't die?"

"Because I was its first, you know? I think it did something to me, it . . . he . . . I dunno . . . he fixed it so that I can't die. If I open my veins, the wounds, they—" She snapped her fingers. "—seal right back up. If I take any pills, I throw 'em back up right away. I even threw myself in front of a car. It hit me real hard and broke a bunch of my bones, but before the ambulance got there my bones and guts . . . they fixed themselves. God, it hurt almost as bad as opening me up does. I keep hoping that maybe . . ." She swallowed with great difficulty as a wave of nausea passed through her. ". . . I keep hoping that maybe somebody will kill me. Maybe they can do what I can't.

"But the worst thing, though, is the things I see while he's taking me apart."

Kirkwood wondered what image could be so horrible that it was worse than not being able to die. "What do you see?"

"I think that's the way he talks to people. He puts these pictures in their heads. I think maybe he shows me the things he's seen, his memories and stuff."

"Can you describe these things you see?"

She shook her head violently, tears coursing down her face. "I never seen anything like what he shows me. The pictures, they're like . . . like . . . you know how they say that if you're drowning, your whole life flashes before your eyes?"

"Yes."

"That's what the pictures are like. They're the end of everything."

Kirkwood checked his tape recorder, made a few more notes, and was surprised when Long Red handed the two rocks of crank back to him.

"Here. I don't want 'em. Wait—I *do* want 'em, want 'em real bad, but maybe if I don't use 'em, I'll get so sick that he can't keep me from dying."

Kirkwood slipped the rocks back into his pocket. This whole damn thing was turning into one big bust. Only the thought of his codeine pills back at the hotel kept him going. The headache was starting to worsen.

"Thanks for your time, miss," he said. "I really appreciate your—"

"You don't believe me, do you?"

"That doesn't really matter. Our job—"

"Don't you even want to see him?"

Kirkwood paused, looked at Nolan, then sighed. "Sure," he said cynically. "Take us to him."

"Don't have to," said Long Red.

"Why's that?"

"Look behind you."

Both Kirkwood and Nolan whirled around.

When Dan Kirkwood was a child, his mother had given a model called *The Visible Man* as a birthday present. Kirkwood had spent two weeks putting it together, slowly and carefully. When it was done, he was amazed at the results. To be able to look at this man with his clear-as-glass skin and be able to see everything inside—the eyes and brain, the muscles and lungs, the organs and veins—it took his breath away in a moment of childhood wonder.

The thing that stood before them now also took his breath away, only now the wonder of childhood was replaced by a near-crippling form of awestruck fear.

It stood at least eight feet tall and a yard wide. Like *The Visible Man*, its skin was almost completely transparent, only there were no internal organs that could be seen. Instead, its interior was filled with a grotesque, roiling form of primordial soup. Bits of bone and skull, wet, shredded tissue, large pieces of lungs and intestines, free-floating hands and eyes, rags of flesh that were once the skin of a face before its owner had been opened up to die, then be absorbed. The cloudy liquid in which these pieces floated glowed like radioactive waste. Once, as the liquid flowed around, Kirkwood could have sworn that one of the faces was trying to form words: *Help me.*

The thing moved forward, pulling itself slowly more erect, amoeba to fish to coelacanth to Cro-Magnon to Man. Its head was roughly diamond shaped, with a small forehead that widened at the jaws and mouth before angling back into its neck. It had no chin that Kirkwood could see. It opened its mouth to reveal no teeth, only a black pit. Kirkwood thought he saw the brief glittering of stars in that darkness.

It looks like a deformed glass ape, he thought.

The pain of his migraine forgotten, Kirkwood found his gaze drawn to the red pupils in the center of its unbelievable silver eyes. They glowed as if replaying the thing's memory of having seen the first fires of creation.

It moved past him toward Long Red.

"Oh, God . . . p-p-please sh-show me my bliss th-this—"

She never finished.

The thing reached out an impossibly long arm and laid a finger of its lithe hand against her chest.

Nolan moved backward but kept the videotape rolling.

The thing began to trace a line down Long Red's center, burning open her dress and splitting the skin and bone beneath, filling the air with the stench of seared flesh.

Long Red threw back her head and tried to cry out but no sound emerged. As the thing continued splitting her open (Dear God does it have to do it so slowly? thought Kirkwood) she managed to turn her head toward Kirkwood, and in her eyes he saw what he thought was a silent, agonized plea.

End it for me, please.

Kirkwood whirled on Nolan but the photographer had seen the plea in Long Red's eyes, as well—or perhaps his fear had finally gotten the better of him—because he set down the video camera and pulled out the 9mm. Taking aim, he looked once at Kirkwood, who nodded. He fired once.

Only he wasn't shooting at Long Red. No, he was shooting at the thing itself, and the bullet connected solidly with its side but that's as far as it went. The bullet lodged in its side as if Nolan had fired into a mass of dense gelatin. The wound puckered like a set of lips and slowly sucked in the bullet, which was then caught in the flow of the primordial soup and vanished into the grotesque, cloudy liquid.

"Jesus Christ!" shouted Nolan. He plowed off two more shots but they were just as ineffective as the first.

From somewhere down the alley came the sound of panicked voices and running feet.

Nolan was firmly in the grip of panic now and fired three more shots directly at the thing's head. It was just as the third bullet hit home that the creature decided it had had enough.

Turning its slick diamond head toward Nolan, it reached for him with its free arm as its other hand continued dissecting Long Red. Before Nolan could turn to run, the thing's hand closed over his skull like a child's hand gripping the head of a favorite doll. It lifted him from the ground. Nolan screamed and kicked his legs frantically. The mouth of the alleyway was suddenly clogged with denizens of the transient camp. Kirkwood ran over, grabbed hold of Nolan's leg, and tried to pull him free.

The thing's mouth opened wider.

The walls of the alley shook as the sound from the thing's throat bounced off the bricks and slammed into everyone. It was the shriek of a million babies doused in gasoline and set aflame. Despite the pain in his head and the screaming in his ears, Kirkwood continued yanking on Nolan's legs, but the photographer was suddenly very still.

The crowd of homeless people began moving forward, staggering, tripping, hands over their ears as they, too, screamed and shrieked with the creature. A few of them held planks of wood, others held empty liquor bottles, still more had sections of pipe or other pieces of detritus grabbed from the alley floor. Nolan's hands went limp, and his gun dropped into a puddle. Kirkwood grabbed the 9mm and scrambled backward on hands and legs like a scuttling crab.

The crowd surged forward, pulled their hands from over their ears, and began to assault the creature. As soon as a weapon connected with its body, its flesh sucked it in, along with the hands and arms of those who did not think to release their weapon in time. It took less than a minute before the creature's body was covered in human beings whose hands, arms, or legs had been drawn into the clear, gelatinous shape. Kirkwood almost laughed at the absurdity of the sight. It was like a dozen or more flies stuck to a strip of flypaper and struggling to free themselves. Long Red was still looking at him. Kirkwood rose unsteadily to his feet. Those who were being absorbed into the creature's body went limp, empty-eyed and lifeless. Kirkwood steadied his hand as best he could and aimed the gun. His gaze met Long Red's. He saw loneliness there, and pain, and confusion, but most of all he saw gratitude.

He pulled in a deep breath and squeezed the trigger. The bullet blew through her right eye and took off half her skull when it exited. The creature jerked and shuddered as if it too had felt the bullet. It yanked its hand away, and Long Red's body slumped to the ground, spilling out its contents. The creature's silver eyes were now almost totally red. It moved toward Kirkwood.

Its lower half was hidden behind the skirt of protruding arms, legs, and torsos that were still being absorbed. Feet dragged through gore. Hands clawed at the mud and puddles on the alley floor. Heads cracked against the sides of the building. The creature picked up speed.

Kirkwood spun around and began to run, suddenly unsure of which direction to take. The alleyways became the Minotaur's Labyrinth to him, but he didn't have the luxury of a lover's silver strand to guide him to safety. He ran, half-blinded by the pain in his head, knocking over trash cans, stumbling over heaps of abandoned clothing, slipping in puddles. Lights exploded before his eyes as the migraine took hold. He staggered, slipped once again, and fell face-first into a heap of garbage teeming with worms and filth. Crying out, choking, and screaming, he rolled onto his back and tried to find the gun. The thing was almost upon him. His hand touched steel and he gripped the 9mm, firing wildly until the clip was emptied. Where are the goddamned police? he screamed within his brain. Even in this section of the city, this much gunfire should have attracted their attention by now.

The creature towered over him. He looked into its eyes and watched, both horrified and transfixed, as the red glow grew smaller and the silver returned to its gaze. There was no longer anger there but a longing, a need, a glimpse of an emptiness that needed to be filled. Kirkwood tried to move but the pain was too much. The creature seemed to sense this. Kirkwood began to weep.

He remembered his parents, his high-school sweetheart, the smile on his sister's face on her wedding day. He remembered his dreams of youth, when he was convinced that he could change the world with his words. He raged against his cynicism and all it had cost him. He pulled in a breath thick with snot and regret and looked one last time into the creature's impossible face. There was no longer any fear in him.

Fear was a luxury reserved for those who had a chance of escaping alive. No option existed for him. The thing looked as lost and confused and filled with regret as he himself was.

"I'm sorry," he whispered to it.

The creature made a gesture as if to say, *So am I. You can't know how much*.

It reached out with one hand and began to slip its fingers inside Kirkwood's skull. The pain of the migraine was replaced by a greater agony. Kirkwood screamed. The drizzle grew heavier. The stinking fog surrounded him, swallowed him.

It did not reveal Kirkwood's bliss to him.

For in the final moments of his life, Kirkwood realized he had never *had* a bliss.

The sound of his scream rose above the alley.

Filled the night briefly.

But no one heard his cry.

So none could answer it.

And no one came.

What seest thou else
In the dark backward and abysm of time?

—Shakespeare, *The Tempest*

Still there are moments when one feels free from one's own
identification with human limitations and inadequacies.
At such moments, one imagines that one stands on some small
spot on an unknown planet, gazing in amazement at the cold
yet profoundly moving beauty of the eternal, the unfathomable:
life and death flow into one, and there is neither
evolution nor destiny; only being.

—Albert Einstein

Heaven wheels above you displaying to you her eternal glories
and still your eyes are on the ground.

—Dante

. . . I saw the hideous phantasm of a man.

—Mary Shelley, *Frankenstein*

chapter
1NE

The neoclassical revival National Archives Building in Washington, D.C. is located halfway between the White House and the Capitol on Pennsylvania Avenue. All public literature relating to the building lists the following statistics: it is three hundred and thirty feet in length from Seventh Street to Ninth Street, two hundred and thirteen feet wide from Pennsylvania Avenue to Constitution Avenue, and one hundred and sixty-six feet tall. It has seventy-two Corinthian columns that are each fifty-three feet high, five feet eight inches in diameter, and weigh ninety-five tons. Two bronze doors that each weigh six and one-half tons and measure thirty-eight feet, seven inches high, ten feet wide, and eleven inches thick guard the Constitution Avenue entrance. James Earl Fraser's famous "Guardianship" sculpture is located on the same side of the building. Sporting a helmet, sword, and lion skin to convey the need to protect the historical records for future generations, it bears the inscription "Eternal Vigilance is the Price of Liberty."

Standing at the base of the stone steps that lead to the sentry-like bronze doors, one cannot help but feel the solemnity of so much knowledge and information crammed into seven hundred and fifty-seven thousand square feet of storage space. The building seems to beckon you, whispering of how much it knows and wishes to share.

But as must be the case with any building in which so much information is housed, it contains just as many secrets.

On this grey morning the outside of the National Archives, like all the other majestic structures in the heart of D.C., was sheened by drizzling rain. Even the face of "Guardianship" shone like an infant newly freed from the womb and still covered with embryonic fluids. Rain dripped from the tip of its marble nose and spattered against its feet, then trickled down onto the plaque bearing its inscription.

A man who looked to be in his early thirties stood before the statue. He held a black umbrella over his head. Water dripped from the edges of the umbrella and spattered against the shoulders of his tan overcoat, darkening them and weighing down the epaulets. He watched as the water cascaded over the words on the plaque and thought, somewhat wryly, that a person of more pessimistic nature might see this as some form of cosmic symbolism . . . a statement of fragile conviction washed away by the waves of time.

The thought made Michael McCain laugh softly as he looked away from "Guardianship" toward the bronze doors at the top of the steps. People filed in and out, or passed by those doors on their way to one of the Archives' other entrances. He wondered how any of them would react if they knew as much he did about the true structure of this building and the things hidden there.

McCain—known since childhood as "Fitz," for reasons that always eluded him—was a field agent for the Intelligence Division of the Hoffman Institute. He had been recruited within days of graduating Yale Law School. McCain's adopted parents were already associated with the Institute and so had helped secure the position for him, which was more than fine with McCain. Not wanting to be yet another smart-ass Yale Law grad with one eye on a fast partnership and the other on his bank balance, McCain wanted to do something more meaningful with his education than advise corporate bigwigs on the best possible tax shelters or sort out high-profile divorce cases. The Hoffman Institute offered him this chance. Besides, it was hard to resist affiliating oneself with an organization whose website proclaimed that its mission was "Improving the Human Condition."

Founded in 1917 with the goal of furthering scientific exploration, the Hoffman Institute was seen by the general population as being nothing more than a private think tank headed by New Age Eccentrics whose research was focused on such fringe topics as alternate energy sources and psychic phenomena.

At first McCain was a bit hesitant to consider the Institute's offer. More than a few of his fellow Yale graduates nicknamed it the "Has-Been Institute" because of its tendency to provide grants and research facilities to scientists who had been humiliated and ostracized by the so-called "scientific community" for espousing their radical theories and ideas. The Institute's director, Dr. Itohiro Nakami, had finally convinced McCain that the institute was the place for him.

"A young man of your considerable talent, intelligence, energy, and inquisitiveness would be wasted anywhere else but here," Nakami had said. "If you truly wish to better the lot of all humankind, that is."

It was this last statement that hooked McCain.

Looking at the bronze doors of the National Archives, something told him that today might just lead to that.

The drizzle grew heavier as he ascended the stone steps, closing his umbrella once he reached the doors. Running a hand through his hair, he then scratched softly at his beard.

Though only a few weeks along, it was nonetheless of sufficient thickness to obscure most of his lower facial features.

The beard had been something of an afterthought, the result of a plumbing fiasco in his house that had left him with precious little hot water during a bout with the flu. It had taken all the hot water—not to mention all of his strength—to simply bathe during the two weeks he'd been sick. Shaving had been out of the question.

To his surprise he found he liked the way he looked in a beard and so had decided to keep it. At least for the time being.

Besides, having one's facial features obscured could come in handy. It made it harder for someone to identify you later if you shaved. A beard also had the dubious distinction of making you noticeable but not particularly memorable. People saw the beard more than they saw the face.

That was going to be helpful today.

He did not want to be remembered by anyone today.

Anonymity was essential.

He looked at the doors and readied himself. If he found what he was after, it would prove the information that had recently come into his hands—information of a very personal and extremely unsettling nature—was true, and not some computer crackpot's complex practical joke.

McCain opened one of the doors. He had not seen the small man who stood across the street watching him with bright, intense, unblinking blue eyes.

"Young sir," whispered the man in a thick Asian accent. "I hope you are ready. The *phyi mi skye ba'i bzod pa* is a hard thing, indeed."

He adjusted the wool cap he wore on his clean-shaven head and wondered how McCain was going to react to his Knowledge of Future Non-origination. Not many could deal with discovering they not only weren't who they thought they were, but *what*.

The man then thought of a passage from Mary Shelley's *Frankenstein*, a book he had only recently read and enjoyed very much. "Did I solicit thee from Darkness to mold me Man?"

He looked down at the strange coin in his hand and thought of the little girl who had given it to him.

He stared at the strange symbol engraved on the coin and thought about its implications, then looked once more at the doors Michael McCain had just disappeared behind.

Will you remember me when the time comes, young sir? he thought.

He moved farther down the street, seated himself on a bus stop bench, opened a newspaper, and waited.

Inside the National Archives, McCain passed under the Faulkner murals as he crossed the magnificent rotunda, and checked in at the downstairs desk. His Researcher Identification Card proclaimed him to be one Dr. Edward Morlan, M.D. He checked to make sure his appointment was listed, was given the research room number on the second floor, and was then asked to place his briefcase, laptop and palmtop computers, watch, and the contents of all his pockets onto the security conveyer for x-ray.

While these objects passed through the x-ray chamber, McCain stepped through the metal detector. Once reunited with his possessions, he was instructed to place all but his laptop, palmtop, and beeper in one of the public storage lockers located to the left. After doing so, he took the massive, winding staircase up to the second floor, then followed the signs to Central Research Room 203. His destination, officially, was the National Archives Library, Room 202, which could only be accessed by going through the Central Research Room.

A library attendant escorted him to his previously reserved

research cubicle and handed him a sealed plastic bag. Inside the bag was a pair of white cotton gloves, as well as a small round filtering mask. He put everything on, then seated himself at the table and readied his laptop as the attendant placed before him three very old leather-bound volumes. These were the handwritten personal research diaries of Dr. Jonas Salk.

McCain thanked the attendant, carefully moved the first volume toward himself, and opened to a random page.

He waited until the attendant had been gone for several minutes before stretching his back. As he did so, he made a quick mental note of the locations of the security cameras surrounding this particular area of the library. One was just outside the cubicle, immediately overhead. The next was several yards down the wall of shelved documents he'd passed on his way here. The third camera—in range, but just barely—was at the far end of the documents row, near the doorway that led into the Central Research Room.

Hunkering back down over the Salk diaries, he gently turned another page, then typed something into his computer. This was for the benefit of the Second Floor Archives' security guards whose job it was to watch the monitors and ensure that no one damaged or tried to steal any of the materials.

He repeated this process several times over the next sixty minutes, stretching his back, crackling his knuckles, turning a page, reading it carefully, then entering information into his computer. Eventually the guards monitoring the area would be used to his routine, so it wouldn't seem the least bit odd to them that he repeated it so often.

McCain reached slowly down to his side and, using only his thumb, pressed down on the back of his pager and slid open the door to the battery compartment.

There were no batteries inside. Instead, a small green button lay beneath the plastic door.

McCain stood to stretch his back again. He faced the camera directly outside the cubicle.

He pressed the green button, and the red indicator light on

the security camera blinked once.

As he made a small show of dropping a pen and bending to pick it up, he turned his body in the direction of the other two cameras. Twice more he pressed the green button, causing the red indicator lights on the other cameras to blink once.

"That should do it," he whispered to himself.

In the security room on the second floor, the images displayed on three of the eleven monitors appeared to roll for a second, then right themselves. The guards on duty made a note of this in their watch logs but thought no more of it. Brief rolling images occurred regularly enough.

What they did not know was that McCain had activated an electronic signal that was now causing the three cameras to enter a looping mode. Until he deactivated the signal, each camera would display only the images they had recorded for the last twenty minutes over and over again. To any watching eye, Dr. Edward Morlan, M.D., would simply be repeating the same tiresome research routine he'd been going through since his arrival seventy-one minutes before.

McCain exited his cubicle, moved quickly down the aisle until he was fifteen yards from the doorway that connected 202 with 203, then veered left down a cramped passageway lined on either side with metal shelves filled to bursting with files. At the far end of this passageway he turned right, walked eighteen feet, then made a quick left into a small, dimly lighted corridor with two unmarked doors. Between these doors a payphone hung on the wall, sporting an official-looking notice that read: TEMPORARILY OUT OF ORDER.

McCain lifted the handset, slid his Researcher Identification Card through the credit card slot on the side of the phone, punched in a series of numbers, then racked the receiver.

As soon as he did this the door to the left of the phone issued a quick, soft series of whirrs and clicks.

McCain removed the filtering mask and gloves, slipped them into his coat pocket, then crossed the threshold, quietly closing the door behind him.

He was now in a six-foot by five-foot room containing only a padded chair, a small table, a wall intercom, and a set of elevator doors.

He pressed the intercom button and said, in a well-rehearsed voice devoid of tone or inflection, "Two-fourteen, seven-B, ten, twenty-four, eleven. Mississippi."

A blue light on the intercom flashed three times in rapid succession. The computer to which he'd just spoken had accepted the security code and acknowledged today's password.

The elevator doors opened, and McCain got on.

Deep breaths, pal, c'mon, he thought. Only one more hurdle and you're there.

There was no security camera in the elevator, nor was there a row of floor numbers above the door. This unit traveled between two points and two points only—from the hidden room on the second floor to the officially non-existent sub-chambers of the National Archives Building, three floors below the Cold Storage Area in the basement where all photographs and video records were stored.

When McCain stepped off this elevator, he would be two hundred feet below Pennsylvania Avenue, in a labyrinthine configuration of warehouse shelves that, along with their contents, comprised the top secret area of the National Archives known as the Tabernacle.

It was a somewhat dignified title for a place whose sole purpose was to keep hidden from the public eye, theoretically forever, artifacts and documents whose existence would prove that the United States government (almost always under the banner of "For Reasons of National Security") had been involved in conspiracies and cover-ups more complex and far-reaching in nature than the child's play of Watergate, Iran-Contra, or Waco.

There were only two ways to get in, this elevator and another door that lay hidden somewhere in the Tabernacle itself. If he had to, McCain would use the second door for his exit.

The elevator made its slow, nerve-wracking descent. The doors opened, and McCain stepped into the Tabernacle.

To his surprise, he found that he could actually feel the weight of the secrecy in this place, for down here lay, among many, many other items, the control panel taken from the Roswell wreckage and the mythic "water engine," whose inventor was disappeared the very day he walked into the offices of General Motors and revealed his creation. Hidden among these shelves in sealed jars were one dozen genetically perfect fetuses—what would have been the true start of Hitler's Master Race—engineered by Joseph Mengele and other Third Reich scientists during their experimentation with Jews in the death camps. The corpse of a creature popularly known as "Bigfoot" stood somewhere down here, preserved forever by a taxidermist's skill. The decapitated head of the so-called "Jersey Devil" was stored here, along with photographs, videotapes, and audio recordings of other-dimensional beings whose unspeakable physical horror was surpassed only by the atrocities they urged others to commit on their behalf (supposedly there was a videotape made by Randolph Anderson, the Ohio Child Flayer, that showed a three-headed demon appearing in the center of his living room, demanding to be fed its dinner of newborns' intestines with a baby's blood chaser). There were weapons here the likes of which no military force on Earth could have conceived, freeze-dried plagues in bomb-proof canisters, blueprints detailing how to build a particle accelerator no bigger than a portable television set, test tubes containing seven different cures for cancer, five for AIDS, an inoculate that would make a newborn's system resistant to any and all forms of infection and that, when administered to an adult, would bring the aging process to an almost complete stop: liquid immortality.

Compared to all of this, McCain's quest seemed almost simpleminded. He was there to find a sealed blue-glass jar among those pieces of evidence from the Kennedy Assassination Records that had never been—nor ever would be—made public.

ple thing, really, just a jar filled with formaldehyde and bits of Kennedy's brain tissue scraped from inside the car he'd been riding in that day in Dallas, waving happily as he passed along the grassy knoll. McCain stepped into a dimly lighted corridor so cold his breath misted in the air. He could hear the deep hum of the air conditioning units that kept the temperature of the Tabernacle at a constant forty degrees Fahrenheit.

He reached into his inside jacket pocket and removed the small palmtop computer, then opened its lid and pressed a key. The screen now displayed a schematic of the Tabernacle's layout. Entering a series of short key commands, McCain enlarged a section labeled E1-7. He was now looking at a map of everything within one hundred yards of the elevator doors.

Whoever had sent him this information must have some very serious—potentially *dangerous*—connections.

Too late to turn back now, he thought.

During his time with Hoffman Institute, McCain's propensity for impulsive acts and rash decisions had more than once come under fire from his superiors. Labeled "reckless" when they didn't work out, but more often than not called "visionary" when they *did* succeed, his decisions had quickly earned him the reputation of being a loose cannon, albeit one with an impressive record of successful assignments.

If this didn't work out, odds were that either Dr. Nakami or Samuel Layacona, supervisor of the Intelligence Division, would be measuring their walls for the best place to mount his head.

But if it *did* work out, if this jar of brain fragments proved what McCain strongly suspected they would, then his next assignment might very well find him part of a much more elite field team.

He moved down the aisles, deliberately not looking at the items that sat on the shelves (wouldn't do to get distracted at this point) until he came to the area highlighted on the palmtop screen. Looking up, he saw that he was among the Kennedy assassination artifacts. He clicked on his penlight and began reading the labels on the boxes and folders until he found what he was looking for: a black medical bag with no label, save for a piece of yellow tape over the lock.

He removed the bag from the shelf, careful to not bump any of the other objects near it. Setting the bag on the floor, he pulled off the strip of yellow tape and opened it.

The bag was filled on either side with large wads of cotton. In the center of this pillow was the jar. McCain gently lifted it from inside and held it up against the dim light. He could see the five fragments of brain tissue floating inside the solution.

Bingo.

He began to place the jar back inside the bag when something small and shiny caught his eye. Using his fingers to move aside the wads of cotton that had been under the jar, he found what at first he thought were round pieces of thin Styrofoam but upon closer examination proved to be some kind of coins. He removed them and examined them with his penlight.

There were three of them. If not exactly coins, they were round and thin, but lighter than any currency he'd ever held. In fact, each weighed about as much as a small piece of Styrofoam would have. He pressed each of them between his thumb and index finger to see if they would bend. When that did nothing to damage them, he bit down on one and nearly shrieked from the sudden, lancing pain that shot up through the top of his skull, causing him to drop them.

They clattered metallically to the floor.

McCain knelt over them and examined them closer under his penlight.

Each was engraved with its own unique symbol. One had what appeared to be a set of conch shells, the second a complex variation of the double helix, and the third was engraved with four circles that overlapped in the center to form a fifth. He gathered them up and put them back inside the medical bag, then replaced the jar and sealed the bag with the same strip of yellow tape.

It was time to get out of there.

He entered another series of short commands, and the schematic on the screen displayed the location of the second entrance/exit—roughly two hundred yards from the spot where he now stood—that would lead him to a tunnel that emptied into the parking garage adjacent the Seventh Street guard station, near the Archives' loading docks. As he made his way to the tunnel's entrance, he nearly tripped over a large rat that scuttled past him.

Your tax dollars at work, he thought, watching the rat dart quickly under a shelf. McCain wondered how much damage the rat had done to the items stored down there, then decided it wasn't his problem.

He found the steel door that marked the entrance to the tunnel and entered the security code into the panel next to it. It was just as the door was sliding open that he smelled something sharp, harsh, and warm.

He turned in the direction of the smell, inhaled deeply, then nearly doubled over from the series of violent coughs that erupted from his chest.

He was smelling sulfur, was suddenly covered in perspiration, and the temperature was getting warmer—a lot warmer.

And very quickly.

He turned and stepped into the tunnel. It felt as if the air inside the Tabernacle was on fire.

He pressed the orange button on the other side and the door began to slide closed—

—then something deep inside the Tabernacle blew apart in an explosion of screaming metal and shattered glass.

McCain caught the first glimpse of rolling flames as the door jammed on its track three-quarters of the way home. Another fiery explosion, much bigger than the first, ripped through the Tabernacle, scattering shelves and searing their contents. McCain turned and began to run as the sound and vibrations of the explosions grew louder and closer. The stench of sulfur was so heavy in the air he could barely breathe, so he pulled in one more breath and forced himself to hold it and not to cough as he continued running.

The next explosion blew away the tunnel door and sent a wave of hot wind blasting through the opening, but McCain not only kept running, he picked up his pace and ran for all he was worth. The air pressure screamed in his ears and the air in his lungs began to escape in slow, agonized wheezes.

I took a wrong turn and ran into the waiting room of Hell, he thought.

His eyes were watering and his heart was trip-hammering in his chest. The emergency lights lining the walls were flickering, causing everything before him to strobe, but as another series of explosions ripped through the Tabernacle somewhere behind him the floor beneath his feet began to ripple and crack, opening small fissures behind and in front of him. He could see the steam rising, and the steam was hot—Jesus, was it hot—but he continued running forward because there was no other direction to run. He was clutching the medical bag close to his chest and praying that the jar had not been damaged when he rounded a curve in the tunnel and had just enough time to look over his shoulder. That was a mistake.

He saw what looked like a wave of fire spilling across the roof of the tunnel and catching up with him. There was no way he could outrun it so he did the only thing that made sense. He dropped down to his knees, then fell forward, facedown on the fissuring concrete as the wave of flame rolled over his head and disappeared up an overhead air vent.

He was back on his feet and running toward the last section of the tunnel, and he could smell the back of his coat smoldering, could see the smoke twisting before his eyes, and in the few seconds before the last and biggest explosion finished things off McCain tried to remember if he was supposed to go to his parents' house for dinner that weekend or—

—the next explosion blew wind and debris down the tunnel, lifting McCain off his feet and slamming him into a buckling air vent. He had just enough time to reach down and press the red button on his pager before losing consciousness and thinking, They're never gonna find my body, not in this mess—

—and Mom had promised to make her famous lasagna, too. . . .

The explosions took out most of the Tabernacle. Debris and flames blew out as far as the Archives' loading docks. Inside the building, the east wall of the first three floors blasted inward, destroying tables, shelves, files, chairs, computer equipment, security monitors, setting off fire alarms and the now near-useless sprinkler system. The elevator that McCain had taken was crumpled like a matchbox, and the flashover from the Tabernacle shot upward, filling the shaft with flames and wreckage.

In the fifty-eight seconds it took for the series of explosions to finish, seventeen people inside the National Archives building were killed and eighty-three seriously injured. Beyond the great bronze doors, a deep, wide crack snaked its way down the majestic stone steps and spread out into the center of Constitution Avenue, where it began to expand like a spider's web.

The street shook. Drivers lost control of their cars and careened into one another. A fuel tanker drove across one of the deepest cracks, fell sideways, and was hit by an oncoming semi. Both vehicles went up in a mushroom cloud of fire. A local traffic helicopter was caught in the updraft of flame, spun out of control, and crashed into the top of the Archives' Pennsylvania Avenue entrance, where its rotor blades snapped against the stone columns and skittered off in three different directions, killing nine people as they boomeranged to the ground. The body of the helicopter fell in flames onto the steps and slid downward into the center of the street, where four different cars, their drivers struggling for control against the violent aftershocks, slammed into it and were consumed as all five fuel tanks simultaneously erupted.

Telephone polls toppled to the ground, their lines snapping. Power lines were severed and whipped around like writhing tentacles, covering the sidewalks with shotgun blasts of sputtering electrical sparks.

Emergency sirens went off all over the area. The Secret Service sealed the White House. Every window within a seven-block radius shattered. People ran. People screamed. People panicked. People died.

When the last body was pulled from the wreckage, the final tally would be thirty-seven dead, one hundred and forty-two injured.

The only bright spot in the whole disaster—and one that the president would emphasize later that night as he went on television to address the nation—was six-month-old Amanda Cummins.

Amanda's mother had been close to the Constitution Avenue side of the National Archives Building when the explosions hit. She had been knocked unconscious by a section of concrete that blasted upward near her feet. When she'd fallen, the carriage in which she'd been pushing her baby daughter rolled away and was carried farther into the street by the momentum of the spreading fissures. Little Amanda cried for her mommy. The carriage was struck by small pieces of debris that shoved it into one of the deepest street fissures. The carriage fell sideways, two of its wheels caught in the crack. Amanda's cries could not be heard.

Seven different cars crashed around her.

Flames from three different explosions scorched the outer material of the carriage.

Its wheels melted.

Its axles buckled.

It dropped farther into the fissure. From a distance, it looked as if a frilly sun-visor was laying in the middle of the street.

When it was finally over it was an unidentified Asian man—described by witnesses as being short and bald—who

37

scrabbled over the wrecked and flaming automobiles and pulled Amanda from her carriage mere seconds before it was completely swallowed by the fissure. He vanished with the baby held safely in his arms.

"I think, Little One," he whispered to her, "that It has begun to awaken."

Amanda was found in the lap of the "Guardianship" sculpture five minutes later, contentedly sucking on her pacifier, not a scratch on her. She even giggled when the police officer picked her up.

Amanda's mother later told reporters that she would be ". . . eternally and gratefully indebted," to the unidentified Asian man who'd saved her little baby.

Amanda's carriage was a lost cause, though, but that worked out all right.

The president himself bought her a new one.

Ten seconds after Michael McCain pressed the red button on his pager, another pager—this one worn by a small, hunchbacked man whose thick grey hair reached nearly to his shoulders—began to vibrate. The grey-haired man adjusted his wire-framed glasses, looked down at the pager's readout screen, and climbed down off the stool where he'd been sitting. He tossed a twenty onto the bar to cover the cost of his club sandwich and Coke, then left the pub and walked a few yards down M Street to an austere-looking antique shop with a **Closed For Lunch—Back in 1 Hour** sign hanging in the window of its front door. He unlocked the door and went inside but did not remove the sign. Instead, he locked the door once again, crossed through the shop proper, and let himself into an office in the back.

A computer terminal sat on the large oak desk. The Shopkeeper sat behind the desk and pressed the "Enter" key on the keyboard.

The screen blinked to life as the system accessed the NFS-net, and the Hoffman Institute logo appeared. The Shopkeeper entered a series of quick commands, and at a transfer rate of 1000 Gb/sec. the orders were received and acted upon.

The institute's D.C.-based Field Agent Emergency Rescue Unit was rolling before the Shopkeeper answered the phone sixty seconds later.

"Yes, sir?" said the Shopkeeper into the phone. "Yes, it's done. They're on their way to the scene right now. The signal?" He checked the coordinates on the screen against the code flashing on his pager's readout. "Near the guard station entrance at Seventh Street. They should have a lock on him in about four minutes. Yes, sir. We felt the vibrations here. I'll keep in touch." He was about to hang up when something occurred to him. "Dr. Nakami? Should I prepare the tele-conferencing equipment? I just thought that perhaps once he's stabilized you'd want to ask him why he was—oh? Is that so?" The Shopkeeper smiled. "I see. Of course, sir. I'll make all the arrangements. I—"

A small alarm began to beep.

"One moment, sir, the unit's sending his exact location." The Shopkeeper pulled up the information and continued, "Yes, sir, the National Archives Building. He's—oh, shit. Sorry, sir, it's just that it appears he's trapped in the wreckage. Would you like to stay on the line, or should I open the link to your office? Right." He racked the receiver and opened a direct link to Nakami's private office.

The Shopkeeper sat back, checked his watch, and waited.

Over the Potomac and past the edge of the Key Bridge, downtown D.C. was choked in chaos as Army and National Guard units were called in to assist the police and emergency workers. Agents from the Secret Service, FBI, and ATF were swarming over the scene, impatient for the fires to be put out so they could investigate the cause of the explosions. More than once the words "Oklahoma City" and "Waco" were whispered.

Elsewhere in Washington that night, several homeless people stopped foot-patrol officers to report sightings of "monsters," or "ghouls," as well as "beasties," and "goblins." One old man claimed that a "big glass ape" had removed his pancreas and "burned away my cancer 'fore he put it back inside me. Hurt like a son-of-a-bitch, but I feel lots better now."

All of the reports were quickly noted but just as quickly dismissed as the ravings of mental cases. It would be several days before any of these reported sightings would be brought to the attention of superior officers in the department. Right now, the sole concern of all law enforcement agencies in the city was discovering how the terrorists (for there was little doubt that the Archives explosion was the work of some grudge-carrying fringe group) had managed to get the bomb into the building and detonate it with such deadly accuracy.

God only knew how much precious history had been incinerated by the blasts. A full one-third of the National Archives Building had been destroyed in less than a minute.

Army and National Guard soldiers worked crowd control and kept looting down to a minimum. Three times riots threatened to break out, but a show of arms quickly dispersed the crowds.

The city was angry and in shock and more than a little afraid. How could this have happened here, in the heart of the nation's government?

Had any of them known (as did the small Asian man who rescued Amanda Cummins) the true nature of what had just happened—of what, in fact, was only just *beginning*, no civil or military force on Earth could have controlled the rioting that would have resulted from the panic.

The Dark Tide had risen.

With a vengeance.

chapter

2 W O

When Jeane Meara was just another young girl living in the Cleveland suburb of Parma, Ohio, she and her father had been insatiable TV cop show junkies. While her father tended to favor the stone-jawed machismo of Mike Connors on *Mannix* and the heightened-sense meticulousness of James Franciscus as the blind detective *Longstreet*, Jeane always openly admired Angie Dickinson on *Police Woman* (she also had a crush on Earl Holliman, Angie's co-star, whose perpetual hang-dog expression just seemed to beg for affection and understanding). Secretly, she'd watch *Charlie's Angels* any chance she got—not because it was in the same league as the other cop shows (not by a long shot) but because it made her feel good to know that a woman could chase criminals, get in fist fights, be drugged by the bad guys for interrogation, fall in mud, then take part in a massive shootout and still go home with her hair and makeup intact. Her father never understood her attraction to the Angels or why she favored the hang-dog Holliman over the chiseled Franciscus. As a compromise, they agreed that Raymond Burr as *Ironside* was one guy you did. Not. Mess. With.

And so was born Jeane's interest in a career in law enforcement. Thank you, Ms. Dickinson.

On the morning after the explosion at the National Archives Building, as she sat impatiently waiting to be admitted to her supervisor's office, Jeane had been with the Washington office of the Bureau of Alcohol, Tobacco, and Firearms for five years. A member of the First Team Arson Investigation Unit, she had been at both Waco and Oklahoma City.

Among her fellow ATF agents, she had earned the nickname (one she wasn't supposed to know about) "Wonder Woman."

There was neither affection nor much respect in the title. Jeane knew full well that she wasn't considered to be very nice, was thought to be too unforgiving, and was often criticized (if not outright condemned) in the field for her expectations of perfection in the performance of duty. Fine. She could live with not being well liked. She'd never really been one of the Warm People, but to be looked down upon because she gave nothing but her best and expected no less of her fellow agents . . . well, that one hurt.

But she'd be damned if she'd let any of them know that.

"Agent Meara?" said the secretary. "Supervisor Travis will see you now."

Jeane got to her feet, made sure that her straight, reddish-brown hair was still tied neatly back in a ponytail (the morning's events had not allowed her much time for her usual grooming routine), and went into Arthur Travis's office.

He was on the phone as she entered. Whomever he was talking with was not at all happy, judging by the volume of his voice.

"I understand, sir," said Travis with more than a touch of apology in his voice. "Yes, sir, I realize that, but you have to understand that Agent Meara is one of our best arson—I beg your pardon? Yes, she's here right now." He cast her a quick, irritated glance. "Would a written apology be sufficient? I see. If you'll allow me to get her side of the story I can—of course. Right away. Thank you, sir."

Travis hung up, gestured for Jeane to take a seat, then rummaged around in one of his desk drawers until he found a half empty bottle of Maalox. He unscrewed the cap and pulled down three deep swallows of the thick, milky liquid, then looked at Jeane and said, "Have you ever woke up with the feeling that you're about to have one of those days that'll start with a hearty breakfast and end with some newscaster saying, 'Before turning the gun on himself . . .'?"

"The man is an idiot, sir."

"The man is a federal fire marshal Agent Meara."

He'd called her "Agent Meara." Not a good sign.

"I am fully aware of his authority, sir," she said. "He's still an idiot."

"He's a close friend of the Vice President of the United States."

"With all due respect, sir, I don't care if he's the pope's partner at the annual Vatican domino tournament. It doesn't change the fact that Fire Marshal Glenn is a pig-headed, tunnel-visioned, borderline-sexist good old boy who has thus far refused any advice or input from me."

"There's a lot of pressure to get answers fast."

"I am aware of that, sir, and let me assure you that until my altercation with Fire Marshal Glenn, I in no way conducted myself in a manner that was detrimental to the reputation of the bureau."

Travis sighed and looked longingly at the Maalox. "I don't doubt that you conducted yourself admirably, Meara. I also have no doubt that Glenn refused to hear what you were trying to tell him, but that does not excuse your calling him a . . . a . . ." Travis began sifting through the piles of notes on his desk.

". . . 'an addled-brained, Neolithic dipshit' is the phrase I believe I employed, sir," Jeane finished for him.

43

Travis sat back and pinched the bridge of his nose. "Care to guess how many phone calls I've gotten in the thirty minutes it took for you to get here?"

"At least one."

Travis almost smiled. Almost.

Checking his watch, he said, "You have fifteen minutes to convince me that your behavior was unduly provoked. In twenty minutes the vice president himself is going to call me and I'm supposed to have an explanation for him. I cannot tell you how much it would displease me if I did not have one to offer."

Jeane looked down at her shoulder bag, then said, "May I speak freely, sir?"

"As opposed to the restraint you've exercised so far?"

"I meant no disrespect."

Travis nodded. "I know, Meara. Just make me understand why, all right?"

"Yes, sir." She quickly consulted some notes.

"One question," said Travis.

"Sir?"

He leaned forward. "How long were you on-site before you ruled out the possibility of a bomb?"

"Well, sir, there were tests on initial environmentals that had be conducted, as well as—"

Travis held up his hand. "Spare me a recitation of the Department Procedure Manual, all right? How soon did you know?"

"Before I was even out of my car."

He seemed surprised—and maybe even a little pleased—by this. "What tipped it for you?"

"The fissures in the sidewalk and street. They were far too deep to have resulted from anything short of a nuclear detonation, and the levels of radiation in the atmosphere were negligible. You'd be exposed to more radioactivity making microwave popcorn. Initial tests and examinations revealed an unidentifiable point of origin. There were no 'V' burn patterns present in or on the area of the building where I began my tests."

"Where was that, by the way?"

"At the Archive's Seventh Street loading docks. A lot of debris had been scattered outward from the air shafts in that location."

"Go on."

"There was evidence of several separate and unconnected fires, as well as unusual burn patterns and high heat stress. All the windows had been blown away from the structure, indicating the flashpoint originated somewhere low in the building. Flameover tests revealed the presence of large amounts of pyrolysate on the debris and covering those sections of the affected areas that were still standing. Radiant heat levels, arcing through char, and arrow patterns were present and measured. It's all here in my notes.

"The vapor density is what began to set off my internal alarms, sir. The ratio of the average molecular weight of the volume of vapor emissions was inconsistent with the average molecular weight of an equal volume tested at the same temperature and pressure. Add to that the vast difference in the heat flux measurements—I employed your personal favorite, sir, Btu/ft2/sec—as well as the patterns revealed in the isochar schematics, and I had no choice but to conclude that whatever caused the explosion was the result of a natural, not man-made phenomenon.

"Among the scenarios that Fire Marshal Glenn wished explored was the possibility that the explosions could have been the result of spontaneous combustion. At first this seemed like a strong possibility to me, as well, considering the variety of combustible materials stored at the Archives, any one of which, under the right circumstances, could have acted as an accelerant. Under a variety of conditions, the temperature of certain materials can increase without drawing heat from their surroundings. If the temperature of the material reached its ignition temperature, spontaneous ignition could very well have been the cause."

"But you ruled that out?"

"Yes, sir." Jeane consulted her notes once again. "Using the portable RITSI Glovebox hardware and allowing for 2D flame spread, I collected and examined several samples of debris, using the infrared radiant heater to ignite the samples. By doing this and recessing the resultant blast into the back wall of the duct to minimize disturbances to the flow, I was able to determine that the blast could not have been the result of spontaneous combustion."

"But Glenn didn't buy that?"

Jeane shook her head. "No, sir. He said he had no need for my 'fancy-assed *Star Wars* toys' to tell him that we were dealing with '. . . a big boom.' "

Travis laughed. "He actually said that? 'Big boom'?"

Jeane neither laughed nor smiled. "Yes, sir, then he proceeded to tell me that I should go amuse myself '. . . like a good little girl.' "

"Oh, brother."

"Would you like me to continue, sir?"

"Yes, Meara, but do me a favor and start phrasing everything in terms that I'll be able to make the vice president understand. He may be a Yale graduate but somehow I doubt he's up on arson technology . . . and speaking for myself, my head hurts too much right now to process the techno-babble."

"Understood, sir." She flipped back in her notes, was unable to find what she was looking for, and so closed the book and recited the rest from memory. "I tried pointing out to Fire Marshal Glenn that in most cases spontaneous heating occurs when a material reacts with oxygen from the air. The reaction is known as oxidation and results in the evolution of heat. In most cases the oxidation process is very slow, and the amount of heat generated in the material is so little that the temperature of the material does not change in a measurable way—a classic example of an oxidation reaction that is not susceptible to spontaneous ignition under normal temperatures is the rusting of iron.

"Many of the materials stored in the Archives, however, are kept in airtight environments and so could not react vigorously with oxygen to generate sufficient heat. In order for the blast to have occurred due to spontaneous combustion, the temperature of any combustible material would have to have increased until the rate of heat generation equals the rate at which the heat is carried away from the material. None of the Archives' materials, to the best of my knowledge, were sufficiently insulated to prevent significant heat dissipation, so the temperature of the material could not have reached its ignition temperature quickly enough to cause this kind of catastrophic damage."

"But spontaneous heating of a substance doesn't always involve reaction with oxygen," said Travis. "If sodium metal is placed in a glass of water, the reaction produces heat and hydrogen. The heat of the reaction is sufficient to ignite the hydrogen being evolved at the surface of the water."

"Yes, sir, but there was nothing in my initial series of tests to indicate that anything of that nature might have occurred in the sealed areas—and I don't believe that any further testing would show otherwise. As I pointed out to Fire Marshal Glenn, Section 10.6 of the ASTM E 1387 standard clearly states that '. . . once a peak starts, it should match a standard until the pattern ends. Peaks missing from the middle of a pattern are usually sufficient grounds for concluding that there is not a match between the sample and the standard, pointing to the possibility that the fire was not the result of human error or interference.' " She shrugged. "Seeing as how Fire Marshal Glenn was the one to point out that there were no peaks present in the middle of the patterns we examined and that he was on the committee that authored Section 10.6, I figured he would see the clarity of my logic. He then accused me of trying to make him look like 'a buffoon' in front of everyone. I tried to apologize to him if anything I said seemed disrespectful. He told me I should go back to Cleveland and 'snag a man with a good job and have lots of smart-ass babies.' I tried once more to show him my test results, and that's when he pushed me out of the way."

Travis consulted some notes. "Let me get that part straight. He physically pushed you away?"

"Yes, sir."

"Where did his hand make contact?"

Jeane sighed. "It was here—" She touched an area between her left shoulder and the slope of her left breast, wincing because it was still quite sore. "—and for the record, his hand was closer to a fist at that point."

Travis nodded. "Then you called him 'an addle-minded, Neolithic dipshit.'"

"That's about the size of it, yes, sir."

"Tell me, Meara, what did you hope to accomplish by that?"

"I wanted his full and undivided attention."

"Because . . . ?—no, wait a second." He turned to his computer. "I want to get some of this down so I can't lose it in this mess—did I mention that I'm not having a blue-ribbon day, Meara?"

"There was some talk of it earlier, yes, sir."

Travis typed some notes into his computer. "For the record, then. All of your preliminary tests pointed away from the possibility of a bomb blast or spontaneous combustion?"

"Yes. In fact, everything seems to strongly suggest an exothermic chemical reaction that is most probably subterranean in nature."

Travis's eyes widened. "You're not saying that—"

"Yes, sir. Everything that I saw and tested indicates that the Archives disaster is the result of a subterranean volcanic eruption."

Travis shook his head and groaned. "Just to clear it up for the sake of my tortured psyche, Meara, this is connected to your insulting Glenn how?"

"I wanted his full and undivided attention, and the only way I felt I could achieve this was to 'get uppity,' as he put it later. If he had bothered to pay attention, I would have pointed out that during the three hours I was on site, I felt no fewer than six aftershocks, each one a little stronger than the one before. In my opinion—and I admit that my knowledge of seismology is less than profound—if there's volcanic activity underneath this city, it's just getting started. He wouldn't listen to me."

Travis blanched. "That would be a reason to call someone a dipshit."

"That's what I thought, sir."

Travis grinned unhappily and took another swig of Maalox. Setting down the bottle, he wiped his mouth on his shirt sleeve and said, "Can you show me anything, *anything* concrete that will convince the vice president to take your conclusions seriously?"

"Yes, I can." She reached down and opened her shoulder bag. "You might want to get someone in here with a video camera, sir. If there's any way to get our hands on a medical scalpel, that would be helpful, as well."

Travis wrinkled his nose and coughed. "What on earth is that stench?"

"I apologize for the smell, sir, but I needed to keep this piece of evidence intact." She placed a wad of plastic wrap in the center of the supervisor's desk and unwrapped it to reveal the badly charred remains of a very large rat.

"Oh, for chrissakes, Meara!" shouted Travis, pushing away from his desk and covering his nose and mouth. "This is your proof?"

"Yes, sir."

Travis glared at her. "It had better be damned convincing. If I have to ask the vice president to look at a videotape of you playing *Operation* with a dead rat on one of this nation's worst days, it had better be just short of a miracle cure at Lourdes. Got me?"

"Understood, sir."

Travis buzzed his secretary and told her what was needed.

Within five minutes a video camera was set up in front of the supervisor's desk with tape rolling.

Jeane came around behind the desk so she was facing the camera. She had put on rubber gloves and was holding the scalpel in one of her hands. Looking at the camera operator, she said, "Get in as close as you can on the corpse without sacrificing focus."

"Whatever you say, Miss Kurosawa."

That got a little smile from her, but the camera didn't catch it.

"If you'll look at the severity of the charring," said Jeane, "you'll see that this rat was very close to the final blast—not close enough to be incinerated, but not so far away that it wasn't killed instantly." She looked at Travis. "I found this rat and another in the same condition while I was attempting to run tests in one of the Seventh Street air vents. Fire Marshal Glenn insisted that the vent was a restricted area and had me forcibly removed."

"He had no right to do that, Meara. That, combined with his later actions, could very well add up to an assault charge. I'll tell the vice president that myself. In my opinion, your actions, while not the most tactful, were justified. Now would you please get this over with?"

"Of course." She turned back to the rat. "Just so you have an idea of the intensity of the heat . . ."

She took one of the rat's paws between her thumb and index finger and, with only the slightest bit of pressure, snapped it cleanly off. When she gently rolled the severed paw between her fingers, all of its tissue and most of the bone crumbled into ash.

"This sort of catastrophic tissue charring can only be caused by close exposure to a nuclear blast or flames from free-flowing volcanic lava. To that end, I want to state that the second rat I found in the air vent was in the exact same condition as this one. Watch carefully." She brought the edge of the scalpel down on the rat's underside and punctured the tissue.

There was a sudden *pop!* followed by a loud hiss as the rat's chest cavity, unaided by Jeane, blossomed outward like the petals of a flower, releasing a quick but very visible cloud of vapor.

"What the hell was that?" said Travis.

"Air in its lungs, sir. The same thing happened to the bodies they discovered at Pompeii and after the Mount St. Helen's disaster. Bodies from Hiroshima and Nagasaki did the same thing when they were assembled for autopsies."

"And . . . ?"

Jeane sighed and said, "Any creature whose body possesses lungs has a built-in defense mechanism when confronted with conditions that threaten to cut off its oxygen supply. It just naturally pulls in a breath and holds it for as long as possible, until conditions allow it to exhale and breathe again. If it's easier to understand, imagine that this rat—like the victims at Pompeii and Hiroshima—was pulling in a breath so it could scream. But the scream, the breath, was never released."

"Meaning what?"

"Meaning the fire that engulfed them was so overpowering, consumed their bodies so quickly and with such an intense level of heat, that they died before they could either scream or exhale. They died with their final breath trapped in their lungs. Just like this rat and the other one I found."

"The other rat . . . *popped* as well?"

"Yes, sir." She leaned down and looked directly into the camera. "Only two kinds of blasts can cause this to happen: a nuclear explosion or a volcanic eruption, and the possibility of a nuclear explosion was ruled out almost immediately." She stood and turned to face her supervisor. "Will that be sufficient, sir?"

Travis waved toward the rat. "Get that thing out of here. Send it down to the lab."

Jeane buzzed Travis's secretary and made the arrangements. A few minutes later, after the rat had been removed and air freshener liberally sprayed about, Travis looked across his desk at Jeane and said, "What do you think should be done now?"

"I'd like to be able to explore that air vent on Seventh more thoroughly. I think that tunnel empties out somewhere very close to the origin of the blast." She shrugged. "But if Fire Marshal Glenn has labeled me *persona non grata*, then I don't see how—"

Travis held up his finger and buzzed his secretary. "Madeleine, get the office of the vice president on the line for me, will you?" He then reached into a desk drawer and removed a bright blue laminated card and handed it to Jeane. "That's an A-Five Security Clearance Pass, same type as the majority of Secret Service Agents carry. In order to get anything higher you have to be one of the Joint Chiefs, the president or vice president, or a member of their families. This will give you access to any area of the site you wish to explore. As soon as the vice president returns my call, I'm going to tell him everything you told me and have a copy of the videotape sent to his offices. I'm also going to suggest it would be best if he pulled Glenn off the site as soon as possible. You done good, Meara, and you've convinced me of the potential danger, but if we're going to tell this city that its ass is parked right on top of an active volcano that could blow us all to smithereens any minute, we're going to need more evidence than what you've shown to me. I want proof out the ying-yang, understand me? I want enough environmentals to choke a whale. I want chemical analyses that'd make a Nobel Prize winner raise an eyebrow. I want isochar schematics that look like fractal patterns. I want vapor emission readings, heat flux measurements, flameover charts, radiant heat levels, arcing through char, arrow and 'V' pattern reports with photographs to back up your conclusions, and pyrolysate samples from every possible surface inside the blast radius."

Jeane was writing it all down. "Anything else, sir?"

"Yes. On your way out, ask Madeleine to send for a fresh bottle of Maalox. I'd prefer the cherry-flavored kind, if they still make it."

"Will do, sir." Jeane started out the door.

"And Meara?"

She turned toward Travis. "Sir?"

"Let's declare a temporary moratorium on the use of 'dipshit' in your everyday conversation, shall we?"

"Can I use it memos?"

Travis blinked. "Was that a joke?"

"Yes, sir."

"I'm not used to that from you. Warn me next time."

"Understood."

Jeane then left her supervisor's office, feeling very much like Wonder Woman and for once not minding it a bit.

As Jeane Meara drove her car out of the ATF parking garage, she took no notice of the small Asian man who stood on the corner and watched her turn in the direction of the National Archives Building. His intense blue eyes watched as she activated her car's siren and portable visibar dome, then disappeared into the traffic.

Once Jeane's car was no longer visible to him, the man once again looked at the strange coin in his hand and thought, The forces are gathering much quicker than I thought. Looking back in the direction Jeane had driven, he asked himself, What part will you play in this?

He considered what to do next. His cell phone beeped, making the decision for him. He moved into the cramped doorway of a business that had closed for the day and answered the phone.

"Dr. Nakami asked me to contact you," said the Shopkeeper.

"Yes?"

"Have you had any further contact with the child since your last check-in?"

"No, but I expect to be seeing her again tonight or in the morning."

"You're certain about the nature of the object she gave you?"

"Yes. There is no question."

The Shopkeeper cleared his throat. "They'll probably come after her because of it. You know that, don't you?"

"Yes."

"Can you handle it alone?"

"No. Now tell me, how is McCain?"

"Still in surgery, but all his vitals are strong."

"Good. Very good."

"That's right," said the Shopkeeper. "You know him, don't you?"

"I know his parents, and I knew him when he was a child. I doubt very much that he would remember me." He stared out at nothing and everything for a few moments, then said, "Will you be in further contact with Dr. Nakami today?"

"Of course."

The small Asian man was silent for a moment, remembering the way he'd watched from a hiding place amidst the wreckage as Jeane had fought valiantly with the foolish men who refused to listen to the wisdom of her young experience. "Please tell him that I may have a new recruit for us very soon."

"Can you give me a name?"

"Soon. Very soon."

The Shopkeeper sighed. "Okay, then. Take care of yourself, my friend. Don't hesitate to call for backup if you need it. Are you all right?"

"I'm fine. Why?"

"I worry."

A smile. "You worry too much."

"It's my new hobby. Watch your back."

chapter

THR3E

Down in the Rusty Room where Buddy lived these words had been written on one of the walls:

> *someone come*
> *i'm tired of naming things*
> *then forgetting their names*
> *the voice in the sky is*
> *loneliness*
> *and the night is*
> *restlessness*
>
> *someone come*

Even though she was only a little girl of six (well, *almost* six), she knew that Buddy had written the words, and that it was some kind of prayer, and that made her sad because she knew what it was like to feel so scared and tired and alone, like you belonged somewhere else but there wasn't anybody listening to you when you asked to leave.

> *and where do I live?*
> *under the tracks of the l*
> *in a cardboard box*
> *that's falling apart*

> *within the cell life is hard, life is long*
> *within the cell, life is hard*

> *someone please come*

Leah was thinking about Buddy and the Rusty Room and the words on the wall as she watched her mother hand the baby over to the man in the dark coat and knew she wouldn't be seeing her little sister again. It always happened this way.

Mommy would go away with the men in the dark coats to the Shiny Place (that's what Mommy called it), and Leah would be all by herself for weeks at a time in the abandoned warehouse that was their home. It was kind of scary for a little while after Mommy left, but it was easier getting the people at the restaurants to give her food when she was by herself—"Oh, you poor child," they all said, stuffing bread and hamburgers and doughnuts and little cartons of milk into paper bags. "What kind of a mother would do this to a child?"—so she never had to dig through the garbage dumpsters like she had to with Mommy, and there was Merc and Chief Wetbrain who were always on their corner a few blocks away, they were really nice and had helped her before . . . but mostly there was Buddy.

She thought it was a good thing that she had Buddy around to take care of her when Mommy was gone. He always made things better.

The dark-coat man took the baby, smiled down at it, then snapped his fingers. Another man in a dark coat and sunglasses

(Leah wondered why none of the dark-coat men ever took their sunglasses off, even at night) got out of the car and handed Mommy a thick envelope. That made Leah feel even worse. She knew there was money in the envelope that the dark-coat man was giving to Mommy for the baby, and Mommy would use it to buy more needle-stuff that would last until the next time the men in the dark coats returned to take her to the Shiny Place, and after a couple of weeks she'd come back all pregnant, then have the baby, then the dark-coat men would be there with their envelopes full of money.

Leah wanted to cry. She hadn't even had a chance to give her little sister a name—and this had been her first sister, too.

She felt a tear forming and closed her eyes, taking a deep breath and Removing herself (that's what Buddy called it) from everything going on around her, watching as silvery shimmer-bursts of light went off behind her closed lids. She did just as Buddy had taught her, she reached out in her mind like in daydream and snagged a ride on one of the shimmers—
—*and saw the Earth and the Moon as they must have looked to astronauts moving through the cold, glittering depths of the cosmos; the dry, pounded surface of the moon, its craters dark and secretive and dead as an old bone; just beyond was a milky-white radiance that cast liquid-grey shadows across the lunarscape while distant stars winked at her, then a burst of heat and pressure and suddenly she was below the moist, gleaming membrane of the bright blue sky, Earth rising exuberantly into her line of sight: she marveled at the majestic, swirling drifts of white clouds covering and uncovering the half-hidden masses of land and watched the continents themselves in motion, drifting apart on their plates, held afloat by the molten fire beneath, and when the plates had settled and the rivers had carved their paths and the trees had spread their wondrous arms, there came next the People and their races and mysteries through the ages, and in her mind she danced through some of those mysteries, Buddy holding her hand as they stood atop places with wonderful and odd names, places like Cheop's Pyramid and the Tower of Ra, Zoroaster's Temple and the Javanese*

Borobudur, the Krishna Shrine, the Valhalla Plateau and Woton's Throne, then they started dancing through Camelot and Gawain's Abyss and Lancelot's Point, then they went to Solomon's Temple at Moriah, then the Aztec Amphitheater, Toltec Point, Cardenas Butte, and Alarcon Terrace before stopping at last in front of the great Wall of Skulls at Chicén Itzá: the skulls awash in a sea of glowing colors, changing shape in the light from above, their mouths opening as if to speak to her, flesh spreading across bone to form faces and her heart—oh, her heart felt almost freed and—

Mommy smacked her on the shoulder and said, "Stop daydreaming, damn you."

The dark-coat man handed the baby to one of his friends, then walked over to Leah, took off his sunglasses, and smiled down at her. His eyes were cold and black and made Leah feel like he'd swallow her up if she looked into them for too long.

"Please don't," said Mommy. "She's all I've got."

One of the other men grabbed Leah's mother and held her back.

"All you've got like my ass chews gum," said the dark-coat man. "You have about as much love in your heart for this child as I do for you, you worthless piece of shit."

"Don't you call my mommy names!" shouted Leah.

"I apologize," said the dark-coat man, kneeling down in front of Leah. "Tell me, sweetheart, how old are you now?"

"I'll be six pretty soon."

"The thirteenth of next month, as a matter of fact," he said. "And you know what's going to happen then?"

"Huh-uh."

"Why, we're going to come back and take both you and your mommy to a birthday party for you."

"Really? In the Shiny Place?"

The dark-coat man shot an angry glance at Leah's mother. "Chatty little thing, aren't you?"

"Screw you."

"And charming, to boot." He looked back at Leah. "Yes, sweetheart, we're going to have a birthday party for you in the

Shiny Place. Then you and your mommy can live there, if you want. It's very nice. It's clean, and you can watch television and play games, and there'll be food every day, and you won't have to worry about ever being left alone again."

"Can I still see my friends?"

Something in the dark-coat man's eyes brightened when she asked this. "What friends do you mean, sweetheart?"

"You know . . . Merc and Chief Wetbrain and Randi—she's a singer who comes around to visit Merc sometimes—and Cain, he's my new friend. Merc, he calls Cain Kung-Fu 'cause he says he looks like some guy who used to be on a TV show. They're all real nice."

"Of course you can still see them, Leah. We'll even bring them to the party if you want."

"Could they live with us, maybe?"

"Maybe. Are there any other friends you want to come to the party?"

She almost told him about Buddy but something in the way he'd said "any other friends" didn't sound very nice, so Leah just shook her head.

The dark-coat man stopped smiling. "Well, then . . . you think about it, sweetheart. If there's anyone else you want to be there, you just tell us where they are and we'll invite them." He reached out and touched her cheek. His hand felt like cold, raw restaurant meat. "Listen, sweetheart, we need to, uh . . . do something to you right now, if it's okay."

"Don't touch her!" shouted Mommy.

"Shut up," said the dark-coat man. Then, to Leah, "Would you do a big favor for me? Would you get into the back seat of my car and let us take a little blood from your arm?"

"W-why?"

"It's all right, Leah. The man who'll do it is a doctor so you don't have to—"

"I don't like needles," said Leah, as much to her mother as to the dark-coat man.

"I know you don't, honey, but we need it . . . we need it in

59

case your little sister gets sick, see? You both have the same blood type—do you know what that is?"

"Uh-huh."

"Good. You both have the same blood type, and it's very rare. You're the only other girl in this part of the country who has it, and if something happens and your little sister needs blood, we wouldn't have any."

Leah thought about it for a moment, then asked, "Will it hurt?"

"Only a little sting, I promise."

Leah's lower lip trembled. "I don't want her to be sick."

"Oh, she's not sick, hon, but if she were to get sick . . ."

"Okay."

"I won't let you!" shouted Mommy.

"That's enough from the peanut gallery," said the dark-coat man, rising to his feet. "She loves her little sister, don't you, Leah? She only wants to help, and if she doesn't, that might spoil things. We don't want to spoil things for her, do we?"

"Will she be there?" asked Leah, pointing at the baby. "At my party?"

"If you want."

"I do. I really do. I never had a little sister before."

"Does she have a name?"

"Huh-uh."

"Ah, well . . . that can be one of your presents. You can give your little sister a name. Would you like that?"

"Oh, yes!"

"Consider it done, then."

Leah got into the back seat and let the nice old doctor with the grey hair take some blood from her arm. It took a lot longer than she thought it would because he had to fill a clear plastic bag. It left her feeling a little dizzy, but he gave her some lemonade and cookies, and she felt better.

As she sat there finishing off the cookies and starting in on the Twinkies ("Maybe you'd better have something more," the doctor had said), she heard Mommy talking with the dark-coat man.

"What're you going to do with her?" asked Mommy.

"None of your business. You've not asked about what happened to any of the others, so why the sudden concern?"

"Because . . . I dunno . . . she's not such a bad kid, y'know? I love—"

"Oh, spare me. God, you're disgusting."

"You can't talk to me like—"

"I can talk to you any way I damned well please. Aside from the fact that it took us three years to find you, the only reason we've let you keep her this long is because she's formed—for whatever bizarre reasons—an emotional attachment to you. She loves you. We didn't expect that. But don't think that means you're safe, bitch. You could be disappeared like *that*"—he snapped his fingers—"and no one would give a damn."

"Maybe," said Mommy. "And maybe not. Maybe I got friends around town, you know? And maybe I gave a couple of them copies of a letter I wrote, and they'll send those letters if I turn up missing."

"Do you really think that means anything to me? Christ! You don't deserve to be her mother."

"What is she to you, anyway?"

"A pinball," said the dark-coat man, then he laughed. "Oh, my, the expression on your face—BoBo the Dog-Faced Boy looked more intelligent. You have no idea what I'm talking about, do you?"

"You never made a whole lot of sense in all the years I've known you."

"And I fear it's prevented us from becoming closer. The heart breaks. Listen, a few weeks ago I was in Jerusalem checking out reports on a little girl who we thought might be like Leah. What happened with her is none of your business and secondary to the point of my story, anyway.

"I was walking through one of the oldest sections of the

city and admiring its ancient beauty, when I got to thinking about how Jerusalem was perceived in medieval times. Many religious groups considered it—and still *do* consider it—the center of the universe, the navel of the world where heaven and earth join. It was there at the center of the universe that God spoke to His prophets and the People of the Book. Jews come to worship at the wall of their temple near the Holy of Holies, Christians come to follow the steps of their Lord in His Final Passion, and Muslims worship at the Dome of the Rock where Mohammed received the Koran.

"In ancient times, there was a center to the old city marked by Roman crossroads that divided the city and the earth into four quadrants—the fulcrum of medieval geography. Most of the roads disappeared long ago, but to this day, at each corner of the crossroads, there still stands a Roman pillar. So I found myself wandering into the very center-within-the-center of the universe. Do you know what's there? Of all the shrines and statues, temples and rocks, symbols and what-have-you that *could* be there to mark the exact, precise center of the universe, can you guess what I found?

"A pinball parlor. Rows and rows of pinball machines. Astonishing. I laughed, I couldn't help it. Determinists think of the universe as a clockwork device. I see it as a pinball machine. Playing pinball requires total concentration, the right combination of skill and chance, an understanding and mastery of indeterminacy as the balls fly about, interacting with the bumpers and cushions. It creates an ersatz reality that integrates into the human nervous system in a remarkable way, and I realized that it was no accident that pinball machines stand at the center of the universe, because in order to know the universe we must observe it, and in the act of observation, uncontrolled and random processes are initiated into reality.

"I can see from that blank look in your eyes that I'm losing you, so I'll make it simple. Children like your daughter will someday soon become the pinballs in the machine of the universe, and whoever has them, whoever controls them, is master of the game and need not worry that the device will tilt on them."

"Man, you are *so* full of shit."

"I take back what I said about you before. You don't disgust me. I pity you too much to feel disgust."

"Feeling better now?" asked the doctor, jostling Leah's arm.

"Yes, sir," she said. "Thanks for the Twinkies. I don't get to have a lot of snacks."

"Would you like some more to take with you?"

"Yes, please."

As the doctor was putting the extra packs of Twinkies into a paper bag for her, he asked, "Tell me, Leah, do you get many headaches?"

"Sometimes."

"Are they bad?"

"Yeah. Sometimes they hurt *real* bad."

"Can you show me where they start, these headaches?"

"Sure." She put a finger on the bridge of her nose. "Right here. I get a runny nose, too. Sometimes my nose bleeds a little."

"I see," said the doctor, then reached into one of his pockets and pulled out a bottle of pills. "What you've got, Leah, is a condition called sinusitis. It's not uncommon for children of . . . for children like yourself. Don't you worry yourself. It's not too serious, if treated properly. Here, you take these pills—and *don't* let your mommy see them, all right? She'd only take them away from you."

". . . 'kay . . . ?"

"The red ones are for your headaches, all right? Take one when the pain gets real bad. The blue ones are for the infection. You should take one of those three times a day. Can you remember all that, Leah?"

"Yes, sir."

The doctor smiled and touched her face. His hand wasn't

at all like the dark-coat man's. The doctor's hand was warm and kind, like a grandpa's hand—or, rather, how Leah imagined a grandpa's hand would feel.

"You're a very pretty little girl, Leah. Has anyone told you that?"

"No, sir."

"And with the 'sir'! So polite."

"Thank you."

"I know a lot of this must be confusing for you, dear, but when we come back and take you to your birthday party next month, you'll understand everything."

"My little sister's gonna be there. The other man said so."

"And so she shall be." The doctor leaned forward, pulled Leah close, and whispered, "Your brothers might be there, as well."

Leah felt her heart skip a beat. "All of them?"

"Yes. And maybe—and you must not tell this to *anyone*— maybe your daddy will be there, too."

Leah was so excited she could barely contain herself. For all her life she'd wondered about her daddy—who he was, where he came from, what he did for a living. All she really knew was that the men drove Mommy to see Daddy whenever they took her away. And now she might maybe get to see her daddy for the first time.

In her heart, wizards, angels, and fairies danced.

"Oh, *thank you*," she said, then gave the doctor a great big hug and kissed him on the cheek. He hugged her back, and there was something sad in the way he did it, something that made Leah think of the words on Buddy's wall: *the voice in the night sky is loneliness . . .*

"You remember about the pills," said the doctor, "and about our little secret about your daddy, okay?"

"Okay," said Leah, stuffing the bottle of pills into one of her pockets and climbing out of the car, the bag of Twinkies clutched to her chest like discovered treasure. She wondered if Buddy liked Twinkies, if he'd ever had them, and looked forward to sharing them with her best-best friend in the whole world.

Mommy grabbed Leah's arm and they ran out of the alley. The only sound Leah could hear now was the laughter of the dark-coat man. It bounced off the alley walls, ugly and mean, coming after her and Mommy like some crazy junkyard dog. The sound wailed and roared in the slick darkness of the rain-dampened streets, and under the laughter Leah could hear her little sister starting to cry and suddenly she felt awful, like she'd just run over a bird with her bike. She felt like a killer. She didn't want to leave her sister in the alley with the dark-coat man. The alley was cold and wet and dark and smelled like somebody threw up.

"Mommy, please go and get her back."

"Be quiet."

"Please? She's crying—hear? She misses us and—"

"I said *shut up!*" screamed her mother, slapping Leah hard across the face. "Shut your miserable little mouth, goddammit, or I swear I'll . . . I'll let Jewel take you up to his room next time!"

Leah went rigid with fear. Jewel was the short little one-eyed man Mommy always bought her needle-stuff from. He was old and wrinkly and sweated all the time and was always trying to touch Leah whenever he saw her. "Young and tasty," he said. "I like 'em when they're young and tasty." Leah didn't know what Jewel wanted to do with her, but she knew it probably wasn't very nice because Jewel had a little girl named Denise who was with him all the time, and she always had bruises and cuts on her face and over her body and sometimes burn marks around her wrists, and she never said anything whenever Leah talked to her, and her eyes were always staring out at something only she seemed able to see, and whatever it was she saw made her empty.

"Oh, no, please Mommy," Leah pleaded, "don't do that!"

"Then be quiet. You've caused me enough trouble as it is."

Leah's face twisted into a tight, hard, painful knot, and she couldn't stop the tears from coming then. She thought that her mommy loved her and would never do something like that. But maybe—

—you have about as much love in your heart for that child as I do for you—

—Mommy only said that because she felt bad about the baby. Leah hoped so but she couldn't ask her mother because Mommy would only get madder, so she decided to wait and tell Buddy about it tonight after Mommy did her needle-thing and rolled her eyes and shook and fell asleep sort of. Buddy would say the right things to make her understand and make it all better.

Leah was glad that Mommy didn't know about Buddy and his secret Rusty Room underneath the warehouse basement.

Buddy didn't like her mother. Not one little bit.

Walking through the cold darkness with her mother, Leah remembered more of the words on the Rusty Room's walls:

> *and where do i live?*
> *in the alleys behind the*
> *cans*
> *abandonment my blanket*
> *no way to slough the fever*
>
> *and where do i live?*
> *in songs unheard*
> *in the flutter of bound wings that*
> *don't know they're bound*
> *where?*
> *somewhere else*
> *not here*
>
> *within the cell, life is long, life is hard,*
> *within the cell, life is hard*
>
> *who will take me?*

chapter
4OUR

Jeane Meara, inside the air vent tunnel near the
Archives' loading docks on Seventh Street, was
placing the last of the pyrolysate samples into the
air-tight containers she'd brought along. True to his
word, Travis's pass had allowed her access to any area
of the site she wanted. Her supervisor had also made
good on his promise to have Fire Marshal Glenn pulled
from the scene. Jeane had been left alone for the last
six hours to gather samples and run tests to her
heart's content.

The vapor emissions in the tunnel were still rather
strong, so she had opted, somewhat reluctantly, to
wear a gas mask as well as a protective helmet. At
least the helmet came equipped with a high-wattage,
battery-operated lantern attached over the rim, so it
was easy for her to see what lay in front of her as she
made her way deeper into the tunnel.

About a hundred and fifty yards down the rubble

and debris formed a solid wall that would have to be blasted open, and the munitions experts on site wouldn't get clearance for that until the rest of the structure was tested for stress levels and deemed capable of withstanding another, albeit smaller, explosion.

Still, the emission readings had gone off the chart when Jeane had come to the wall of rubble. That, combined with the heaviness of pyrolysate samples that covered the roof and walls of the tunnel, confirmed in her mind that the blast had originated deep in the bowels of the building. The only thing that troubled her at the moment was the inconsistency between the Archives' blueprints and the flame- and flashover patterns she'd measured in this tunnel. In order for the flames to have formed these patterns—not to mention the explosion being able to blow so much debris so far—the blast would have to have started well beyond two hundred feet below the building's basement. Okay, fine, that only strengthened her volcano theory, but the flash- and flameover patterns were so focused that the flames would have to have had room to roll and expand.

That meant that beyond this wall of rubble and debris, there had to be some sort of subbasement not shown on the official blueprints.

She wasn't too surprised her. In D.C., every building had its "secret" rooms. What bothered her was knowing that any secret storage space was going to require a higher security clearance in order to gain access. Red tape and more of the Bureaucratic Cha-Cha-Cha. Just ducky.

She checked her watch and saw that it was nearly midnight. Time to break for a very late dinner before continuing. She began packing up her lab equipment and samples, very pleased with herself that she'd managed to accumulate so much hard evidence in so short a time—as she knew she'd be able to do if left alone—and was making a last check of the area when the light from her helmet flashed over something that caught her attention.

About six feet to her left, half buried in rubble but close enough to the surface that its door could still be seen, a small wall safe lay in the wreckage. Never one to let a curiosity go ignored, Jeane walked over and slowly began to dig the safe from the rubble.

As it turned out, there was no need. Its door had been blown loose by the explosion.

She examined the burn patterns on its sides and quickly concluded that this safe had not only not been installed in a wall but that it had been blown to this spot by the explosion.

So let's see what sort of secrets they're hiding down here, she thought, and pulled open the door.

The safe held only one eleven-inch by seventeen-inch fire-proof box. The keys to the lock were taped to the back of the safe. Leah unlocked the box and opened it.

Inside was a single file, rather thick, that bore the NASA logo on its front above the stapled sign-out sheets.

It was also stamped **TOP SECRET**.

Examining the names and offices listed on the sign-out sheets, she discovered that the contents of this file had passed through the hands of officials from the Pentagon, dozens of members of the Joint Chiefs—past and present—several notable scientists, and no fewer than four past presidents.

"Jesus," she whispered to herself. "What don't they want anyone to see?"

She opened the file, looked at the first three of the twenty-one photographs, and had her answer.

All three photographs were in rich, clear, vibrant color—the kind that could only have resulted from the use of high-end digital equipment.

The first photograph was one she'd seen reproduced on television and in magazines many times, a picture taken in the back yard of a home in Trenton, New Jersey in 1962. It showed a large disc-shaped object hovering over the trees. The only difference between this photograph and its public reproductions was that here, the symbols engraved on the craft's hull were clearly visible. There was a symbol that looked like a variation of the double-helix, another that resembled a pair of conch shells, and a third in which four overlapping circles formed a fifth in the center.

"What the . . . ?"

The second picture was an aerial photograph. The words **Tibet/Bhutan Border: Monastery of Inner Light** were typed onto a white label that had been pasted in the corner. The photograph clearly showed Air Force One flying just below a craft similar to that in the first picture. That in itself was enough to unnerve Jeane, but it was the mountain peaks behind the crafts that succeeded in sending chills down her spine.

They were covered in tall, lithe, large-headed beings who bore only the most passing resemblance to anything human. They stood like sentries, staring upward. Even from as great a distance as this photograph had been taken, their large, black, almond-shaped eyes could be seen.

Behind them, only partially visible because of the low cloud formations that were moving in, was a device the likes of which Jeane had never seen before. Not a craft of any kind, it looked like a series of towers and satellites constructed from bones . . . only the bones were made of glass, or a glasslike material. Inside this device she could make out a fantastic, complex network of metallic strands and what looked like multicolored ice sculptures.

How is this so clear? she wondered. She knew she shouldn't be able to make out so much detail.

She turned the photograph over and read the words written on the back: **A gift from the Greys to the people of Earth: The Frozen Museum of Central Motion**.

Jeane then looked at the third photograph.

Again, this one was marked **Tibet/Bhutan Border: Monastery of Inner Light.** It showed three incredible beings standing at the organic-looking base of the bone-glass device. Snow swirled around them, but not enough to hide any of their features. Large, oval-shaped heads with black-almond eyes on tall, lithe bodies. Arms that were so long they nearly touched the ground. Hands with seven fingers of varying lengths, the shortest of which—in the place where a human being had a thumb—was at least six inches long.

The tallest and oldest-looking of these beings stood a bit farther front than the other two. Next to him, dressed in heavy mountain clothing, his face encircled by the thick fur that rimmed the edge of the jacket's hood, smiling as if this were the greatest moment not only of his life but in the history of the human race, President John F. Kennedy was looking directly into the camera as his small, puny hand was gripped by the gigantic hand of the miraculous being that stood next to him, towering over the President.

There were other men in the background but Jeane didn't bother concentrating on their faces. She opened her side-pack and removed her hand-sized digital camera and began taking pictures of the photographs. The light from her helmet would help bring out the colors, which was good. The camera itself employed a hybrid of infrared and Starlight technology which, while ensuring the pictures would be sharp and clear, would have developed in simple sepia tones had there not been another source of light.

This had to be some kind of joke. Okay, so they'd stored this stuff down here for God only knew how long, but didn't the government investigate—officially or otherwise—all of those lame-brained UFO reports? And if there was someone with the know-how and technology to doctor up photos like *these* in 1962 . . . it would make sense that someone High Up might take a passing interest.

This all suddenly seemed a bit silly to her, but her curiosity was piqued, nonetheless.

Besides, it might give her a good story to tell someday. It would at least provide some private chuckles, and after the day she'd had, a few private laughs would come in handy.

Jeane took two pictures of each photograph for a total of forty-two. She set her camera down next to the safe in the rubble, and was preparing to put the photographs back in the file when a hand came over her shoulder and snatched the pictures away.

She jumped to her feet and whirled around, kicking up dust and knocking her camera into a crack in the rubble around the safe.

Three men stood before her. All of them wore long black coats and sported equally dark sunglasses.

"Who the hell are you?" she shouted. Inside the confines of the gas mask, the sound of her voice became an ice pick in her ears.

The man in the middle snapped his fingers. The man who had taken the photos from Jeane handed them to the man in the middle.

"Agent Meara, I presume?" he said.

"Identify yourselves," she said, reaching under her coat for her 9mm.

The other two men produced Uzis and pressed the business ends into each of her sides.

Jeane froze.

"Well, well, well," said Middle Man. He held up the photo of Kennedy and the creature. "We should have done this first. I think she would have liked to've seen a picture of her Daddy." He smiled then. The expression writhed across his face like a worm squirming on a summer sidewalk under a magnifying glass.

"What do you want?" asked Jeane, the words crawling out of her throat as if they were afraid of the night.

"A pinball machine that doesn't tilt," said Middle Man. Then, to the others, "Bring her."

They began to drag Jeane out of the tunnel.

None of them made a move to retrieve her camera.

That was something, at least.

"By the way, Agent Meara," said Middle Man. "If you make any noise or in any way attempt to break free, we will not hesitate to kill you. It's not something I like, but . . . there it is."

Jeane cooperated.

What else could she do?

They loaded her into the back of a long black sedan. A grey-haired man dressed like a doctor was waiting there. He stuck a needle into Jeane's arm and sank the plunger. She was unconscious before the last of the liquid entered her system.

The car drove away.

For several minutes, there was no movement, then the small Asian man with the intense blue eyes moved from behind a large pile of rubble and stared in the direction of the sedan. He moved quickly and silently across the loading dock, pausing only a moment by Jeane's abandoned car to look inside.

He pulled a gas mask from the pocket of his coat and headed into the tunnel.

Morning.

Leah smiled as Chief Wetbrain drew a chalk circle around himself, scooted into its center—he had to scoot everywhere because he didn't have any legs—and started playing his saxophone. Leah thought it was too bad that people called him Chief Wetbrain (she did it, too, and always felt bad afterward) because it was such an ugly name and they only used it because he got drunk a lot on account of the pain in his leg stumps. His real name was Jimmy Nighteagle, and Leah wished he'd tell more people to call him that. It was the name of a king, and that's what Jimmy was in her eyes.

Mommy was down the street at Jewel's apartment buying her needle-stuff and had said it was okay for Leah to go visit with her friends. Leah liked listening to Jimmy play his saxophone. His music made her feel less scared and sometimes, if she closed her eyes and

listened real hard the way Buddy had taught her, she could
hear the unspoken words in Jimmy's songs: *Who will take me?*
I don't belong here.

(. . . someone come . . .)

Listening the way Buddy had taught her, she heard Jimmy's
song cry out a tale composed of notes that became Kachinas
and Crow Mothers and They Who Breathed the Land Into
Being. She heard it turn round in the breeze and catch raindrops
that held his memories of nights on the plains, soaring above
the heads of the people as they passed, sprinkling them with
hints of things he still knew and they had long ago forgotten,
secrets of the Earth and time hidden in the silences between the
notes. A breath, a beat, songs of the Elders and their tales of
the Fiery-Sky Ones, another breath, another beat, and the notes
multiplied like the birds of the sky after solstice, power,
strength, and courage in his grip as he pulled the sax closer to
his ruined body, breathing his soul into the reeds like a fine
medicine man should—and over there, a glint in a passing pair
of eyes, yes, as the song banked on the winds and came back to
him, more than it was before, making him feel that he was back
among his people again, back where he should have been all
along, grace covering him like tree-fallen leaves in autumn, so
good, yes, I am ready. The time is upon me to fly.

Jimmy stopped playing as a young man in a three-piece
suit walked by and threw some change into a tin cup sitting
between his stumps. Jimmy smiled and lifted his hat to the
young man in thanks, then looked into the cup.

"*Sokelas!*" he said, taking out the three quarters and jin-
gling them in his hand. "And my folks used to worry about me
making a living as a jazz musician." He looked at Leah, then
gave her one of the coins. "That's just for being a pretty sight
to these tired eyes."

Leah reached into her pocket and took out one of the coins
from Buddy's Ice Bank money and gave it to Jimmy.

"*Another* one?" he said, taking the coin in his hands and
examining it. "Where do you find these?"

"I got a secret place I get 'em from."

"Really? Secret, eh?" He looked at the front of the coin, then the back, then slipped it into his pocket. "It looks different than the one you gave to Cain."

"It is. All of 'em are different."

Leah didn't want to talk about it any more. Buddy's Ice Bank was down in the Rusty Room, and she knew it was supposed to be a Big Secret between them. Buddy had told her it was all right to take out a few coins at a time—which was all Leah could handle, because they were always so cold when they came out. Buddy said she should find people who were nice to her—"worthy" was the word he used, but she figured he meant people who were nice to her—and pass the coins along to them as gifts.

She wanted to ask him why but figured he'd tell her when he felt like it. They were friends, after all.

Jimmy stretched his back and let fly with a whopper of a yawn.

"How come you're tired?" asked Leah.

"*How come I'm—?* I'm sorry, I didn't mean to snap like that."

"S'okay."

"No, it isn't," said Jimmy, taking hold of her hand. "I'm tired because I've been having too many bad dreams lately. I'm tired because I feel more and more like *eceyanunia*—a fool—every day. I'm tired because no one answers the music."

He pulled her a little closer, putting his arm around her waist. Leah liked it when Jimmy hugged her. It wasn't at all like when Jewel touched her—moist and chilly and sick-making. Jimmy's hugs were gentle and kind and made her feel loved.

"There was a time, Leah, before I left to be educated in the white schools, when I would play my music at night under the stars and know that it would be heard by *Matotipila*, would linger in the heart of *Wanagitacanku*, answered by *Tayamni*, but not here, not in the city. There's too much noise, too much anger and violence, and the buildings block out the heavens. Sometimes I find myself wondering if the heavens are still really there." He shook his head. "Does any of this make sense to you?"

"Uh-huh, some."

"I like you very much, Leah. You're a good friend and I will miss you when I'm gone."

"You're not leaving, are you?"

"Oh, not right now, probably not for a while, but I've been thinking about it for a long time. Especially since the dreams started."

"What kind of dreams? What happens in them?"

Jimmy laughed but there was no humor in it. "You see, that's the thing, I can't really say what happens because I don't know, exactly. It's not so much what happens in them, anyway, as it is . . . the impression they leave when I wake up. I feel like I don't belong here, but I can't go back home because I don't belong there anymore, either. Not that they'd have me, and if they wouldn't, then . . . who will take me?" He reached out and massaged one of his stumps. "Get drunk and pass out under one trailer, have it back over you and crush your legs— do this once, and people think you're incompetent."

Leah giggled.

"Ah, good girl," said Jimmy. "There was a time when you wouldn't've realized I was making a joke."

"But it was only half a joke. It was still funny, though."

"I'm glad you liked it. I like hearing you laugh. It's a lovely sound. I wish you made it more often."

"I know. Buddy says that I—" She gasped, then covered her mouth with her hands, eyes wide. Oh, God! She'd never mentioned Buddy to anyone before and now.

"Buddy," whispered Jimmy. "So that's his name? In my dream he was called *Peye'wik*: It-Is-Approaching."

Slowly, Leah pulled her hands away from her mouth. "You know about Buddy?"

Jimmy reached into one of his pockets and took out a folded piece of paper that he handed to Leah. "There was one image from the dreams that I remembered early on, and I drew it on that paper. Take a look and tell me if those're—tell me if it looks familiar to you. "

Leah unfolded the piece of paper. Most of it was blank, except for two large, dark, slanted, opposing almond-shapes in the middle. "Buddy's eyes," she said.

" 'Someone come,' " said Jimmy.

"Wh-what?"

" 'Someone come.' Buddy wrote those words on a wall somewhere, didn't he?"

"Uh-huh."

"He's very lonely, isn't he, your Buddy?"

"I guess. But with him it's like . . . it's like with Denise, that girl who lives with Jewel?"

Jimmy closed his eyes and nodded his head. "A Hollow House. More pain than person. *Goddamn* that little pervert."

"With Buddy, it's like he's so lonely he don't even know it."

"Oh, I doubt that," said Jimmy. "I think he knows exactly how lonely he is. He's just like us, Leah. He should be somewhere else."

Just then Merc came around the corner pulling something behind him that made a funny *thunka-thunka-shisk! thunka-thunka-shisk!* noise. It was an orange crate nailed to a set of planks that were supported by roller-skate wheels.

"Oh, *man*," said Merc, coming to a stop next to them. "I read this article in the science section of the paper yesterday about that damn wooly mammoth they found up north a couple weeks ago—you know, the one that was almost completely preserved? Anyway, these science dudes, they were makin' all this brouhaha over the buttercups that were in the thing's mouth. Seems these buttercups were as totally preserved as the mammoth, right? But what makes everything so righteously fu—oops, sorry, Leah, gotta learn to watch my mouth—what makes it all really weird, right, is that buttercups evidently release some kind of chemical into your system when you eat them that acts like a natural anti-freeze, y'dig? The mammoth had itself a bellyful of buttercups, so they're saying that's why it was so well preserved, but—whoa, almost lost track of where I's going with this—but the thing is, butter-cups can only grow in a moist, warm climate, like around seventy-eight degrees or so, and these buttercups in the mammoth's belly, they weren't dehydrated, and neither was the mammoth. You know what that means? That means in order for the mammoth to've been preserved so well and without dehydration, the temperature had to've dropped from around eighty degrees to something like three-hundred *below zero* in a matter of seconds! And these science wizards, they got no idea what happened, let alone how it could've hap-pened, and if they can't speculate on what happened, then they got no way of being able to predict if or when it might happen again. Man, I tell you, that *messed up* my breakfast big time! Knowing that at any given second we could all be slammed into the fu—uh, friggin' deep freeze and there's nothing we can do about it. It could all be over"—he snapped his fingers—"like that, and I spent ten minutes trying to decide what to wear today. Not that I got what you'd call an *ex-sten-sive* wardrobe. That game on your head, or what?"

"Do you ever just say 'hello'?" asked Jimmy.

"Uh, yeah, right. Forgettin' my manners left and right today. Hello."

"What'cha got there?" said Leah, pointing at the orange crate.

"Huh? Oh, this?" He stood back and gestured with his arms like a model at an automobile show. "This here's the new Chiefmobile, first one off the line."

Jimmy stared. "You . . . you made this for me?"

"I get kinda tired of watching you do the Stumpy Dance when you walk. Them little short steps give me a pain. Takes forever to get anywhere with you. I figure this way, you hop in the Chiefmobile and we'll be burnin' up pavement. Do wonders for clearing up my schedule. So, you like it?"

Jimmy shrugged but gave Leah a quick wink and said, "It's all right, if you like that sort of thing."

"That sort of thing? I been digging through dumpsters for the last two weeks trying to find four sets of wheels that're all the same size and all you got to say is, 'If you like that sort of thing'? Talk about your ingrates. Here we got you *trans-portation*, Chief. You hear what I'm saying? Take your act on the road. Make 'em Big Wampum . . . go truckin' on down that Happy Trail in style."

"It is perhaps one of the ten most wondrous sights I have ever beheld in all my life. Why, in all the history of history itself, there has never been a more resplendent orange crate chariot. I think I'm safe in saying that, yes."

Merc cocked his head to one side as if trying to decide if Jimmy was yanking his chain or not, then gave a quick nod. "Well, that's more like it. Man needs to know his labors're appreciated."

"Very much," said Jimmy, reaching out and patting the side of Merc's leg. "Very much. Thank you."

Merc knelt down and clapped Jimmy on the shoulder. "No *hombre* of mine's gonna be stumpin' round and giving himself more pain."

The two of them looked at one another for a moment.

In the silence, Leah heard the song of two hearts: friendship.

She ran over and gave Merc a big hug and kiss. She couldn't help it.

"What's that for?" asked Merc.

" 'Cause you're a sweetie."

"Uh-oh, this's starting to get too warm and fuzzy for me—but thanks for the hug and smoochie, darlin'. Nice to know the Merc's still got it for the ladies. Speaking of—you seen Randi around here today, Chief?"

"No, but I heard she's selling—uh, I heard she's *singing* at some club in the East End."

"Singing?" Merc looked from Jimmy to Leah, then back to Jimmy again. "Oh, yeah, right. I forgot about her, uh, *singing* engagement."

"I know what a hooker is," said Leah. "You don't have to talk around me like I'm stupid or something."

Jimmy and Merc burst out laughing.

"Here I thought we were being so *co-vert,*" said Merc.

"It's okay," said Leah. "I tell everybody that Randi's a singer so they won't know."

"Well, that's darned thoughtful of you." Merc touched the side of her face. "Where's your mom today? No, wait, don't tell me." He looked at Jimmy. "Jewel's place?"

Jimmy nodded.

"Jeez Louise." He looked back at Leah. "You two still squattin' in that warehouse down by the fish market?"

"Uh-huh. It's not too bad there."

"She's got no business keeping you in a place like that and usin' her money to buy—"

"*Merc,*" said Jimmy; a warning.

"I can't help it," shouted Merc, rising to his feet. "Shit, when I was workin' over in Panama a couple years ago, we'd been hired to blow a worthless piece of crap like Jewel right out of his socks. Him, and about forty of his boys. I enjoyed it a little too much, y'know? Won't do for a merc to start takin' sides. That's how come I got out."

"I know," said Jimmy.

Merc smiled—and it wasn't a nice smile. "Still got me a little firepower." He looked around, nervous, then pulled open one side of his jacket to reveal a large silver 9mm semiautomatic tucked into the waist of his pants.

"Oh, great," said Jimmy, "look at this. *Son of The Equalizer*—close your coat, for chrissakes. People will think you're flashing us."

"Hey, if I decided to whip out the man-meat," said Merc, closing his coat, "you'd *know* you been flashed. Didn't mean to shock you, Leah."

"You didn't."

Jimmy laughed.

Merc pulled himself up straight. "Gettin' off the point here a bit, ain't we? I'd just love to dust our little Jewel. 'Bout the only way we'd ever get Denise away from him. And you know, don't you, Chief, that it's gotta be us. Nobody else gives a rat's ass. We're just partial people to all of them, and you don't pay no attention to a partial person."

"My father had a term for us," said Jimmy. "He called people like us 'Hollow Houses.' We are the Unbelonging—vessels with homeless spirits."

"We don't belong here," said Merc.

"We should be somewhere else," whispered Jimmy.

And Leah thought: *Someone come.*

"Well, Darlin'," said Merc, laying a hand on top of Leah's head, "I imagine your mom's gonna be havin' herself a private little party tonight. Maybe Jimmy and me—bet'cha didn't think I knew your real name, did'ya, Jimmy?—maybe the two of us'll cruise on by in the Chiefmobile later and see how you're doing. Can't never tell how a person's gonna act after they shoot that crap in their veins." He saw something behind them, then rolled his eyes. "Speaking of . . ."

"Watch it, Merc," said Jimmy. "I'm serious."

"Yeah, well, if old King-Fu was around, I'd ask him to introduce the business end of a roundhouse kick to the side of her skull."

"*Merc,*" whispered Jimmy, the threat strong in his voice.

"Leah!" shouted Mommy as she came around the corner a few yards away, trying to sound nice and almost making it. "C'mon, hon. Time to get something to eat."

"Bitch's gonna buy her daughter some real *food?*" whispered Merc to Jimmy. "Sorry state, when junkies start thinking of others. Almost enough to make you believe there's a God."

"Put a sock in it, will you?" said Jimmy.

Mommy came up behind Leah and grabbed her arm. "Say good-bye to your friends, hon. You can maybe come back tomorrow."

"How's Jewel doing?" said Merc.

"Fine," snapped Mommy. "He said to send his regards."

"I'll bet," muttered Jimmy.

"You see Denise?" asked Leah.

"Oh, she, uh . . . she wasn't feeling too well today, hon. Jewel was making her stay in bed."

Jimmy snorted a nasty laugh. "What a tactful way to put it."

Mommy pushed Leah behind her. "All right, assholes, you've had your fun. I don't need this from the likes of you. Nice crate, by the way."

"That's the Chiefmobile, Mommy!"

"It's a goddamned orange crate, for hauling garbage." And she turned around and pulled Leah along.

Leah managed to turn around and wave at Jimmy and Merc. They waved back but didn't look very happy.

As they got to the corner, Leah looked over at Jewel's building and saw Denise standing at her window. She looked pale and empty and sad. The lower half of the window was foggy with steam, and Denise was drawing patterns in the condensation with her finger. When she finished her drawing, she knelt down and looked out through the two opposing almond-shapes.

Below the almonds, she'd written: *Someone come.*

Leah wanted to touch her, to tell Denise that she'd be her friend.

Buddy would like Denise. Merc and Jimmy and Cain, too.

Partial people. Hollow Houses.

"Who will take me?" Leah whispered.

"*What?*" snapped Mommy.

"Nothin'."

"Christ Almighty. Freakin' *starchild*. Airhead's more like it."

"I'm sorry, Mommy."

"Not half as much as I am. C'mon. I suppose we should get you something to eat. Just eat it quick. I need to get back."

"Yes, Mommy."

chapter
6 I X

The sharp glow of a penlight shone into McCain's right eye, then his left, and at last he blinked and pulled in a deep breath, feeling the slick pressure of the tube in his nose running all the way down into his stomach.

The doctor made a last check of McCain's pupils with his penlight, then clicked it off and slipped it back into his pocket.

"Nice of you to join us," he said, taking McCain's pulse.

McCain tried to speak but found that his throat tissue had been replaced with sandpaper. He glanced to the doctor's left and saw an IV stand that held at least three clear plastic bags, two of which were emptying into him and one that was filling with a dark semi-liquid that was being drawn from his stomach.

"Here," said the doctor, picking up a cup of crushed ice and holding it to McCain's lips. "Don't swallow, all right? Just let the ice lay in your mouth and melt."

It took McCain three more helpings to empty the cup and allow the blissfully cool chips to coat his throat enough to summon a whisper, but when at last he was able to dredge up a semblance of his voice, he touched the doctor's hand and said, ". . . ong?"

"What was that?"

". . . how . . . long . . . ?"

"Close enough to three days to call it. Do me a favor and look at my finger. That's right. Now follow it with your eyes—no, don't move your head, okay? Just your eyes. There you go . . . now over here . . . now back. One more time. There you go. Good." He looked over his shoulder at someone McCain couldn't see and said, "His tracking is fine, pupils equal and reactive." He looked at McCain again. "Now, squeeze my hand. Very good. Now with your left, squeeze. Excellent." He went to the foot of the bed and pulled back the sheet, then removed a tongue depressor from his pocket and ran it up the inside of McCain's left foot. "Can you feel that?"

". . . tickles . . ."

"It's supposed to. What about your right foot? Feel that?"

McCain looked down and saw the metal brace encircling his right leg. ". . . no . . ."

"That's because I cheated and didn't do anything. How about now?"

"Tickles."

He put the sheet back, then stood next to McCain. "Can you tell me your name?"

". . . gotta be . . . kidding . . ."

"Yes, I'm famous throughout the institute for my Noel Coward-like wit. Dr. Nakami hires me to entertain at his parties, so I'll milk this gag for all it's worth and ask you again: Do you know your name?"

"McCain." He swallowed painfully. "Michael McCain."

"Do you know what day it is?"

"Not really—no, wait . . . if I've been out for three days,

then it has to be . . . Thursday?"

"Wednesday, actually, but a good try. Do you know what year it is?"

"Two thousand."

"Do you know where you are?"

"Making a cameo in the new *Alien Autopsy* sequel?"

"He's fine," said the doctor, patting McCain's shoulder, then checking the dressing on the head wound. "For the record, though, you're in a mobile emergency medical facility used exclusively for Hoffman Institute field agents who are injured in the line of duty. Don't you feel special now?"

"I guess . . . ?"

"We gotta stop meeting like this or people are going to talk." The doctor made a notation on the chart, then said, "Not too long, all right? He needs his rest."

The doctor left the room and a small Asian man with intense blue eyes came up beside McCain's bed. "It's good to see you again, Michael."

McCain looked at the man and tried to recall where he'd seen him before. "Do I know you?" he asked.

The man shrugged. "You did, once, long ago."

McCain caught a whiff of jasmine incense clinging to the man's clothes—

—and in a rush it all came back to him, those summer and autumn afternoons when he was a child and Mom and Dad would get all excited because McCain's uncle was coming to visit—McCain knew that the man wasn't really his uncle, just a friend of the family, but everyone called him "Uncle"—and when he showed up he'd be dressed in simple clothes that smelled of jasmine, and he'd play with young Michael in the back yard, tossing him high and catching him, making him squeal with gleeful laughter, and Michael would always cry "Again! Again!" and his uncle would grin as the sunlight made glissandos of light over his bald head and his bright blue eyes would sparkle, then he'd toss Michael even higher, so high he thought he might sprout wings and fly away, then it was

"Again! Again!" and higher and higher, the laughter so strong and sweet he thought it would never end—

—"Again?" said McCain. "UncleAgain?" He said it all as one word because that's how he'd said it as a child.

"I didn't think you'd remember me," said the small man, taking hold of McCain's hand and squeezing it with deep affection. "My name is Ngan Song Kun'dren. Your parents used to call me simply 'Ngan.' You couldn't pronounce it, so 'Ngan' became—"

"—Again." McCain smiled and pulled Ngan down. "UncleAgain."

The two men embraced, then Ngan pulled back and brushed some hair from McCain's face.

"You were very lucky, Michael. You suffered only a broken leg, three fractured ribs, a dislocated shoulder, and several cuts to your face and torso."

"What the hell happened in there?"

"A terrible explosion."

"Is there such a thing as a 'wonderful' explosion? Never mind." He tried recalling some of the details of the events moments before the blast but couldn't. He blanched and asked, "Terrorists?"

Ngan shook his head. "No. Something much more dangerous. You need to rest so I cannot explain all of it now, but you have to understand this much: we have very little time. You and I must work together."

"What's happening?"

Ngan stared off to the side as if considering something, then looked directly into McCain's eyes. "Have you ever heard anyone connected with the institute use the phrase 'Dark Matter'?"

"Yes. I always assumed that it referred to secret information of a dangerous nature . . . or something like that. You know, a code phrase."

Ngan thought about something for a moment, then said, "We live in a world where suspicion has displaced trust, where belief in the strange and unexplainable is replacing belief in the normal. When pressed, most will laugh off such claims or at least ignore the greater implications of such beliefs, but have you ever noticed, Michael, that every now and then something occurs that cannot be easily explained by governments or scientists? Something that should not have happened the way it did or surely cannot mean what it seems to suggest? It is precisely at those moments that the facade of reality drops away and we cannot help but wonder if it's all true. What if all of the so-called crackpots are right? What if the unknown, the terrifying, the strange and unexplainable is all around us? And what if it's getting worse?

"Ghosts, UFOs, ancient creatures seen swimming through Scottish lakes, all of them are part of the Dark Matter, Michael. All are part of the world of the unknown. And all of them are components of the Dark Tide that is rising in the world. Are you familiar with any Native American mythology?"

"No."

"Many Native American clans passed down stories of a race of beings who were monstrous gods who existed before the beginning of time. According to these myths, these gods— so horrible to look upon that a man's mind would crumble from a simple glimpse—co-exist with us. In this space, at this time, we are separated from them only by a scrim of perception. Lift that scrim, and these gods will consume us, will move back into this layer of reality and claim the world as their own once again."

Ngan leaned close to McCain. "These myths are true, Michael. These creatures, these gods, do exist with us. They're in this room right now. All that protects us from their wrath is that simple, thin scrim of perception. That scrim is a piece of Dark Matter. Do you understand?"

"Uh . . . yes . . ."

"Do you believe what I am telling you?"

"I don't know."

Ngan gripped McCain's hand. "When I was a child being

raised by the Kha-glor monks at the Monastery of Inner Light, the Ascended Masters there taught me the sacred art of *rjes su shes pa'i bzod pa*—what is commonly referred to as 'astral projection.' I am able to free my mind and spirit from this shell called a body and move between worlds, Michael—and there are worlds within worlds within worlds that you pass through every day. Only the scrim of perception separates you from them.

"I am going to show you something now, Michael. I need you to open your mind to all possibilities, all right? There is not much time, I fear, so I have no choice but to show this to you. Can you deal with it?"

"I don't know, I . . ."

Ngan smiled. "When you were a child and I used to toss you into the air in your back yard, did I ever once drop you?"

"No."

"Then believe me when I tell you, I will not drop you now. Close you eyes. There. Now come with me, Michael, just for a moment, beyond the scrim. . . ."

It happened in the moment between McCain's closing his eyes then opening them again for just a second—for one terrible second in which he feared he'd be forever frozen. The pain in the back of his head came snarling forward, turning every muscle in his body to concrete and gluing his eyelids open, and he saw Ngan *alter*. Suddenly UncleAgain's eyes bulged forward and outward like an insect's, far too large for his head, too large for any human head, and McCain stared in horror at those inhuman almond eyes following his every move, their deep blackness filled not only with coldness but something more underneath, something he dared not try to identify because it would mean staring into them, and he knew if he did that he'd be swallowed in their gaze and spend the rest of time as a prisoner screaming behind them, trapped, pounding his fists against the inner tissue, a child sent away to summer camp pressing his face against the rear window of the school bus as the thing took off while Mommy and Daddy grew smaller and smaller as he was spirited away into the horrifying Unknown where no friends waited—

—but it didn't end there. Suddenly these creatures were all around him, slipping out of the walls like sentient bas-relief sculptures and filling the room. Behind them were other creatures moving from behind other scrims of perception, some fantastic, some too horrible for McCain to look upon. He turned away from them and saw only blackness and stars and the deep country of empty space, as if he were looking through the observation portal of a space shuttle. The view from here told him that he was light-centuries from Earth so don't bother trying to deny it. He couldn't even find any of the familiar constellations that, from the beginning of history, had been friends and compasses to humankind. He sensed for a terrifying moment that the stars blazing around him had never before been seen by the unaided human eye. Most of them were concentrated in a glowing belt, broken here and there by ebony bands of obscuring cosmic dust. He wondered if he weren't being given a glimpse of the center of someone's interior galaxy—perhaps even his own—whose true form lay only in the prehistoric depths of the unconscious, but that was bullshit because everything within and without told him that he was *physically* disconnected, so inconceivably removed from the Solar System that it mattered not a tinker's damn if he were exploring his own interior cosmos or one that had never been glimpsed by even the most powerful of radio telescopes—

—and all of the creatures moved back into his line of sight, merging, bleeding into one another, *melting* into one another, becoming both Here and There, Everything and Nothing, Within and Without, and in a blink McCain found himself staring into the center of a falling light, catching glimpses of rock formations and stalactites and fissures in stone and almost turned away for fear of what he sensed he might see, then the light bounced off a cluster of stones somewhere and spun sideways—

—and for a moment that threatened to sear his mind forever

he saw It, he stared down on part of the slumbering form of a god or monster, and seeing a section of Its face he screamed within himself as he'd never before screamed. No nightmare, no titan from storybooks, no grief, no euphoria, no imagined childhood bogeyman could have prepared him for facing something this sacred, for sacred it must have been, as anything so mythic and extreme and unimaginable must be sacred. It was both terrifying and compelling, a thing beyond All Things, a being above All Beings, beyond love and bliss or their sum, beyond grief and violence or their total, beyond grace and prayer or their cumulative effects on the psyche, beyond even the place in humankind's unconscious where the monstrous and depraved joined hands with the majestic and beautiful to begin the dance, one which ended with physical evil and moral goodness forever intertwined like the strands of a double helix encoded into the DNA of the universe, and, finally, beyond the capability of McCain's mind to comprehend and catalogue its hideous grandeur. He tried to force himself to close his eyes, to blank every detail of the sight from his memory and lock it away and bury it so he'd never have to look at it again, but he could not look away—

—it snaked out one shiny, thick, grotesque tentacle and ran the tip down the side of McCain's face, leaving a trail of something cold, thick, and gelatinous on his flesh—

—and in an instant it was over. Ngan pulled his hand from McCain's and the hospital room returned in slow but strong degrees. This wall. That chair. This bed. This breath. This moment.

When McCain was at last able to fully focus his eyes again, he saw that Ngan was shaking.

"Are you all right?" he croaked.

Ngan nodded his head, then exhaled a slow, staggered breath. "And you saw only a fraction of it."

McCain shuddered. "You can't mean it was all real?"

"Touch your cheek."

McCain did. He felt the slick, cold, gelatinous trail. When

he pulled his hand away, his fingers glistened with it. "Oh, God. . . ."

Ngan removed a handkerchief from his pocket and cleaned McCain's hand and face. "Do you believe me, Michael?"

"Yes." There was no hesitation, no doubt, no suspicion.

"The world as you knew it is lost to you forever now," said Ngan. "But that is how it needs to be. You have been touched by Dark Matter, my dear friend, and it is now your duty to help us protect the scrims of perception."

Ngan reached into his pocket and removed a clear plastic bag. Inside it were the three coins that McCain had discovered inside the black medical bag. He reached into another pocket and brought out a fourth coin.

"This was given to me by a little girl I met while living on the streets of this city," said Ngan. "It is of the same nature as those in the bag. She has given other . . . 'coins,' we'll call them, to several other people. I know this child, and I can find her, but we have to find the people to whom she's given the other coins before it's too late."

"Too late for what?"

Ngan was visibly agitated. "Have you ever read *Frankenstein*?"

"Yes."

Ngan held up the bag. "Think of each of these coins, then, as being Frankenstein's monster—completed, but not yet given life."

It was almost too much for McCain to grasp. "Freeze-dried monsters? Just add water and one of those will—?"

"Yes," snapped Ngan. "You've simplified it as a child would, but, yes. These objects are the essence of beings like those you saw during our journey. Their creator trapped them in this state before he grew too ill to watch over them. He is called the Keeper, and he has slept for centuries. As long as he was asleep, these beings remained trapped in this state.

"But he has begun to awaken, Michael, and his power over his creations is still very weak. As long as they are not in his possession, he cannot control what happens with them. The little girl who gave this coin to me knows where the Keeper is. We have to find the other coins and return them to the Keeper, and we have to protect that little girl. The institute has many enemies, and one of them is coming for her."

"Dear Lord . . ."

"I have to leave for a little while, Michael. You'll need to rest. You will need all your strength for what is going to come at you over the next few days." Ngan leaned over and gave McCain a quick but firm embrace, filled with strength and deep affection. "Rest now. Your questions will all be answered soon enough."

McCain gripped Ngan's forearm. "The bag that the coins were in? What—"

"The contents of the bag are at Central Lab, Michael. And once the tests have been completed, the results will tell you what you wish to know."

McCain stared into Ngan's intense eyes.

"You know, don't you?" he said. "Tell me, Ngan, please."

"Yes, I know."

"You're the one who sent me the encrypted files, aren't you?"

"Yes."

"Why?"

"Because it was time for you to know the truth. I have great respect for the Hoffman Institute, but I do not fully trust it. You would do well to view it the same way."

"The schematics, the maps and security codes . . . you sent those to me, as well?"

"Yes."

His grip on Ngan's arm tightened. McCain's stomach was in knots and his head felt as if it were going to implode. "Is it true, then?"

A beat, then, "Everything you have suspected for the last ten years of your life is just as you thought it was." He gently removed McCain's grip from his arm. "I have to go, Michael, but I'll be back soon. You rest. We have much to do, and much to talk about."

Ngan left the room. McCain lay back in the bed and was nearly blinded by the pain in his head. A few moments later a nurse came in and gave him a shot for the pain. McCain began to drift away. He had wings. He was shiny. UncleAgain was here with him, tossing him high in the air. He was flying above it all. He was free. No pain could touch him.

And at last he knew the truth about himself. His parents had adopted him, yes, but he had not been abandoned by his birth parents when he was an infant.

His birth began in a test tube, and ended with a fertilized egg that was placed into the womb of the woman he knew as his mother.

Fitz. What a joke.

McCain forced himself to say it aloud before he surrendered to the painkillers; if he could make himself say it aloud, then it would be Out There, part of the world, taking its place in reality.

Say it, he commanded himself. Get it the hell over with and you can deal with it when you wake up.

"Clone," he whispered, the sad absurdity of the word almost causing him to laugh.

Almost.

Leah finished untying the funny rubber band from around her mother's arm and threw it on top of the box they kept all their clothes in. Leah didn't understand why her mother always left that thing around her arm. She had lots of time to take it all the way off after the needle-thing but she never did. She just loosened it enough so the vein would go back down after she stuck the needle in, then she shook a lot and made weird noises, sighing and growling at the same time. A lot of the time Leah even had to take the needle out of her mother's arm after Mommy went to sleep sort-of, and that made her nervous because she was afraid she might slip and Mommy would start to bleed too much and maybe die. She didn't like these nights because Mommy wasn't her mother anymore, she was like some zombie from those old black-and-white horror movies Jewel watched on his TV. Mommy knew a lot of zombies. They always came around to see her after the dark-coat man gave her money for her babies.

They all had black eyes and runny noses and were shaky and smelled like old hamburger. Their skin was grey and crusty and all of them had the same little hole-bruises on their arms. They would give Mommy a little money or food or something for a "taste" of the needle-stuff then light the candles. Leah thought that part was kind of pretty; all of them sitting huddled over the candles, heating up the shiny spoons and lighting the sticks that smelled like Christmas trees. They would laugh and tell jokes, and the candle flames made them all look like broken dolls, and it was kind of soft and glowing . . . but then they'd take out the needles and those funny rubber bands that they wrapped around their arms and it wasn't pretty anymore.

That's when Leah would leave to go see Buddy.

Just like tonight. She was glad that Mommy had done the needle-thing by herself because that meant Leah didn't have to worry about someone else trying to stop her, so she wadded up some old clothes and put them under her mother's head for a pillow, covered her with an old rug so she wouldn't get too cold, and silently crept to the bottom of the stairs. This was fun, like she was in one of those old movies where they were escaping from jail.

She reached the bottom of the stairs and walked straight ahead into the middle of the basement where a bunch of barrels were stacked up, then pushed one of them aside and crawled through the opening, careful not to jostle anything and make the stack come crashing down. In the middle of the floor was a loose board, and Leah slid it to one side. This part was never hard to do. The warehouse was all stinking and falling apart, anyway, like all the buildings around here. There were probably all kinds of loose boards that she could rip up, but she didn't want to. This was her special board, her special secret. She had first seen Buddy's lights glowing from underneath this loose board, and because she wanted to keep it a secret, she had stacked all the barrels around it like a bunch of pop cans so no one else would be able to find it. She didn't ever want Mommy to find out about Buddy because then she'd probably tell the dark-coat man about it, and Leah just knew that dark-coat man had been talking about Buddy when he asked about her having any other friends.

Sometimes she felt like she had to be scared all the time.

She couldn't stop thinking about what Mommy had said to her, about letting Jewel take her up to his room. That hurt Leah because she loved her mother. She loved her mother very, very much.

She squeezed through the opening left by the missing board, turned around once she was inside, and pulled the board back into place. This way, no one would ever be able to find her. The way she felt right now, Leah wasn't sure she ever wanted to go back to her mother. Maybe if she didn't come back, Mommy would know how she felt when she was left alone all the time.

In the darkness Leah could hear the sounds of rats running back and forth. That was good, because it meant the rats were scared and that meant that Buddy was waiting for her.

She scooted over onto her butt and slid down the dirt incline. This part was fun, too. It was like going down the slide at one of the playgrounds Mommy let her play on once. Even though she'd only been able to go down the slide one time, Leah never forgot what it felt like because it made her think she was going home. The speed, the feeling that she could take flight at any moment, the wind pressing against her—wherever she was supposed to be instead of here, she'd found some small part of it that day on the sliding board.

She hit the bottom of the subbasement with a moist thud and heard the rats screech and run deeper into the darkness. It was hard to see down here, so she got on her hands and knees and moved forward very slowly. This was the hard part, making sure she didn't get all mixed up in the dark. She slid her hands forward, then dragged her legs, once, twice, three times. On the third time she felt the cold metal under her fingers.

The door to the Rusty Room.

She took a deep breath and rose up on her knees—she had to be strong for this because the door was heavy—and worked her fingers into a crack right along the top and pulled.

The door came up with a loud *screech!* sound that felt like an ice pick stuck in her ears. She fell back, panting, then held her breath and listened. When the door made that noise she always expected Mommy to wake up and come looking for her, but she never did.

She crawled forward once again and peered down. There was a little light tonight, sort of red-blue, and that was enough for her to see the rounded walls of the metal tunnel, so she scooted around, slid her legs in, and pushed forward, sliding down the metal tunnel and laughing. She couldn't help laughing. This was fun, even more fun than the sliding board.

She landed on the floor and slid forward a few more feet because the floor of the Rusty Room was made out of black glass. At least, that's what it looked like to Leah. In the middle of the room was a tall pillar that narrowed in the center and supported part of the domed ceiling. The walls were made out of some kind of metal that was very old and had started rusting over the years. The room smelled like dust and copper, and sometimes when Leah would touch one of the walls, the rust came off on her hand, revealing layer upon layer of much older rust underneath.

In one of the corners of the room—and it puzzled Leah that a room so round would actually have squared corners—was a hole that looked like something had exploded there. One time she stuck her head through the hole and saw the River of Ash People that went on and on, farther than she could see even with a flashlight. Buddy had told her that the Ash People weren't all people, some of them were animals and other creatures that "didn't quite work out as planned."

She wasn't sure she knew what Buddy meant by that, but, still, they were all pretty neat, like sand sculptures people made at the beach in summer. From what she understood, the

Ash People had all gotten caught in some kind of fire-flood, like volcano lava, and had been washed down here where they were forever frozen in one position when the lava hardened.

It seemed kind of sad to her that all of the Ash People looked like they were reaching upward, hoping someone would pull them out and take them home because they didn't really belong here. She wondered if that mammoth Merc talked about had been reaching up when the scientists found it.

She decided not to say hello to the Ash People tonight, and hoped they'd understand. She had important things to talk about with Buddy.

Then she noticed that Buddy had written some more words on the wall above the hole.

> *someone come*
> *be there in the morning*
> *when I*
> *wake up*
> *with your silver thread*
> *to lead me out*
> *I don't belong here*
> *who will take me?*
>
> *someone come*

A few feet away from the central pillar was a doorway, and above the door there was a sign of some sort, printed in raised letters (she guessed they were letters, anyway; she'd never seen anything quite like them) that shone with an almost eerie phosphorescence, just like all those neon signs downtown where Jewel lived. The red-blue light she'd seen from above came from those letters, and gave off enough light that she could make her way around the Rusty Room without banging into anything. Not that there was much to bang into—just a large white table like in a doctor's office and a bunch of things that looked like leather coffins stacked one on top of the other.

"Buddy?" she called softly.

She waited to be answered by music that was both primitive and majestic. Clicks, grunts, wheezing whistles, then a series of trills, arpeggios, and multitoned flutings, all parts of Buddy's language. A long time ago, when she'd first met him, Buddy had put her on the table and done something to her head with a gizmo that looked like one of those things doctors looked in your ears with, only Buddy's gizmo had a kind of liquid spring attached that uncoiled like a snake and went into her ear, then deeper. It tickled a lot, but ever since then Leah had been able to understand what Buddy was saying to her.

"I know I'm late. I'm sorry, but Mommy . . . Mommy sold the baby, then we had to go and get some of her needle-stuff."

Still, she was answered by silence. That was all right, though. Sometimes Buddy didn't feel like talking or even showing himself. It was enough for Leah to just know he was around. She could feel him near.

"I got a bag of Twinkies the doctor gave me!" She pulled the crushed bag from under her shirt. "Uh-oh. They got squished. But that's okay, they still taste real good, they're just kinda messy." She worked the remains of one from its package and held it out. "You want one? I saved a package for you."

Silence.

"Okay, if you're sure. I'll probably eat 'em all. I'm still kinda hungry. Mommy bought me a hamburger, but I didn't get to eat it all 'cause she was in a hurry." She shrugged. "It was kinda greasy, anyway."

She devoured the first package of cakes, then opened the next one. "I wish you weren't so quiet tonight. I missed you. Mommy, she . . . I dunno. I think she does that needle-thing because she's sad about something and it won't leave her alone. Sometimes, when she talks about how she first met my daddy, she gets all sad, then mean. I don't really understand a lot about it. I don't get what a metal cave is supposed to be, unless it's something like your place. Buddy. I guess maybe that's it, and maybe that's what makes her sad enough to do the needle-thing. I bet that's why all of them do the needle-thing, to make the sad go away. I just wish . . ." She wiped her eyes, surprised that she'd started crying again.

"I just wish that she didn't have to give the babies to the dark-coat man for money. She gave him my little sister. I never had a little sister before, and I didn't even get to name her.

"I wish you'd say something. You're my best-best friend. I love you, Buddy."

She was answered only by silence, but in that silence she felt Buddy's confusion—not at her being sad, or hungry, or about Mommy and the babies and the needle-stuff, but at one word: love. It wasn't that Buddy didn't know what love was, because he did, in his way. What confused him was that Leah felt such deep and strong affection for him.

"Okay, I guess you don't feel like company tonight. I'll come back again tomorrow night, okay? I'll save you some of the Twinkies, in case you change your mind."

She made her way over to the metal tunnel and saw that Buddy had, as usual, turned it into a ladder so she could climb back up.

She started up, then swung out, one hand still gripping a rung, and waved good night to the Ash People.

Above the hole, some new words had been written.

> *and where do I live?*
> *in the empty spaces where*
> *a spirit should be*
> *among the odd, damaged ones*
> *in hollow houses of flesh*
> *and bone*
> *that the Belonging will not*
> *see*

someone come
one last time
I will wait for you
you ask who will take me?

someone come
and answer

soon.

tomorrow.

within the cell, life is long, life is hard.
within the cell, life is hard.

and home is a cruel joke.

someone come.

"Okay," said Leah, smiling. "I'll come back tomorrow."

When she emerged several minutes later from her hiding place inside the stacked barrels, someone was waiting for her.

chapter
8 IGHT

$\int$eane regained consciousness to find herself lying on a cot in a semidarkened room. The only source of light came from a small bulb plugged into a wall outlet—a child's night-light—and the slash of light that bled in from under the closed door several feet away from her. She tried to sit up but was still too dizzy from whatever it was they had shot into her.

She lay her head on the hard, uncomfortable pillow and began to slowly pat herself down.

No cell phone, no 9mm, no pager, no keys, zip. They'd cleaned her out.

And she still had no idea who "they" were.

No matter. When she didn't report to Travis in the morning—assuming that morning hadn't already come and gone—someone would be sent to find her.

Maybe they'd find her camera in the tunnel, and maybe they'd develop the pictures and see what she had—

The sound of a key being inserted in the locked door stopped her from continuing down that particular path of thought.

Two of the three men from the tunnel—she'd come to think of them as Tweedledum and Tweedledee—entered the room and pulled her to her feet. One of them broke open a capsule of smelling salt and rammed it under her nose and Jeane started gagging, but at least she was starting to feel her body awaken, and that was something.

Dum and Dee took her from the room and into a brightly lit hallway that looked familiar to her. Next, it was to an elevator, then another hallway. It was only as they veered left and entered a security code into a panel next to a steel door that Jeane realized where they were. They'd been keeping her in one of the several fallout shelters under the ATF building.

Jeane kept fading in and out—enough that she was aware only of moving and not her surroundings—but when she caught a whiff of the perfume worn by Travis's secretary, she opened her eyes.

Dum and Dee were leading her through the darkened reception area—the clock on the wall told her that it was a little after three in the morning—into her supervisor's office.

She was dropped into a chair and given a swig of very hot coffee.

It took a few moments for her to clear her head and get her bearings.

Dum and Dee stood on either side of Travis's desk. The third guy from the tunnel—Middle Man—stood beside her supervisor, who had looked far better in his day.

Travis had been badly beaten. He had two black eyes, several abrasions on his face, and a broken nose that was still bleeding.

"Sir," said Jeane.

"You're in a great deal of trouble, Agent Meara," Travis croaked. "The Bureau doesn't take kindly to agents who assault their supervisors and steal security clearance cards."

His eyes. There was something in his eyes that told her he was being forced to do this. She made a quick scan of the desk and the men who stood around it.

Bingo.

The small framed photograph of Travis's wife and children was lying facedown on the desk, surrounded by small sections of broken glass.

They'd beaten him, then threatened his family if he didn't cooperate with them.

"What do you have to say for yourself, Meara?" asked Travis.

"Nothing, sir."

"Good girl," said Middle Man. "You neither confirm nor deny the charges. Excellent. Might I suggest that—oh, but where are my manners? Would you care for another sip of coffee, Agent Meara?"

"That would be nice, thank you."

Tweedledum poured a little more coffee into a cup and held it while Jeane took a few more sips.

She was starting to feel the buzz—and it had little to do with the caffeine.

During her combat and defense training, her instructor—a former mercenary rumored to have assassinated no fewer than nine world leaders—had told Jeane's class, "Most people don't know it, no reason they should, but every person on Earth has buried, deep inside their skull, a throwback brain. It's a remnant from an earlier epoch, and over time what we have come to think of as our brain has grown over and on top of the cells of the throwback brain . . . but the throwback brain remains inside us. No surgery, law, or religion can ever remove it from us. It has only five urges. It wants to eat, sleep, fight, screw, and kill. That's it. There are no cells for caring in the throwback brain, no cells for love or compassion or friendship—we get all that from the surrounding brain. I tell you about this because there is going to come a time in your career when you're going to start feeling a little buzz somewhere in the back of your skull. Odds are you'll start feeling this when you're in a kill-or-be-killed situation. There's nothing you can do about it. That buzz is your throwback brain taking control. My advice to you is, when that happens—and it *will* happen eventually, trust me on this—do not fight it. Give it control. If the situation is dire enough that the throwback brain has been awakened, there is no other way out for you. For the record, I can tell you from experience exactly how long it will be in control: fifteen seconds. That's how long it takes before the outer brain realizes what's happened and takes steps to regain power. You can do a lot of damage in those fifteen seconds, folks, if you don't fight it."

The buzz was moving from the back of her skull to the front now. Jeane sat back in the chair and let it move through her body, shoulders, arms, chest, and legs.

She looked at Travis. His eyes said, "I'm so sorry," though he didn't speak.

So that was it. They were going to kill her and make it look as if she'd flipped out in her supervisor's office and attacked him.

All right, then . . .

"Something you wish to say, Agent Meara?" asked Middle Man.

"I would like to be on my feet when I die, if you don't mind."

Middle Man arched his eyebrows. "Well, well . . . you're much sharper than I gave you credit for. You may stand."

Jeane fingered the small St. Christopher medal that hung from a chain around her neck—a First Communion gift from her mother—then rose to her feet and moved away from the chair.

The buzz was roaring in her ears, sending erotic, electric shocks through her body.

Tweedledum moved behind her.

This was a good thing, this was what her throwback brain wanted.

"Does he have to be here?" she asked, gesturing toward Travis.

"Yes, unfortunately. Your supervisor understands that his presence is necessary to make our little scenario believable to the authorities."

"Just checking." The buzz engulfed her totally now.

The throwback reared up its ugly head—

—and she gladly gave it control.

The first second began with nothing unusual about it, at least on the surface. In fact, no one but Jeane knew that it had begun at all. Tweedledee stood on one side of Travis, Middle Man on the other, and Tweedledum behind her. Travis was staring at her with fear and regret. Middle Man watched her with interest, his head cocked to the left. Tweedledee was reaching under his coat for his weapon when he heard a sound—a grunt, to be more precise. The reason for the sound was this:

Jeane had just snap-kicked backward with her right foot, aiming and hitting Tweedledee's kneecap. Her shoe wasn't the heaviest thing in the world, but it did have a sharp metal heel and Jeane had always been good at this sort of kick. She knew two things from the sound of her heel connecting. Tweedledum was going to scream, but not until second three, and his kneecap was gone.

During second number two, Travis remained seated at his desk, hearing the grunt but not quite understanding its meaning. Middle Man, on the other hand, seemed to pick up on its significance right away. His head was still cocked to the side and all he managed to do was blink several times in rapid succession. Tweedledum, for his part, seemed to be removed from everything. The pain had not yet registered with him. Tweedledee quickened his reach for his weapon while at the same time turning his body away from the two other men at the desk in order to get a clearer look at what exactly was going on. Jeane took a leisurely step away from Tweedledum toward Tweedledee, yanked the St. Christopher medal from its chain around her neck, and second number two passed quickly into oblivion.

If second number two had seemed somewhat uneventful, then most of second number three was downright boring by comparison. Jeane continued to move, only now she brought her left hand up to the middle of her body, then to the side of it. Middle Man's eyes widened into a stare. Travis's mouth began to open as if he were going to say something or shout a warning to her, but she knew there was nothing behind her to be warned about. Tweedledee had his gun—a Bulldog .44— almost halfway out and was nearly finished with his turn. The information concerning what had happened to his kneecap finally reached Tweedledum's brain and he began to scream and scream and scream.

Second number four was a fairly important one all the way around. It was the first time Middle Man realized the need for action and began to move. Tweedledum, screaming to beat the band, began to buckle to the floor. Tweedledee had the Bulldog out of its shoulder holster and was starting to take aim. Travis began to move his chair. And Jeane, in a smooth, fast, arc, brought her left hand up as she took another step toward Tweedledee and used the jagged eye at the top of the medal to slash a deep cut across his forehead, sending a curtain of blood down into his eyes and, for the moment, blinding him.

The fifth second was even more crucial. Jeane stepped back and began to squat, reaching behind her and grabbing Tweedledum's arms and wrapping them around her waist. Tweedledee cursed as he tried unsuccessfully to blink the blood from his eyes. Middle Man began to move from behind the desk. Travis pushed his chair to the left.

In second number six, Tweedledum was still screaming from the pain of his kneecap and so did little to try to pull his arms from around Jeane's waist. Middle Man shouted, "Shoot her!" but Tweedledee was busy wiping the stinging blood from his eyes. Travis remained still in his chair. The only thing Jeane did was to drop her chin down onto her chest.

The seventh second Jeane snapped her head back with all the strength she had, her skull careening into several sections of Tweedledum's face, most notably the nose and cheekbone. Middle Man reached under his jacket for his weapon. Travis reached forward to open a desk drawer. For his part, Tweedle-dee continued to swear in blind frustration.

Second number eight began with Jeane stepping away from Tweedledum, who collapsed to the floor, his face shattered. Middle Man now had his weapon halfway out. Travis had his desk drawer open. Tweedledee still swore incoherently but managed to get a shot off that missed Jeane by a mile but was fatal to a glass decanter of whiskey on Travis's wet bar.

The ninth second was a busy one for all concerned. Travis pulled a pistol from his desk drawer. Middle Man's weapon was fully exposed now. Tweedledum rolled over on his side and began to grab for Jeane's ankle, and Tweedledee got off another shot, this one closer but still missing.

Second number ten was when Jeane launched into her dive, because that's when Travis did not one but two things. He tossed the weapon into the air and moved the chair back so that one of its wheels rolled directly onto Middle Man's foot. Middle Man let out with a shriek and began to double over. Tweedledee moved forward and fired once more, the bullet passing through the space where Jeane had been standing just before her dive.

The eleventh second began when Jeane caught the pistol that Travis had thrown, then fell toward the floor so that she'd hit with her right shoulder. Travis grabbed a paperweight from the center of his desk. Middle Man drew back the hand holding his gun to strike at Travis's skull. Tweedledee reached into another pocket with his free hand.

Jeane hit the floor with her shoulder in the twelfth second and went into a quick roll up to one knee. Tweedledee had the knife out now and dropped his gun as he threw himself forward, the hand that had been holding the gun grabbing for Jeane's hair or face, whatever he could get a hold on. The paperweight in

111

Travis's hand connected solidly with the side of Middle Man's skull, but not before Middle Man managed to slam the butt of his pistol into Travis's shoulder.

Second thirteen began with a bang as Jeane came up on her knee and fired off a shot that blew away half of Tweedledee's knife hand. Travis—dazed but far from out of the game—pushed his chair back even more and there was an audible *crack!* as the bones in Middle Man's foot shattered under the weight.

Almost over now, the fourteenth second was marked by Jeane's turn to perform double duty. She came up on her feet and spread her arms out. With her left, she jabbed her knuckles into Tweedledee's throat, hammering his windpipe. He gasped and clutched at his throat. With her right hand, Jeane fired off another shot and hit Middle Man in the shoulder.

Fifteenth and final second: Tweedledee went down on his knees clutching at his throat. Middle Man fell backward and vanished behind Travis's desk. Jeane whirled around just as Tweedledum began to crawl toward her and kicked him in the side of the neck.

Jeane was perspiring heavily as she turned in a circle, looking at the two figures on the floor. Then she glanced at Travis, who was busy delivering a second and less severe blow to Middle Man's skull.

She and her supervisor stared at one another.

"You okay?" she asked.

"Jesus, Meara. I'd forgotten just how dangerous you can be."

"That makes two of us."

Travis pulled several items from his desk. Her cell phone, her beeper, ID, and gun. Jeane grabbed everything except her St. Christopher medal—there was no time to find it in this mess. One of the things she learned in her combat and defense training was that if you had to take the offensive in a situation, you did not stick around any longer than necessary once your opponent was down.

Besides, security would be all over this place in about thirty seconds.

She and Travis ran from the office to the stairwell. Travis veered back for a second, punched the elevator button, then followed her into the stairwell.

"Why'd you push the elevator button?"

"That's the first thing security will check for. It bought us maybe thirty seconds. Keep your gun pointed at me."

They took the stairs three at a time on the way down.

"Sir, why are we running like this?"

"Because right now you're a very wanted person, Jeane. They made me issue a Code Seven on you about twenty minutes ago. I guess they wanted to cover all the bases in case you did something like this."

They exited the stairwell at the parking garage level. Travis pointed toward his car and they ran to it. Once inside, Travis used his emergency security clearance key card to exit the garage. Jeane knew they'd both be in big trouble, one way or the other. The security cameras had recorded their every move since leaving the office.

And she was Code Seven—Armed and Dangerous, Apprehend with Extreme Prejudice.

"Listen to me, Jeane," said Travis. "I don't know what the hell you found that has those guys so worked up, and I don't want to know, got me? As of right now your career with the Bureau of Alcohol, Tobacco, and Firearms is over. I'm sorry as hell about this, but there's nothing I can do. My family is in danger right now, and that's all I care about. As far as the security cameras will show, you had your gun on me the whole time, so when we left the garage, I was a prisoner. My guess is that agents have already been dispatched to my house— that's what I'm counting on." He turned down a side street and pulled over. "I need to make sure my family is safe, Jeane, then I'll do whatever I can to help you, all right? But for the moment I need for everyone to think you kidnapped me and I managed to get away. Keep your cell phone turned on. Two

113

rings, then one, then two, that'll be my signal. Do not answer it otherwise, understand me?" He reached across and opened the passenger side door. "Get out, and keep yourself hidden until you hear from me, all right?"

"Yes, sir."

"Good luck, Jeane."

"Thank you, sir."

He drove away, leaving her alone on the darkened street.

Jeane had never felt more vulnerable or afraid in her entire life.

"**C**ain!" shouted Leah as she emerged from within the stack of barrels.

Ngan smiled at her as she ran into his arms and hugged him as if he were a much-loved grandfather. He liked the way this felt. A child belonged in the arms of someone who cared about her well-being, who did not wish to exploit or abuse her, whose only concern was that this small, vulnerable, trusting person be happy, safe, and healthy.

Ngan looked around the warehouse and asked, "Where is your mother?"

Leah looked away and whispered, "She's sick again."

"Ah." Ngan knew very well that "sick" was a code word Leah used, and insomuch as he was capable of genuine hatred, Ngan hated that a child so wonderful as she should have to know enough of the seamy side of life to invent a code word.

"I hope she will be feeling better soon," he said to

her. Leah kissed his cheek and pulled away but did not let go of his hand.

"I'm real glad you're here," Leah said. "It was weird tonight. Down there, I mean."

"You were visiting Buddy?"

"Yeah, but he wouldn't come out from his hiding place." She leaned toward Ngan. "I think he's real sad about something. Or maybe he's sick. I dunno. It was weird."

"I see."

"You do?"

"Yes, Leah, I do."

The child regarded him for a moment, her head cocked to the side, a spark of wonder in her tired eyes. "Did you . . . did you ever know someone like Buddy?"

"Yes, I did."

"Was it weird?"

Ngan thought for a moment about how to answer her question, then decided that she should know the truth. There was no greater vessel for the storage of truth than the soul and mind of a child.

He sat down on the dirty floor of the warehouse and patted the ground next to him. Leah came over and seated herself beside him, leaning against his side. Ngan put a protective arm around her.

"Do you remember when I told you about the place where I grew up?"

"The . . . the mon'stery?"

"Monastery," said Ngan. "Yes, it was high up in the mountains of Tibet. The Kha-glor monks live there—very holy men, Ascended Masters. They raised me. I am told that, as a very young child—younger even, than you—I was carried away by a yeti. Do you know what a yeti is?"

Leah nodded her head, eyes wide. "Uh-huh. A 'bominable snow monster, like Bumble in *Rudolph the Red-Nosed Reindeer?*"

Ngan smiled at her innocence. "Yes, I suppose that's one way of describing it."

"What was it like? Did they hurt you at all?"

Ngan brushed some hair from her face. "That's just it, Leah. I don't remember. As I said, I was very young. There are times, though—mostly at night when I am about to drift off to sleep—that I remember . . . impressions of them. Do you know what that means, 'impression'?"

"Huh-uh."

Ngan thought carefully on this before going on. "Do you ever get the feeling sometimes that someone is staring at you, even though you can't see them doing it?"

"Oh, sure! I feel that way a lot, 'specially when Mommy falls asleep after doing her needle-thing. It's real hard for me to get to sleep 'cause it's dark, you know? And I feel like maybe somebody's hiding out there, watching me."

Ngan swallowed back his anger, fought away his sadness for her. "That's an impression of sorts. It's more of a feeling than anything else." He began now to gently tap his thumb against her right temple. *Tap, tap-tap . . . tap, tap-tap . . .*

She began to relax in his arms, unaware that he was beginning to hypnotize her.

"I feel that way all the time," she whispered. "I don't like it very much."

"Does it make you afraid?"

"Uh-huh."

"Does Buddy ever feel that way?"

"Sure he does—and lonely, too. He misses his home, but he knows he can't ever go back there."

Tap . . . tap-tap . . . tap, tap-tap . . .

"Does he ever tell you why he can't go back?"

"Yeah. His real home, it isn't there any more."

Tap, tap-tap . . . tap, tap-tap . . .

"I know how he feels," whispered Ngan. "He's very lucky to have a friend like you."

"Were you friends with the 'bominable snowmen?"

"I think I was, yes, but as I said, I have only the impressions, the ghosts of memories, if you can understand that. I remember the cold, but I remember being kept warm. I remember strong, furry arms, and echoes from inside caves, and singing."

"You sang songs to them?"

"No," said Ngan, "but I think they sang songs to me."

Tap, tap-tap . . . tap, tap-tap . . .

"I wish Mommy wouldn't sell the babies," whispered Leah. "I wanna have a baby brother or sister to take care of. And I could, too. I'd take real good care of them."

"I'm sure you would."

"If Mommy wouldn't spend all her money on her needle-stuff, maybe we'd get a 'partment and live there."

"An apartment? Don't you want a house?"

She looked directly into his eyes. "You mean, there're *real* houses?"

"Yes."

"I only seen pictures of houses in magazines. I never seen a real house. A house would be nice."

Tap, tap-tap . . . tap, tap-tap . . .

She was having difficulty keeping her eyes open.

Ngan knew he would have to be very careful once she was under. He did not like having to sneak into her mind this way, but Leah's unconscious undoubtedly held impressions given to her from Buddy that her little girl's mind and vocabulary could not possibly begin to articulate.

"Do you want to take a little nap, Leah?"

Tap, tap-tap . . .

"Uh-huh . . . so tired . . ."

Tap, tap-tap . . .

"Shh, then, you just snuggle against me like this. There you go. I'll stay right here, Leah. I'll watch over while you sleep."

"Mommy might get worried if she wakes up and I'm not there . . ."

"You'll be fine, just fine."

" 'Kay . . ."

Tap, tap-tap . . . tap, tap-tap . . .

She sank into him, wilting in exhaustion. Ngan continued with his rhythmic tapping until her breathing came slowly, deep and steady.

Finally he whispered, "Can you hear me?"

"Yes," she replied.

"Are you talking with Buddy?"

"Uh-huh."

"Does Buddy have a name?"

"Yeah . . ."

"Will he tell you what it is?"

"Ylem."

"Ylem," whispered Ngan.

An old physicist's term given to all theoretical matter that existed in the universe prior to the Big Bang.

He whispered to Leah, "Can you tell me what is happening here?"

"Dunno . . ."

"Leah?"

"Yeah?"

"We're going to go to your secret spring now, okay? You remember your secret spring?"

"Uh-huh . . . pretty water . . ."

"May I take your hand?"

"Sure . . ."

"Okay. I'm going to join you now, all right?"

"Uh-huh . . . come on in . . ."

Ngan closed his eyes and slowly, steadily, took himself into a state of deep meditation, all the while making a series of soft, melodic sounds in the back of his throat, concentrating all his power and will on synchronizing his breathing with Leah's.

The rhythm of one's breath was the first step. After that came the changing of one's heart rate to match that of the other person's. Finally—and this was the most difficult step, one that could only be taught by the Ascended Masters—it was a matter of directing the flow of information to one's brain to join hands in the rhythmic dance and thus merge one's own streams of consciousness with the subject's, in essence merging two minds into one.

The Kha-glor monks had believed in the "vibration metaphor." Throw a pebble in a pond, and the vibrations ripple outward in concentric circles. Strike a bell, and it vibrates in waves of sound. Meditate on a thought, and it will echo through the realm of the collective unconscious. In his travels since leaving the monastery, Ngan had learned that if one were to theoretically apply the vibration metaphor to some recent discoveries about the susceptibility of brain-wave patterns to nonphysical stimuli, then it was possible to employ a blended and sequenced series of binaural sound pulses to induce a frequency-following response in the brain, creating a ripple effect that could alter EEG wave patterns and generate expanded states of consciousness. Given those conditions, resting-state alpha activity was suppressed and replaced by synchronous slow wave activity in the median of the central cortex. Increase the amplitude and frequency of the sound impulses, and the resting-state alpha and slow wave activity could be induced to operate simultaneously, accompanied by temporal gamma brainwave activity, enabling an individual to perceive nonphysical energies outside the confines of the physical law belief system. Not only that, but the individual would perceive these nonphysical phenomena as constituting his or her whole field of awareness—not unlike a waking dream, stimulating alternate brain wave patterns to produce a shared transcendent-state experience.

Ngan had done this many times in his life, but only twice with Leah. The first time was shortly after he met her, when he found her sleeping between a couple of trash cans not far from the fish market. Left to her own devices once again by her mother, Leah had fallen asleep after an encounter with Buddy. When Ngan picked her up, the echoing energy of her encounter was so strong that Ngan was actually forced into a state of Merging with her. It had taken all of his mental energy to break the connection, but what he'd sensed during those few crucial seconds had never stopped haunting him.

Buddy—Ylem—was using portions of Leah's mind as a repository of information.

It became necessary then for Ngan to give a subconscious physical form to this area of Leah's mind. He found her to be a child with a remarkably rich fantasy life, and so he had invented and designed her secret spring. Now that he was merging with her, the place began to slowly appear around them, a developing time-lapse photograph.

In this place where their minds were now merged, Ngan took hold of Leah's hand and smiled at her.

"Ready?" he asked.

"You bet!"

She looked so much healthier and alive here in her mind, than she did in the corporeal world. Ngan wondered if she ever had the impression that she was lying to herself here . . . or perhaps it was just a child's wish fulfillment.

At the moment they stood in the center of a topiary garden of cherry and rose bushes. Masses of foliage created a circle around them, trimmed in tall, willowy, semi-human shapes with large oval heads. These figures, sculpted representations of the classic extra-terrestrial being, were holding hands.

The circle of figures opened at every other handclasp, and beyond one such opening a large oblong opening in the ground manifested itself. Leah and Ngan stepped into the circle and approached the hole in the ground by stepping onto a stairway formed of stratified rock that led down and around the inner perimeter of the hole. At the base of the stairway stood another level of topiary garden, hidden from above and accessible only by descending the stairway and passing through the hole in the ground.

They began their descent, and as they took each stair slowly, other sculpted figures appeared, only these were beings created from hardened volcano ash, their hands reaching outward as if trying to touch the old man and little girl walking past them.

The figures whispered to Ngan and Leah.

"We are approaching the Meeting. Between ourselves and the Last Ones. The source of The Creation."

Ngan asked one of the ash figures, "Why is this happening now?"

"Because we have reached too far."

". . . the end of expansion . . ."

". . . snap-snap, the band snaps back . . ."

". . . trapped inside this darkness . . ."

". . . withering in pain . . ."

". . . and loneliness . . ."

". . . lonely . . ."

". . . lonely . . ."

". . . lonely blackboard sky of eternity. . . ."

Ngan continued, "Who tells you these things?"

". . . the Last Ones . . ."

". . . who were the First Ones . . ."

". . . before the Life of Darkness became the Death in Light . . ."

". . . They tell us . . ."

". . . sing us their songs . . ."

". . . give us things . . ."

". . . comfort us in sickness . . ."

". . . all this sickness . . ."

". . . make us well again after Seeing, after Becoming . . ."

"Becoming what?" asked Ngan.

". . . what we should have been all along . . ."

". . . what we should be now . . ."

". . . if only we had been worthy . . ."

". . . if only we had not reached too far . . ."

". . . too far . . ."

". . . so far . . ."

". . . so far into loneliness . . ."

". . . lonely, lonely, lonely . . ."

". . . They have been protecting us until now, but we're too close . . ."

". . . trapped inside this darkness . . ."

". . . withering in pain . . ."

". . . They have touched some of us . . ."

". . . a warning . . ."

". . . turn back, turn back now . . ."

". . . maybe a long time coming, maybe very soon . . ."

". . . They won't tell us . . ."

". . . because . . ."

". . . because it would frighten us too much . . ."

". . . so They show us . . ."

". . . reveal Themselves to us . . ."

". . . peekaboo . . ."

". . . say hello . . ."

". . . look up . . ."

". . . say hello . . ."

"I think they're scared and lonely, just like Buddy," said Leah.

"I think so, too," replied Ngan.

They reached the bottom of the stairway, stepped through the hole in the ground, and found themselves in the second topiary garden.

Ngan knew it was here that Buddy—Ylem—had hidden its most precious knowledge in Leah's subconscious.

And for some reason, that made him feel very afraid.

chapter
1 0 EN

McCain awoke just as the doctor was injecting something into his arm.

"What's this?" he said, nodding toward the hypodermic.

"Syrinx," replied the doctor, then offered nothing more.

"Well, well . . . that's informative."

The doctor smiled. "It's an experimental strain of albumin that attaches itself to certain receptors in the brain so that pain stimuli fail to register."

"In English?"

The doctor removed the needle. "Okay, I'll give you the full version. This brace around your leg is holding roughly thirty pins in place. Those pins are keeping your bones together. If you were to simply lie here for the next three weeks and not move, then everything would heal properly and, with physical therapy, you'd be almost as good as new in about a year. We don't have that kind of time. I got a call from Nakami himself, and our fearless leader wants you on your feet within the next seventy-odd hours."

McCain laughed. "You're kidding, right?"

The doctor shook his head. "We've already covered my sense of humor in our previous conversation, so I'd really appreciate it if you'd stop asking me that question every time I tell you something you find difficult to believe."

"Sorry. Go on."

"I knew as soon as you were brought in that Nakami was going to want you up and about as soon as possible, so you've been getting steady injections of Syrinx since you arrived here. The pins and brace used on your leg can withstand up to three thousand pounds of pressure, so unless you plan on getting run over by a monster truck, there's little chance anything can happen to further damage your leg. Three more doses of Syrinx and your brain will register no pain whatsoever."

It took a moment for McCain to process all of this. "So you're telling me that after three more injections, I'll be able to walk?" he asked.

"Not without the benefit of a crutch—and forget about running any marathons anytime soon—but, yes, you'll be mobile. You'll be able to stand up and move around without passing out from the agony."

"Incredible . . ."

"That's what they pay me for, the incredible." The doctor checked the leg brace and pin settings once more, gave McCain's leg a little jiggle, and said, "Feel anything?"

"Your hands are cold."

"I'm surrounded by flaming wits, God help me. *Pain,* do you feel any pain?"

"A little ache—like a sore tooth—but that's about it."

The doctor nodded and said, "Good. The stuff's working."

"You mean you weren't sure?"

"No, that's not what I mean. I know it works. I engineered

the stuff. It just happens to be working exactly as it should, that's all, and I am pleased with the results because it reaffirms my genius in my own eyes, ergo I make a little comment like, 'Good. The stuff's working.' Do you find any of this confusing?"

"No."

"Relief abounds." The doctor rose and walked to the door. "You have a visitor, by the way."

McCain sat up slightly. "Ngan?"

"No. Some fellow with a private message from Nakami. Don't know his name, don't know what the message is, nobody tells me nothing, nobody loves me except my mother, and she might be jiving me, too."

"B.B. King. Great song."

The doctor looked out at the man who waited on the other side of the door. "Cloak and dagger and secrecy, oh my. Shall I send him in?"

McCain slumped back down into the bed. "Why not?"

The doctor left. A few seconds later a small, hunchbacked man whose thick grey hair reached almost to his shoulders entered the room. He had an envelope. He handed it to McCain, then—saying not a word—sat down in a chair by the side of the bed.

"Hello, yourself," said McCain.

The man smiled. His eyes were blue and warm; kind eyes, but the kind eyes of someone who was, at the moment, in the midst of carrying out a professional task and so allowed no room for small talk.

"I assume I'm supposed to open this?" asked McCain.

The man nodded.

McCain opened the envelope. Inside was a letter on official Hoffman Institute stationary, from Dr. Nakami's office.

Dear Michael,
  First I wish for you to know how relieved I was to hear that your injuries, though serious enough, will not

be life-threatening. We are, of course, professional colleagues, but I have always thought of myself first and foremost as a friend of your family's, and, thus, of yours as well.

The man who has brought this letter to you is most trustworthy. He's been a close associate of mine for many, many years, so please do not be put off by his manner. I instructed him to tell you something. You may take what he says as absolute truth. He will answer no questions, so I suggest you pay close attention. This information is of a nature so delicate that it is neither recorded nor encrypted nor written down anywhere.

Only five people within the Institute know what he's going to tell you. Ngan is one of them.

You may not discuss this information between yourselves.

I am aware that you have recently discovered the truth behind your birth. I realize that you must be hurt, angry, and confused, and that you must have many, many questions—not the least of which has to be "Why?"

"You can say that again," whispered McCain.

The hunchbacked man looked up and grinned, but said nothing.

McCain read on.

It had always been my intention to move you into the Dark Matter branch of the Institute in slow degrees—there is much one needs to learn and train for to be an effective agent—but circumstances now dictate that you be thrown headfirst into the fire, and for that I apologize.

Listen to what he has to tell you. We shall speak very soon.

—N.

McCain put the letter aside—still surprised by the compassionate tone used by the usually coolly reserved Nakami—and turned to his visitor.

"Something you wish to say to me, then?"

The Shopkeeper smiled, then cleared his throat and rose to his feet, crossing to the side of McCain's bed.

"In 1947, a pilot flying near Mt. Rainier in western Washington state saw a number of flying crescents skipping like 'saucers' across water. The name 'flying saucer' stuck, and thus began the modern era of UFO sightings. Later that same year, an even more significant event occurred, though there are many versions of what actually happened. One story indicates that an alien spaceship developed a systems failure and crashed near Roswell, New Mexico on July second, 1947. Another version claims that the U.S. government shot the craft down with an anti-aircraft battery but immediately realized its terrible blunder. In either case, the government has kept the ship secret ever since. The craft and its dead occupants were taken to Groom Lake Air Force base in Nevada, also known as Area 51 and commonly called 'Dreamland.' "

He spoke in a steady rhythm, his voice flat and colorless.

"Try not to get so excited about this," said McCain.

The Shopkeeper raised an eyebrow and almost smiled. "Please don't interrupt me."

"Sorry."

"A second craft, perhaps sent to rescue survivors from the first crash, met with equipment failure itself and fell to Earth not far away. Investigators discovered this vessel at San Augustine Flats near Magdelena, New Mexico on July third, 1947.

"This incident spurred the first organized contact between humans and aliens—known as the Greys—in modern times. Alien technology and physiology were now available for human scientists to study. Whether mankind was alone in the universe was no longer even a viable question, at least to those in the know. In response, the Greys contacted certain government officials and worked out a treaty. The humans who formed the committee that communicated with the aliens called themselves Majestic-12. Later, some members of M12 would join with covert agents of the Office of Naval Intelligence to form a secret group called COM-12, which exists to combat a covert, possibly alien-backed, organization within the government. Only fractions of COM-12 got . . . out of hand, you might say, and have devised a plan with the codename Aquarius. These fractions are working with forces in the United Nations to establish a world government, a perverted form of New World Order, dedicated to seeking out and destroying all Greys and Grey influence on human culture.

"As of at least twenty-four hours ago, COM-12 has classified you and an agent from the ATF by the name of Jeane Meara as 'possible risks.' "

"Meaning?"

"Meaning that until the present situation is resolved and you can safely be moved elsewhere, your life is in danger, as is Agent Meara's."

"Has she been brought in?"

"No."

"Are Ngan and I supposed to—?"

He didn't bother finishing the question. He saw the answer on the Shopkeeper's face.

The Shopkeeper put his hand against his chest as if experiencing the onset of a heart attack, then removed a vibrating cell phone from his pocket, listened for a moment to what was said to him, and replied, "Yes, sir, we have just finished our talk. Of course."

He offered the phone to McCain.

McCain took the phone. "Hello?"

"Michael," said Nakami. "I think perhaps you might have a question or two for me?"

chapter

ELEVEN

As Ngan and Leah entered the second topiary garden in the depths of her unconscious mind, the landscape around them changed dramatically. No longer were they surrounded by sculpted figures and rose and cherry bushes. Now they were in the middle of a maze of cracked and leaking pipes, panes of shattered glass that littered the ground, moldering cardboard boxes, and other reminders of the urban decay that Leah called home.

Interspersed throughout the garbage around them, Ngan caught sight of something very curious. It was a new-looking pinball machine whose steel legs were overgrown with, of all things, buttercups.

He wondered if these were images from Leah's mind, or if they were symbols of something Ylem was trying to convey.

Leah knelt down by the edge of her secret spring and gestured for Ngan to do the same.

"This's where Buddy hides all his best secrets," said Leah.

She reached out a finger and touched the water—which was, Ngan now saw, liquid lambda—and a small ripple began spreading outward.

Ngan felt damp all over. He looked down at himself. His shirt was soaked, his shoes were soaked, even his heart felt soaked. Everything was washing away. The ripples were flooding him, passing through him and coming out the other side. Black drops fell from his watchband onto his hand, grey drops fell from his shirt sleeves onto his arms. Behind him the stairway had melted away. His shirt was running in heavy grey rivulets down onto his tan pants, his pants were trickling onto his shoes, and his shoes were flowing away in inky streams. Everything was washing away. His cheeks were running, flesh-colored streams fell from his shining fingertips, he was dissolving into the ripples. He looked at Leah. She, too, was washing into the secret spring in ripples of black and grey and tan and flesh. They flowed outward into the spring.

"Buddy does this," she said, taking hold of Ngan's hand. "Don't be scared. He says . . . he says that our bodies are too weak to understand what he wants us to know, so it has to be this way."

"Does he turn you back later?" asked Ngan.

"You bet." She was little more than a running stain now, as was Ngan, and they bled into one another, became one stream, and flowed into the spring.

"You gotta go over there," said Leah.

Ngan was puzzled. There was no "over there" for either of them now. Water and space were no different than death and emptiness. All physical reference points had vanished.

Before Ngan could ask what Leah meant, he felt himself being separated from her, as a drop of ink will break apart when placed in water.

He scattered, then reformed elsewhere.

Over there.

Away from Leah.

He knew in an instant that Leah had been instructed by "Buddy" to bring him here, for only an adult could comprehend the information Buddy had hidden away in this place.

I understand now, Ngan said to Buddy/Ylem.

As I knew you would, came the reply.

And in an overpowering flash, Ngan learned Ylem's history and purpose.

The pursuit of knowledge was the only endeavor worthy of intelligence, the Seekers had taught, and the pupil Ylem believed without question. . . . Theirs was a dying world, one that lay far too close to the edge of Forever, the place where the expanding universe began to contract. . . . For this reason, all of their efforts were directed toward finding another place where their race might be able to sustain itself and, eventually, prosper. . . . It was a time both exciting and frightening to young pupils, and Ylem knew that his destiny lay in the fulfillment of this most important task. . . .

As time passed, the pupil Ylem achieved high status—not yet a Seeker, but already a Sentient, and together he and the Seekers created a Device to search for other life among other stars in other galaxies, unseen but known. . . . The Device passed through interspace and back as it was programmed to, but in the messages it now sent were uneven waves that emerged as streaks of clashing colors, mud-grey splotches, even a black spray that swelled and shrank, appeared and vanished. . . . With regret the Seeker Wished it Undone. . . . The fountain of multihued lights that recorded the Device's existence dimmed and faded. . . . The messages ceased. . . . The second Device, much altered, did not send any messages after its passage through interspace, but now a column of blackness marred the fountain of lights. . . . This black column did not waver, nor did it grow. . . . It shifted, first here, then there. . . . It persisted despite all their efforts to remove it. . . . Again the Seeker Wished it Undone. . . . The column of darkness continued to lash within the fountain of lights. No messages were forthcoming. . . .

Reviewers were appointed to examine the work, test the equations, study the methods. . . . They could find no flaw, yet the fountain of many colors remained disfigured and hideous, marred by darkness that had become the darkness of ignorance, then the shadow of fear. . . . "We cannot find the Device," *the Seeker said at the review hearing,* "Once it passed through interspace, it was lost to us. We know it still exists somewhere. We know it is seriously flawed, perhaps fatally flawed. It will pass out of the galaxy eventually, and until it does, it poses a problem, perhaps even a threat to any life form it locates. It does not respond to the selfdestruct command. It is beyond our ability to stop it or to correct it. We have tried to no avail. . . ."

The reviewers gazed at the marred fountain of light, a pale, sad flicker here and there the only visible reaction among them. . . . After the adjournment, the Seeker's own lights dimmed and faded. . . . before the Sentient Ylem could follow his example, the reviewers intervened. . . . "Sentient Ylem," *the Seeker of reviewers said,* "the pursuit of knowledge is to our race the highest order of intelligence, second only to love and respect for intelligence itself. You and your Seeker have brought dishonor to this pursuit, and a threat to life. However, in doing so, you have also alerted us to the dangers of unknown hazards that lie in interspace. We thought ourselves ready to travel among the stars, and we find instead that we must be resigned to roam no farther than the reaches of our own star system until we have solved the problems your Device has revealed. This knowledge is most precious to us, for we now know that our race is doomed to die here, so we must now concern ourselves with preserving our knowledge and casting it to the stars in hopes some worthy race will discover and interpret its meanings. But there still remains the matter of your failure. . . .*

"Because the good you have brought to your own race is overshadowed by the evil that you may have brought to other life forms, it is the decision of this review panel that you must complete the project you have begun. . . . Until the lights of the Device fade, you will monitor them, for however long the Device continues to exist. . . ."

Ylem's own lights dimmed and flickered. . . . "May I," he asked in a low voice, "continue to work on the Device in order to try to solve this mystery?"

"Yes, Sentient Ylem. That is the only task you will have for as long as it exists. . . ."

The Device emerged from interspace in the star system of a primary with five satellites. . . . One by one it orbited the satellites until it found life. . . . When it completed its examination of the new place, it left behind a trail of destruction, death, and madness. . . . Sentient Ylem prayed to the intelligence that ruled all life to destroy it, but the fountain of many lights remained undiminished. . . . The blackness at its heart continued. . . . It did not respond to shadowing of the destruct panel. . . . It did not send any messages. . . .

(On the planet Earth, fur-clad hunters pursued shaggy mastodons across the ice sheets to the steppes beyond, and some kept going south, always south. They came in waves, seeking better hunting, more hospitable territory, then the ice crashed into the sea, and the retreat vanished. Somehow the Device had been watching this . . . or something spawned by the Device had watched for it.)

In time, Ylem's people launched an interspace life-ship, then another, and another. . . . Some of them even searched for the tiny Device, but they could not find it in the immensity of space. . . . Ylem continued to monitor the fountain of lights with the blackness of evil at its core. . . . He knew exactly when it emerged from interspace, when it reentered. . . . He could not know what it did in the intervals. . . . He no longer saw the multihued lights, all he could see was the blackness, the evil. . . .

Sentient Ylem often gazed at the glowing heavens, with the three pathways of stars that looked like ribbons, and his own lights pulsed in harmony with the gently pulsing lights from above. . . . Those nights his shame drove him to renew his efforts to find the evil he had launched, the ugliness he had injected into such beauty. . . . Each time he knew the Device had emerged from interspace he prayed that this time it would be destroyed. . . . Three times he had been offered the release of pardon and total annihilation, and

*each time he had refused. . . . From his laboratories had come the
theories that propelled his people through the mysterious interspace
and out to other star systems with myriad life forms. . . .*

*Each time the fountain of lights with its hideous black heart
appeared and disappeared, he pulsed the data into his computer,
and possible trajectories were formulated, only to be discarded
with new data, as new paths were hypothesized. . . . Some of these
were not rejected. . . . From a number that had been so large it had
been meaningless, there were now fewer than a hundred possible
courses that the Device might be traversing. In charting the emer-
gence of the Device from interspace and back in again, he was also
charting planetary systems, more than anyone had imagined,
could imagine. . . . No race could explore them all. . . . one might
as easily examine every grain of sand on an infinite beach. . . .*

*His theories became even more abstract and abstruse. . . . That
no one read them any longer was a matter of indifference to him. . . .
The pursuit of knowledge was the only endeavor worthy of intelligence, he told himself now and again, and could not remember if he
had made this up, or if he had heard it from someone else a long time
ago. . . . Eventually even the desire for knowledge faded, and for long
periods he was motionless, a pale flicker the only indication that he
still lived. He had been made a subject of study himself, and his
observers reported that sometimes following his pale interludes, he
almost blazed with an incandescence. No one knew how to interpret
this. He no longer talked or wrote scientific papers. . . . The observers
also reported that sometimes after his pale interludes, he flared with
the gaiety of laughter, and this left them uneasy. . . . The Seekers
would have put him to rest, but they did not dare. He had become a
legend. . . . None knew that Ylem had been experimenting with the
genetic makeup of his own race in an effort to ensure their continued
existence once the craft containing all their knowledge had been
launched into space. . . . Only a few observers were with him when it
happened. . . . For a long time the Device had presented its fountain
of lights with the black lashing column at its heart, and Ylem had
been observing it. . . . This was his pattern when the Device emerged
from interspace. . . .*

He watched and pulsed data into the computer, then faded back into his pale lethargy when the Device reentered interspace. . . . This time something changed. . . . The fountain of lights with the unquiet black column was glowing one second, then it flickered, dimmed, and faded out. . . . The observers turned to Ylem for an explanation, only to find him gone also. . . . He flared with laughter. . . . Folds, he thought. . . . Of course, space did not fold by itself, one had to fold it. . . . Ylem had folded himself into the Device and brought with him all the knowledge of his race as well as their genetic codes. . . . Folds!

He had tried to explain this to the Seekers and they had not understood. . . . He had told them in language made as plain as possible that at the moment of destruction of the Device, he would be able to locate it. . . . He had waited for that moment. . . . He folded space and interspace and time and stepped through to enter the Device. . . .

How little it had changed, he marveled, centered in the midst of the ever-rising, ever-falling torrent of light that ranged the spectrum of colors. . . . How beautiful it was!

They had done their work well, better than they had known. . . . Had they planned for it to be self-repairing? He did not know, but evidently it had that capability, as well as many others it had either learned, assimilated, or taught itself throughout its journeys. . . . There was a dead creature being probed by the photoscan. . . . Another creature walked without grace through the darkness. . . . This creature was alive, but tired. . . . So tired. . . . So alone. . . .

Ylem touched the creature, and knew at once its origin. . . .

The Device . . .

The Device had been gathering its own knowledge, sampling its own genetics from other races, merging them with its own organic structure to create a new race, one descended from Ylem's yet very much its own. . . .

The Device had learned to create life and instill that life with knowledge. . . .

Grey, this race was, and somewhat crude by the standards of Ylem's planet, but still far advanced from any other form of life found in the solar system thus far. . . .

"We have found another race, my Maker," said the grey one, recognizing Ylem from the secrets revealed to it by the Device.... "We have been in contact with this race and think they may someday become Worthy...." Ylem looked beyond it, and found himself outside the Device, surveying the world it had been probing.... A lovely planet, with clouds, seas, obviously with an intelligent life form. Ylem knew he could fold space/time again, if he chose, and have enough time to explore the galaxy and still return to learn everything there was to know about this planet, but then something happened, the Device sputtered, and there was a mininova in Ylem's mind....

Ngan was jolted from the vision by the sensation of Leah moving.

No longer liquid lambda, Leah had flowed backward onto the shore beside her secret spring and was assuming human form once again.

"I gotta go," she whispered to him, "or Mommy'll be mad. She always gets so mad when she wakes up and I'm not there. You'll be okay, though. Buddy, he wants to tell you a secret. I'll see you in a little bit, okay?"

Ngan tried to speak, tried to form words but could not. He tried to send the question to Leah: *Where will you be? Where in this terrible place do you live? I must be able to take you with me when I*—but he could not do even that much.

She was gone, and he was alone here.

His heart sank. He should have simply taken her and made this contact elsewhere, in a safe place where she would have been protected by the institute's security, but she had seemed so vulnerable, had climbed right into his lap like a trusting child who was happy to see a grandparent, and Ngan had chosen to seize the opportunity while her encounter with Buddy/Ylem was still fresh in her mind.

Now he'd lost her.

He faced the Impossible Being that was now forming itself in the liquid lambda.

He stared into its large, dark eyes and understood.

I am dying, it told his mind. *This body is dying and I must find another in which to live. There is much room in the Little One, many hollow places that she will never use or even be aware of. I intend to make my new home with her, so that I may right this terrible wrong.*

What terrible wrong? asked/thought Ngan.

The Travelers I have created.

The Ash People?

That is what the Little One calls them, yes. Vain attempts by me to re-create my race. They are little more than monstrosities. They are failures, but their essence is strong. I can no longer contain their power as I once could. I must find a new home before the signal reaches the Device.

What signal?

The self-destruct signal I sent out into space eons ago. A signal does not die, Friend of Little One, it merely travels from point to point indefinitely.

Or until it comes into contact with the thing that was supposed to receive it in the first place?

Yes. The Device has begun to shut down. It has detected traces of the signal. The signal itself has found traces of the Device's last entry point into interspace. It will not be long now before the signal reaches the Device and it is destroyed.

And you with it . . . unless you can find a new and worthy home?

Yes.

Does she know?

She has an impression of my intent, yes.

And what will you do once you have a new home, a new life in her body? Ngan asked.

I will continue the work that my creations—the Greys—have begun.

And what work is that, exactly?

Another flash, this one so brief Ngan barely had time for its full impact to register . . . the cure for cancer.

Despite my misgivings, my children's work is focused on preventing your arrogant race from committing genocide, Ylem though/said. *You are not much, but the Greys, my children, think you Worthy, and so Worthy you shall be made.*

And if we are judged to be unworthy?

Ylem said nothing.

And that silence told Ngan everything he needed to know.

When he awoke sometime later, Ngan found himself wandering the streets, miles from Leah's warehouse.

This had never happened to him before, and it frightened him.

Ylem—even sick and dying—possessed almost incomprehensible powers.

Ngan steadied himself, found his bearings, and quickly ascertained where in D.C. he was.

Not far from the institute's mobile hospital.

Ylem had to have done this on purpose.

Ngan looked at the sky.

Almost morning.

One way or another, they were running out of time.

chapter
2WELVE

"**W**hy did you do it?" asked McCain into the cell phone.

"Would it satisfy you if I were to say I did it because the man from whom you were cloned was my friend?"

"Not really, no."

Nakami sighed. "My dear Michael, always the suspicious one, always looking out for the hidden agenda or the unspoken truth. You're very much like him in that way."

"I'm very much like *who* in many ways?"

Nakami laughed. "Shave your beard and see if you remind yourself of anyone. I think you should shave, anyway. The beard makes you look somewhat sinister."

"Lucky me."

Silence, then, "Your sarcasm is out of place, Michael, not to mention a bit disrespectful."

"I apologize, sir."

"Please don't 'sir' me."

"I don't quite know how to talk to you at this point. In the last twenty-four hours I've been damn near blown apart, given a glimpse of the Dark Matter, and now discover that I came out of a test tube. I've had better days."

"Do not get so melodramatic on me, Michael. You're an intelligent young man, you're fully aware of how the cloning process works. You were born just as any other child is born. Your mother, like millions of women before her, stuck her legs into a pair of stirrups and bore the pain of labor in order to bring you into this world."

"Why does this not cheer me up?"

Again, silence from Nakami's end.

"Doctor Nakami?" said McCain.

"I'm sorry you had to find out this way, Michael. I had every intention of telling you the truth when the time was right. There were—and *are*—reasons for keeping you uninformed on certain matters."

McCain was hurt and angry and damn near heartbroken. "Oppenheimer and his boys had their 'reasons' as well. Look where that got us."

"Michael—"

"No, sir. My life, my *entire life* has just been proven a grand lie, and I'm upset as hell about it, so if my tone is somewhat less than grateful that's just too damned bad." He pulled in a deep breath. "So my parents were in on it?"

"Don't use such an archaic phrase as 'in on it.' There was no complex conspiracy involved here. The cells were taken from the donor's body, the process performed, and your mother was the willing surrogate."

"My mother . . ."

"She *is* your mother, Michael. She and your father love you very much. They accept you for who and what you are, not who you were cloned from."

"Which brings me back to my original question. Why?"

"Despite his flaws, the man from whom you were cloned was my friend and I loved him."

"Don't take this the wrong way, Dr. Nakami, but you're not much of a sentimentalist."

"Meaning?"

"Meaning, sir, that I suspect there is another more important reason this was done."

"Your suspicion would be correct."

A beat, then, "If you'd like to let me in on it, sir, this would be a good time."

Nakami exhaled heavily, then—after several moments of tense silence—said, "Both the Greys and this being called Ylem have senses beyond the five we as human beings attribute to all living things. Specifically, they have a psychic ability to recognize someone not by how they look or sound or smell or behave, but on a genetic level. The Greys are fully aware that humanity can be a deceptive creature, so they employ this particular sense in their dealings with human beings.

"They can recognize an individual by his unique base DNA code. Are you following this, Michael? They recognize people on a *cellular* level. That is the other reason for your existence. When you encounter a Grey, it will at once recognize the donor's specific DNA in you, and know you can be trusted."

McCain swallowed. "And their possible maker, this Ylem?"

"Ylem knew the donor, as well. It is my fervent hope that you and Ngan can find Ylem, and that Ylem—recognizing the donor's DNA in you—will once more reveal to his friend those same secrets he revealed over forty years ago."

McCain was silent for a moment.

"Are you still there, Michael?"

"Yes . . ."

"Do you understand now?"

"I think so, yes. I think it's unfair as hell that no one will tell me who—"

"Think, Michael, *think*. What does it matter? It has thus far in no way changed who and what you are. Knowing that you are a clone may somewhat alter your perception of your life—fine. I accept that and will once again offer my apologies for my part in the deception, but knowing specifically who the donor cells came from . . . that might change things drastically for you. Forever.

"Someday, when you are ready, you'll be told. In the meantime—will you trust me, Michael? Will you let this matter of 'Who?' drop?"

"Why should I, sir?"

Nakami sighed, this time with noticeable impatience. "Ylem has information that may very well be vital to the continuation of the human species. We need to know what it is, and the man whose cells you carry is the only person he will reveal that information to."

Silence, then, "I know who I am. I'm not an idiot. I want to hear you say it. I want to hear you say the name."

"*Do* you?"

"Yes."

Nakami said, in a gentle tone, "You are still your own person, Michael, that much has never been in question. Do not doubt for a moment that you are not unique, for you are, despite your genetic origins. You are as much a part of the world as anyone you pass on the street—possibly more so, for you can help to bring about great and positive changes."

"He didn't."

"Didn't he?"

McCain closed his eyes for a moment. "I'm a little . . . a little worn out right now, sir."

"Understandable. Syrinx creates a strain on the immune system during its initial introduction. I will let you rest for a while—but we'll be speaking again very soon.

"Do not despair, Michael. You are needed. You are loved. You are respected."

"Thank you."

"Rest for a while, my friend, and we'll discuss the rest of this soon."

"Yes, sir."

Nakami gave a short, dry laugh. "Again with the 'sir.' "

"Sorry."

"Rest now, Michael."

McCain gave the phone back to the Shopkeeper and fell asleep almost immediately.

When he woke a few hours later, Ngan was at his side and the doctor was administering the third, and final, dose of Syrinx.

"Time to take your body out for a spin," said the doctor.

Ngan looked deeply into McCain's eyes. "So you know."

McCain nodded.

"Then you know that things are now . . . uncertain?"

"What a lovely euphemism."

Ngan held up the clothes he had gathered together for McCain. "Then you know we probably don't have a great deal of time."

"Wouldn't be an automobile wreck without innocent bystanders."

"I beg your pardon?"

McCain grinned unpleasantly. "Never mind."

chapter

TH1RT3EN

ommy was awake when Leah got back from her visit with Buddy and her nap with Cain, but there was a man with her, and they were doing the grabbing-thing. Leah hated that because Mommy always screamed a lot when she did the grabbing-thing with a man, but she knew that the grabbing-thing was how babies were made because Randi told her about it once, because that's what hookers did, except they didn't want to have babies so they just did it for fun or money. Like Mommy sometimes did with one of her needle-friends.

Leah sat in a dark corner where they couldn't see her and thought about what Cain had said about living in a real house. She thought that would be great. Especially if Mommy got all better and wasn't sick anymore and didn't want to do the needle-thing or the grabbing-thing. Maybe Mommy and she would even learn how to cook, and they could make dinner. Leah liked that idea.

She hated being hungry so much of the time—and cold and scared. She hated the . . . *impression* that she was always being watched or that someone or something was going to come out of the shadows and hurt her or take away what little she had.

"Ooooh, God, baby," croaked Mommy, ". . . feels so good . . ."

Leah pulled her knees up against her chest and folded her arms across them, then put her head down and cried, wishing that Buddy had felt like company or that she'd waited until Cain was awake.

After it was over, Leah watched as her mother and the man lay naked in the candlelight, sweating. She hoped that the grabbing-thing was over because she was getting hungry again. Maybe Mommy would be in a good mood now and give her some money so she could buy a hot dog or a taco or something. She walked out of the darkness, and the man laying next to her mother sat up and smiled.

"So that's her, huh, babe?"

"Yeah. . . ."

"Wow. I ain't never seen a . . . a whatchamacallit—space-baby before."

"Not much to look at, is she?"

"Hey, I think she's real pretty. Like her mom."

"Mommy's just a former abductee."

"Yeah, but them saucer-men must've got themselves a real taste for you, what with them always asking those dudes to bring you back so they can have some more."

They laughed, and Leah laughed, too, then came over and stood next to Mommy and said, "Can I have some money to buy a hot dog?"

"You already ate once today."

"Please?"

Mommy jumped up and slapped her hard across the mouth, knocking Leah back into the boxes.

"I said *no!*"

" 'Kay," whimpered Leah, wiping the blood from her chin and trying hard not to cry.

"Her blood's the same color as ours," said the man.

"So what?"

"So, I dunno . . . it's interesting, that's all."

"Shit. Only reason I keep her is because they give me more money each time to make sure I don't accidentally leave her someplace. But that ends next month. She'll be six then, and I guess there's something that happens to them when they turn six—something important, so they're gonna take her to the Center."

"But you said they was gonna take you, too."

"Do I look stupid? I know damn well that when they show up to get us, there'll be *two* cars 'cause they'll want us to ride separate, and *hers'll* be the only car with a passenger when they get there. I mean, it ain't like they couldn't still use me, but Mr. I'm-In-Charge, he don't like me so much."

The man *hmm*'d, then picked up one of the needles. "And this shit don't have no effect on the babies?"

"Nope. They've all been real healthy. I guess that's one of the things they're doing all the tests on at the Center. I guess maybe all the stuff I take ought to hurt them, but it don't, and they wanna know why."

The man looked at Leah. "You ever do any experimentin' on her?"

"Like what?"

"Ever send her trippin'?"

Leah wondered then, for the first time, if the needle-thing was their way of Removing themselves from what was going on around them.

Mommy looked at her and smiled. "It's not like I have to take care of her now, is it? They won't be giving me any more money."

"I hear Mexico's real pretty this time of year. You 'n me, we take your money and your stash, we maybe hit Jewel's for some extra, then head on down. We could set ourselves up pretty good down there."

Mommy threw off the rug she'd been using for a blanket. "She's been nothing but a pain in the ass since she was born. Let's do it."

Mommy's eyes looked just like the dark-coat man's and Leah tried to get to her feet and run away but she was still dizzy from being hit so hard and Mommy and the man were on top of her before she could even stand up straight and one of them hit her real hard in the mouth with a fist and everything went white and she felt the rubber band being tied around her arm then a sting and she cried out for Buddy to come and save her but then the world went liquid and runny and numb . . .

. . . *she was back at the Wall of Skulls, only now the skulls had grown flesh and become faces again, and all of them were talking but no sound emerged from their mouths. All she could hear were* tings! *and buzzes and beeps. Climbing on the faces, she made her way up to the top of the wall where a wooly mammoth stood in front of a pinball machine, concentrating for all it was worth. She said hello and it looked over its shoulder at her. It had Buddy's black-almond eyes.*

"Come on," it said. "I'm getting tired. You take over for me."

Leah stood in front of the pinball machine and placed her hands on the buttons. Even though she wasn't doing anything, the machine went crazy—lights blinking, silver balls shooting all over the place and bouncing off the bumpers, the score ding-ding-dinging higher and higher, and she began to remove her hands but the mammoth said, "No, just keep a grip on the machine and it'll continue to work." So she did.

The pinball machine told her things, but not like the mammoth or Buddy or Cain or Jimmy or Merc. It spoke to her from somewhere deep inside, and even though she didn't understand all of what it said—okay, maybe she didn't understand any *of it—it made her feel good to listen as she played pinball.*

. . . COMMUNICATION WITH EXTRATERRESTRIAL INTELLI-GENCE MAY EMPLOY THE ELECTRO-MAGNETIC SPECTRUM

AND MOST LIKELY THE RADIO WAVE LEVEL OF THE SPEC-
TRUM OR NEUTRINOS OR TACHYONS BUT WHATEVER THE
CHANNEL IT WILL REQUIRE MACHINES THAT ARE A PERFECT
FUSION BETWEEN THE MECHANICAL AND THE ORGANIC COM-
PUTER-ACTUATED MACHINES WITH ABILITIES THAT
APPROACH IF NOT EQUAL THE HIGHEST FORM OF HUMAN
INTELLIGENCE THE NUMBER OF ADVANCED CIVILIZATIONS
IN THE KNOWN AND UNKNOWN UNIVERSE HAS BEGUN LONG
BEFORE THE FIRST AMOEBA WRIGGLED TO LIFE NOT AWARE
THAT BEFORE IT BILLIONS OF YEARS OF EVOLUTIONARY
TIME AND TRIAL AND ERROR WAS AVAILABLE FOR THE WOR-
THY THE WORTHY THE WORTHY THE PRECISE SEQUENCE OF
EVENTS THAT HAVE TAKEN PLACE ON YOUR PLANET FROM
THE EXTINCTION OF THE DINOSAURS TO THE RECESSION OF
THE PLIOCENE AND PLEISTOCENE FORESTS HAVE NOT
OCCURRED IN EXACTLY THE SAME MANNER ANYWHERE
ELSE IN THE UNIVERSE AND THAT MAKES THIS PLANET AND
ITS INHABITANTS UNIQUE IF NOT IMMEDIATELY WORTHY
WORTHY WORTHY THE ENTIRE EVOLUTIONARY HISTORY OF
YOUR PLANET PARTICULARLY THE SECRETS CONTAINED IN
FOSSILIZED ENDOCASTS DEMONSTRATES A PROGRESSIVE
TENDENCY TOWARD THE WORTHINESS THAT COMES FROM
INTELLIGENCE SMART ORGANISMS SURVIVE BETTER AND
LEAVE MORE OFFSPRING THAN UNINTELLIGENT ONES BUT
THAT MATTERS LITTLE BECAUSE ONCE INTELLIGENT
BEINGS NO MATTER HOW HIGH OR ADMIRABLE THEIR GOALS
ACHIEVE TECHNOLOGY AND THE CAPACITY FOR SELF-
DESTRUCTION OF THEIR SPECIES THE SELECTIVE ADVAN-
TAGE OF INTELLIGENCE BECOMES MORE UNCERTAIN . . .

The mammoth stood next to her and pointed with its trunk to
a field that lay beyond the wall.

"Everything dies," it said, "but we only know about it as a kind
of abstraction. If you were to go out into that field and stand in the
middle, almost everything you can see is in the process of dying,
and most of those things will be dead long before you are. If it
weren't for the constant renewal and replacement going on before

your eyes—even though you can't see most of it—the whole world would turn to stone and sand under your feet. Everything dies, but there are some things that do not seem to die at all. They simply vanish totally into their own progeny."

The mammoth paused for a moment to munch on a few buttercups.

"Single cells do this," it said. "Not eat buttercups, but vanish into their progeny. The cell becomes two, then four, and so on, until after a while the last trace is gone, but you can't look upon that as death. Barring unnatural mutations that should be gotten rid of, the descendants are simply that first cell, living over and over again. And sometimes, if things go as planned, eventually the descendants will grow back into their original form. They will rebecome the first cell.

"Do you understand what's happening right now?"

"No," said Leah, watching as the stars above came closer, grew colder.

"Buddy is what you were before you became what you are, and he is also what you will become again one day, if things go as planned."

"Why didn't I just stay like Buddy?"

It was so cold, suddenly. So very, very cold.

"If I knew the answer to that, none of this would have ever happened, but I think it has something to do with worthiness."

The mammoth did not scream as the ice came but instead seemed to welcome it happily. . . .

Cold. Alone. Dark. Confused. Frightened.

Helpless.

For most of her life, Jeane had considered herself to be a strong, independent person, one who did not have to worry about being left to her own devices, but now, working her way slowly through the dirty back alleys of Washington, D.C., at close to three in the morning, she felt more like a scared little girl than she'd ever felt in her life.

And she hated it.

The oncoming paranoia didn't help much, either, truth be told.

Everywhere she looked she saw long black cars. Every corner and storefront, every pay phone and bus stop seemed to have some figure in a long, dark coat lurking nearby. Yes, it had crossed her mind that D.C. during this time of the year was overflowing with people in raincoats, and odds favored some of the raincoats would be dark, but after what had happened at the National Archives, then at her supervisor's office, she didn't dare take any chances.

She knew no one to call, couldn't think of anyplace to go where they wouldn't already have someone looking for her.

Plus it was getting damned cold.

So, as she emerged momentarily from an alley that lay in an area between North Capital and First Street, she decided to make her way to the subway entrance near Union Station.

It seemed to her that the best way to go "underground" was to physically go underground.

She was less than a block away from the subway entrance when she noticed that the echo of her footsteps on the pavement didn't sound quite right.

She whirled around and looked behind her.

Was that a shadow she saw retreating into a doorway back there? One wearing a long, dark coat?

She increased her pace.

The echo of her footsteps sounded just fine for a few dozens yards, then whoever was following her fell out of step with her rhythm. This time she didn't bother turning around.

She simply ran.

The lights that illuminated the stairs leading down to the subway were in her sights, and she concentrated on those, running for all she was worth. Once she reached the stairs she took them three at a time. She jumped the gate and continued running.

A train was just pulling out, and she was alone down there. She pressed herself against the far side of one of the marble posts, facing away from the stairs.

She listened.

Footsteps.

Getting closer, then stopping.

She listened carefully and heard the sound of a cell phone being activated.

Of course he'd have to do that before coming all the way

down. His cell phone—and hers, as well, it occurred to her—was useless underground.

She leaned a little to the right and listened very carefully.

She was able to catch only bits and pieces of what the man was saying.

". . . followed her for several blocks . . . spotted me then ran . . . Union Station . . . no, I can't see her . . . I agree, she can't get far, has to be hiding down here . . . wait for backup on street level, yes, sir . . ."

Then the sound of retreating footsteps.

She waited a minute, then removed her weapon and jumped out from behind the post, ready to fire if she needed to.

No one.

She was alone, but for how much longer?

She couldn't chance waiting for the next train—God knows by now they'd probably have agents riding the trains, keeping an eye out for her—so she holstered her weapon and considered her severely limited options.

In the end, there was only one thing she could do.

No one was there to see her ease off the platform and slip down onto the tracks. The electrified rail was across the roadbed, and she could easily avoid it, but ahead of her the black tunnel hung open like the mouth of some great, ancient beast waiting to devour her. Driven by a need to find one of the underground service ladders that she knew must be somewhere along here—ladders that led up to the street—she walked forward into the darkness, trying not to think about what would happen to her if a train came screaming down on top of her.

As she made her way carefully along the path, she started to think about all she'd seen in the last twenty-four or so hours—not the least of which were the alien photographs. She remembered as a child watching a special on television where numerous experts were asked about the so-called "drawings" that existed on mountainsides throughout Europe, and how every last one of them had stated that these drawings—carvings, actually, embedded into the sides of the mountains—were thousands, possibly millions of years old. From the ground they made no sense, just ruts and endless ditches . . . but from the air, thousands of feet above, they formed definite shapes—spiders and deer and circles and figures of men wearing bulbous head-gear. All of the experts agreed that there was no way this construction could have been supervised from the ground. It had to have been directed by someone or something that was thousands of feet in the air, and since primitive man had no means of flight, that led many of the experts to hypothesize that these drawings were directed by otherworldly visitors . . . ancient astronauts.

Aliens.

Little green men.

Bug-eyed monsters from outer space.

As a child Jeane had giggled at such notions—alien visitors were the stuff of bad Saturday afternoon science fiction movies—but now . . .

Now she wasn't so sure.

Scratch that. She was sure—sure that there had been more truth in those theories than she'd given them credit for.

What else could explain those photographs or why the men in black had been so hell-bent on keeping those photos a secret? Why else had they tried to kill her? If it wasn't true, then they wouldn't be after her now, but they were after her now, ergo . . .

Ergo.

She kept going.

A moving target was harder to hit.

The tracks curved to the left and soon the lights from the Union Street station were completely obscured. Jeane found herself moving in total darkness, the kind of pitch black, impenetrable darkness that stands at the entryway to every child's nightmare, beckoning *come, little one, and scream for me.* There was not even the dim eye of a signal semaphore to give her direction, and she felt her stomach tightening as she moved clumsily, keeping her left hand in touch with the cold, moist, slimy wall of the tunnel. She lost all sense of time, becoming engrossed with the darkness, the uneven roadbed, and the dead touch of the wall. She felt more terribly vulnerable than she had in her entire life, and she knew in her gut that she was walking to a place where no civilized human being had ever freely chosen to walk before.

Something was taking shape ahead of her, rimmed by faint light. She saw that it was the outline of a support girder along the wall. Another came into view, then another. With each step the light grew stronger, and she could see the shine of the rails ahead. She knew she had to be careful. There were places where the subway tunnels had collapsed in earlier years or been sealed off when the routes where changed and new tracks laid. Somewhere beneath this city were dozens of abandoned platforms, their entrances sealed off with concrete years before she'd even been born. They were tombs, these places, isolated and deep and dank, and it wouldn't matter a damn how loudly you screamed, there would be no one to hear you, no place for the echo of your cries to go.

Way to keep a positive attitude, she thought, then took a deep breath and continued making her way forward.

The wall curved to the left again, and she walked toward a rectangle of light suspended in the darkness. It looked unreal, like a stage devoid of props and actors. She pressed forward and pulled herself up over the edge of the platform, instantly aware of a coldness about the place that transcended temperature.

So she'd found one: an abandoned, sealed-off platform.

Could a person be more alone than she were if she found herself in a place like this?

As bad as it was, it still beat holy hell out of facing however many of the men in dark coats were swarming farther down the tracks at this moment, all of them armed to the teeth and looking for her.

She took in her dim, dank, oppressive surroundings.

It was a chilling sense of timelessness that touched her

mind rather than her flesh. Looking around, Jeane saw that the platform was not deep, nor were there any exit stairs—so much for finding a service ladder here—only a seamless wall of cold tiles trailing off into the shadows beyond the perimeters of light from the solitary bulb.

Odd, she thought, that there would still be power running through the electrical wiring down here. Odder still that someone would think to keep a fresh bulb in the overhead fixture.

The homeless, she thought.

Perhaps there was group of homeless people who'd discovered a way down here, and they'd decided to use this abandoned, cut-off subway platform as their shelter against the rain and cold.

She knew that she must walk into the shadows, and as she did so, she became more acutely aware of the silence of the place. The mechanical clop of her shoes seemed so loud, so obscenely loud. She should have felt fear, but it was replaced by a stronger emotion, a need to know this place for whatever it was—then there was something touching her face.

Out of the shadows it languished and played about her cheek like fog. It became a cold, heavy mist that swirled and churned with a glowing energy of its own, and it became brighter the deeper as she probed it. She could sense a barrier ahead of her, but not anything that would stop her, but rather a portal through which she must pass.

She stepped forward to find herself standing on a narrow, rocky ledge that wound across the sheer face of a great cavern. Above her, like the vault of a cathedral, the ceiling arched, defined by the phosphorescent glow of mineral veins. To her right a sheer cliff dropped off into utter darkness. To her left was a perfectly vertical wall. Jeane followed the narrow, winding path, each step bringing her closer to an eerie sound.

At first it was like a gently rising wind, whispering, then murmuring, finally screaming through the cavern, an uncontrollable, eternal wailing. Jeane recognized the sound—it was the sound of utter loneliness. It was a sound made by something totally alien and simultaneously all too human. It was a sound that until now she had heard only in the depths of her own mind. Such a primal, basic sound. She became entranced by it, moving closer to its source, until she saw a group of shadows assembled in a semicircle, each of them holding lighted candles.

A series of boxes and crates had been arranged to form something like a large table, and this table had been covered with several sheets of moldy tarpaulin. Atop this structure were several other candles that had been lit and placed in various holders to keep the hot wax from setting the tarp aflame. In discarded menorahs, broken sections of glass and plates, a piece of something porcelain that looked as if it might have been taken from a shattered toilet, the candles snapped and burned. In other places cones of old incense filled the air with heavy, spicy scents.

It was only as she drew closer to the crowd and this structure that she realized part of the sound she'd been hearing was their chanting. She also realized that the structure around which they all stood was a makeshift altar.

For a moment she feared that she'd stumbled upon some bizarre underground cult of devil worshipers or something worse, but then she noticed the offerings that were scattered about the altar. There were old pictures of children and families, some coins probably begged from passersby, broken radios, small television sets whose tubes had long since been shattered, pieces of automobile engines, fragments of broken telephones, and other items that—except for the photographs, some of which were framed—were all somehow electronic in nature.

The crowd was composed of several ragged homeless people, their faces ghostly in the flickering light of the candles.

Jeane pressed herself against the wall and listened to the words they chanted.

"Someone come . . ." said an old man in a tattered duster who seemed to be their version of a celebrant.

"Someone come," answered the others.

"And where do I live?" asked the celebrant.

"Under the tracks of the L," replied the worshipers, "in a cardboard box that's falling apart."

They bowed their heads.

"Within the cell life is hard, life is long," they chanted as one. "Within the cell, life is hard. Someone please come."

The tattered celebrant produced from one of his oversized pockets a tin can, their version of a chalice. He also produced a pocket knife with which he cut a small section of his thumb, squeezing the blood into the tin can.

He went around the circle and, using his knife, made a small cut in everyone's thumb, squeezing their blood into the can to mix with his own.

When everyone had been bled, he returned to his place before the altar and held the can high.

"And where do we live?" he asked of the congregation.

"In the alleys behind the cans," they replied. "Abandonment our blanket, no way to slough the fever. No friends to live in our hollow houses."

Jeane leaned forward very carefully and saw then that the altar stood a few yards away from a massive opening that resembled a drain pipe, only it was far too large to be a drain pipe. It looked almost like a section of subway tunnel whose construction had been abandoned. You could easily drive a semi into the thing and still have some room at the top.

She peered closer.

Not a drain pipe or tunnel at all—those would have been made from concrete and brick—this opening was constructed of some kind of metal, now giving away to rust. As the celebrant moved around the group and Jeane's eyes adjusted to the candlelight, she saw that the tunnel extended inward for several feet, perhaps even yards, perhaps even farther.

What the hell is that thing? she thought.

Maybe, just maybe, it was some kind of service tunnel.

She slowly, carefully stepped from the shadows and made

her way toward the congregation. She still had her gun, so she might be able to get through them if they tried to stop her.

"And where do we live?" intoned the celebrant.

"In songs unheard," replied the congregation.

Jeane stopped moving.

Was it just her anxiety, or was there some kind of heavy, rhythmic thumping coming from somewhere deep inside the rusty metal tunnel?

"And where do we live?"

"In the flutter of bound wings that don't know they're bound."

"Where?"

"Somewhere else, not here."

The lights that bounced off the interior of the metal tunnel were swallowed by something massive, dark, and shifting. A shadow.

The thumping grew louder and harder.

Jeane suddenly realized her mouth had gone dry.

"Within the cell, life is long, life is hard," chanted the group. "Within the cell, life is hard."

The tattered celebrant held the tin can of blood even higher and sang, "Who will take me? Where is my Creator? When will a Protector show themselves to us?"

She moved forward, removing her weapon out of habit.

A moment later, the thing emerged from the tunnel.

Jeane gasped.

No nightmare, no titan from storybooks, no grief, no euphoria, no imagined childhood bogeyman could have prepared her for facing something this sacred, for sacred it must have been, as anything so mythic and extreme and unimaginable must be sacred. It was both terrifying and compelling, a thing beyond All Things, a being above All Beings, beyond love and bliss or their sum, beyond grief and violence or their total, beyond grace and prayer or their cumulative effects on the psyche, beyond even the place in humankind's unconscious where the monstrous and depraved joined hands with the majestic and beautiful to begin the dance that ended with physical evil and moral goodness forever intertwined like the strands of a double helix encoded into the DNA of the universe, and, finally, beyond the capability of Jeane's mind to comprehend and catalogue its grandeur. She tried to force herself to close her eyes, to blank every detail of the sight from her memory and lock it away and bury it so she'd never have to look at it again, but she could not look away.

Its arms and legs gave it a vaguely human form, but its true shape was amorphous, indistinct. There was a shimmering, almost slimy aspect to its body as it writhed and strained against her perception.

It resembled, in a way, all of the drawings of so-called "aliens" that she'd seen over the years, only where these depictions had shown the aliens as being small, thin, almost willowy, the incredible thing that stood before the underground congregation was massive, its body covered in thick muscles. Its skin was grey and mottled, and its oval-shaped head was easily the size of any automobile, maybe even bigger.

The creature paid no attention to Jeane's approach, continuing with its task in dead earnest—gathering up the offerings placed on the altar and slipping them into a pouch near its hip.

It was wearing some kind of belt—only now, as Jeane grew closer, she saw that it was no belt at all but an organic pouch like that of a kangaroo that was part of the creature's anatomy.

The celebrant moved forward and offered the can of blood.

The creature took the can, then removed a clear test tube—easily the size of a normal human's arm—from its pouch and poured the blood inside.

The congregation began to kneel before it.

It was only now that Jeane saw that many of them were hurt, crippled, or deformed; burned faces, missing limbs, twisted backs or legs.

The creature—dear God, she couldn't believe how huge it

was—moved toward the people, hunched over, reaching out with one of its massive hands, quintuple-jointed fingers bending as if readying to grasp something.

One by one, the creature laid its hands on the heads of the afflicted.

A bright, near-blinding blue light emanated from its fingers and coursed over the people. One by one, each person it touched was healed of his affliction. Deformed backs were made smooth and straight, burned tissue was rejuvenated, broken limbs were made strong and healthy again, hands and feet that were missing fingers or toes were made whole.

Jeane was so stunned she didn't even realize there were tears in her eyes.

The creature looked down upon each of the afflicted with large, black, almond-shaped eyes whose onyx depths could not, for some reason, hide its empathy, its interest, its intent.

Its loneliness.

The kneeling congregation began to sing, over and over, "And where do I live? And where do I live?"

The creature seemed to understand that they were worshiping it.

Just as Jeane realized she had stepped into the glow of the candles, the creature looked up at her.

It regarded her with a calmness that seemed to say: *So you have come at last.* Jeane looked into its eyes, dark and oddly human and yet inhuman, seeing the eons of suffering, millennia of pain and loneliness. Deep within the eyes she could also see the disillusionment, the brooding coals of hate and retribution waiting to be unleashed.

So few are worthy, whispered a voice in her head, *but these ragged ones, they are the worthiest of all. Do not harm them.*

There was a sensation of warning mixed with longing that radiated from those monstrous eyes, and Jeane could feel a bond with the tortured figure. The emotions in its eyes seemed to alter, grow stronger, hinting at an impatience—a task nearing completion.

The creature sent her mind a series of images—

—and she saw the Earth and the moon as they must have looked to this being as it moved through the cold, glittering depths of the cosmos—the dry, pounded surface of the moon, its craters dark and secretive and dead as an old bone. Just beyond was a milky-white radiance that cast liquid grey shadows across the lunarscape while distant stars winked at her, then a burst of heat and pressure and suddenly she was below the moist, gleaming membrane of the bright blue sky, Earth rising exuberantly into her line of sight. She marveled at the majestic, swirling drifts of white clouds covering and uncovering the half-hidden masses of land and watched the continents themselves in motion, drifting apart on their plates, held afloat by the molten fire beneath, and when the plates had settled and the rivers had carved their paths and the trees had spread their wondrous arms, there came next the People and their races and mysteries through the ages, and in her mind she danced through some of those mysteries, Buddy holding her hand as they stood atop places with wonderful and odd names, places like Cheop's Pyramid and the Tower of Ra, Zoroaster's Temple and the Javanese Borobudur, the Krishna Shrine, the Valhalla Plateau and Woton's Throne, then they started dancing through Camelot and Gawain's Abyss and Lancelot's Point, then they went to Solomon's Temple at Moriah, then the Aztec Amphitheater, Toltec Point, Cardenas Butte, and Alarcon Terrace before stopping at last in front of the great Wall of Skulls at Chicén Itzá. The skulls were awash in a sea of glowing colors, changing shape in the light from above, their mouths opening as if to speak to her, flesh spreading across bone to form faces and her heart—oh, her heart felt almost freed and—

—and Jeane knew—she could not say how—that she was not the first human being with whom the creature had shared these images.

Who else knows? she asked it silently.

The little one. My friend.

The little one? asked Jeane.

When she dared meet its gaze again there was no sound of

pain this time, no agony in its eyes, which remained fixed upon Jeane.

Help set me free, said its eyes, *and I shall right the wrongs*. Jeane understood, nodding, almost smiling. Slowly she approached. Jeane was beyond fear now. She had peered into the eyes of the thing, sharing its greatest pain, the confusion, and the loneliness. Jeane could feel these things pulsing out of the creature, especially the loneliness, which had been bubbling like lava for untold ages. It reached out with its mind and touched Jeane's consciousness, suffusing her with strength, and she stepped closer to the congregation, her left foot sliding on the cavern floor. Hearing the sound, the celebrant paused, turning his skull-like head, cocking it to the side, to regard the intruder that stood nearby.

"The Protector has come," he said, pointing toward her.

The congregation turned and, seeing the gun in her hand, smiled and offered their thanks to both the god who stood before them and the one above who could not be seen.

Stepping forward, Jeanne could feel an energy radiating from the creature.

The last of the afflicted healed, it began to move toward her—

—and something happened. It doubled over as if in great pain and opened its mouth and screamed. The sound grew like an approaching storm, filling the cavern with a terrible static charge and the sound of a billion people doused in gasoline and set aflame.

In her mind Jeane heard the creature's cry: *THE LITTLE ONE! MY FRIEND! WHAT ARE THEY DOING TO HER?*

It was a cry born of eons of humiliation and isolation and loneliness and defeat. The cavern walls shook from the power of the cry, and the altar exploded in a shower of wood and metallic fragments. Jeane backed away, for the first time awed by the power of the thing, seeing that its facial features had changed into something dark and nameless. For an instant, the thing's eyes touched her, and she felt immediately cold.

There was an eruption of light and a clap of thunder. Jeane fell backward as the great thing whirled around and ran back into the tunnel, past the congregation, and toward the source of its pain and anger.

Darkness and cold settled over Jeane as she ran after it, the congregation parting for her as she headed into the tunnel. She knew where the thing would be going, that this was the buried entrance to the ship that had brought it to this planet, and she knew what terrible lessons it would wreak upon the world if the "Little One" were to come to any further harm.

"Give thanks to the Protector!" cried the celebrant.

"The Protector has come at last!" shouted the congregation.

Jeane grabbed one of the menorahs and, using its light to show her the way, entered the tunnel, the creature's deafening, furious wailing echoing around her.

cCain looked at himself in the mirror and said, "Where'd you'd get these clothes, anyway— 'Hoboes 'R' Us'?"

"It's important that you blend in with the other street people," replied Ngan, checking the brace on McCain's leg. "How do you feel?"

"Like I haven't had a bath in four days."

"I think he means your leg," said the doctor, who stood over to the side checking the three bottles of medication he was about to give McCain.

McCain put some weight on his injured leg—as much as he could while using the aluminum crutch—and winced.

"Pain?" asked the doctor.

"No, nothing hurts, it's just I can . . ." McCain shook his head and exhaled heavily. "I can feel the pins holding the bone together . . . I can feel the muscles surrounding the bone—hell, I think I can even feel the cartilage."

The doctor nodded. "You'll experience some sensation of minor shifting for a little while, but it's nothing to worry about." He pointed to the leg brace, which, to McCain's eyes, anyway, looked like something out of a science fiction movie, an attachment for a Mechanical Man Under Construction. "It would take a rocket launcher to knock that thing out of place."

"He exaggerates a little, I think," said Ngan.

The doctor grinned. "Okay, maybe a little, but not by much." He put the three bottles of pills into a paper bag, along with a detailed set of instructions on how and when the medications should be taken, and slipped everything into the pocket of McCain's shabby coat. "You won't need to take the first dose until later today."

"That reminds me," said McCain. "What time is it?"

"A little before four a.m." replied Ngan.

"You're kidding."

"Have you ever known me to make many jokes?"

"No."

"It is now one minute closer to four a.m., Michael, and what have we to show for the passing of that time?"

McCain smiled. "Fishing hours."

Ngan stared at him. "I beg your pardon?"

McCain looked at Ngan. "Fishing hours."

"I heard you the first time, Michael. I did not need for you to repeat your statement but rather to clarify it."

"Remember when I was a kid and you and Dad would take me fishing? We always got started somewhere between three and five in the morning."

"I remember," said Ngan. "For I was always the one who had to pull you out of bed."

"Feet first, as I recall."

"Yes. You frequently bumped your head on the bed post—which explains many things, now that I think about it."

McCain looked at the man he'd always thought of as "UncleAgain" and asked, "Was that a joke?"

"What do you think?"

"This isn't some multilayered Zen riddle, is it?"

"No. Just a question."

"It sounded like a joke to me."

Ngan nodded. "It was an attempt at one, yes."

"I thought it was pretty good," said the doctor.

Ngan faced the doctor. "Is everything in order?"

"Yes, God, please, take him."

McCain turned around. "Hey, I haven't been *that* bad a patient."

"In your opinion," said the doctor, "but how can you be trusted, what with all those serious fishing-related head injuries as a child?"

Before McCain could respond, the doctor left the room and Ngan was guiding him toward an exit door in the other direction.

"Are we going after Meara?" asked McCain.

"Yes."

"You think she knows about the Greys?"

"Yes. Right now, even her own people are after her. It doesn't matter if they find her first or the COM-12 agents do. Either way, she'll be killed unless we get to her before they do."

"Do you know where she is?"

"Her cell phone signal was last detected near the Union Station subway entrance. I believe that she was pursued underground."

"Do you think she'll be safe until we get there?"

"I don't know."

Jeane was perhaps twenty yards into the tunnel when she saw the first rat.

It was easily the size of a mole, with milky blind eyes but no back legs. It lay across a nest made from old newspapers and bits of string. As Jeane lowered the lighted menorah for a closer look, she saw that it was guarding several small newborns, all of them pink and shiny.

Jeane had never been particularly frightened of rodents but knew to use caution.

She gently stepped around and over the nest—no small feat, considering that the curved floor of the tunnel gave her little room. It was almost like being in a funhouse tunnel—one that rotated constantly—only the vertigo here was caused by her anxiety and the fact that she could only see three feet in front of her.

That creature was in here someplace . . . or it waited wherever this tunnel ended.

She glanced back at the mother rat and her offspring and thought of the rats she'd found at the explosion site, then became acutely aware of the stench in the air.

Something down here had been in a fire recently.

Or an explosion.

She moved slowly forward, using her free hand to press against the wall of the tunnel as her feet—both now turned outward as if she were attempting to imitate the walk of Charlie Chaplin's Little Tramp—moved slowly forward.

It might be a goofy way to walk, but at least she could maintain her balance.

She could still hear the distant echo of the homeless congregation and felt her heart go out to them. Jeane understood their plight—at least spiritually—better than most people would understand. She'd always lived with a feeling of being odd, of never quite fitting in, and so often hid this vulnerability behind a hard scrim.

But there were reasons.

Until she'd been seventeen, Jeane had grown up with esotropia—what most people referred to as a "lazy" or "traveling" eye. As a result, her face had always had a slightly comic, cross-eyed look, and children, being children, had been merciless in their taunting. "Which one of us you looking at now, Jeane?" they'd teased because she could not focus her eye. It had taken six years and three operations to correct the problem, but by then she was spiritually an outsider. She never really understood or connected with the pretty and successful girls and boys. She mostly hung out with the nerds, the overweight, the crippled, and the unpopular. She felt a bond with them, much like the bond the homeless congregation felt with each other. Even when she began to expand her social circle—mostly at the insistence of her parents, who worried that their daughter would be labeled a "weirdo" for the rest of her life—she still felt like more of a mascot when she went to the places and parties where all the pretty people gathered. She would always be an observer of a world to which she would never fully belong.

Law enforcement had been a natural outlet for her. It gave her a sense of protecting the outsiders—be it from others or from themselves. Even before everything that had happened to her in the last thirty hours, she'd begun to feel a free-floating sense of dissatisfaction with her work at the ATF. It seemed lately that the department spent as much time coming up with ways to cover its ass as it did actually enforcing the law. That didn't set right with her. Any body of law enforcement should never fear the truth. But that was idealism speaking, and she knew it.

Still, there were times when she wished she'd sought a position with something like the World Health Organization, or the Peace Corps, or even something as odd and high-minded as the Hoffman Institute.

She slipped and nearly dropped the menorah. Three of the candles fell out and rolled away, fizzling into darkness as they hit a puddle of something wet and thick that Jeane was glad she couldn't see. If she was wading through part of the city's sewage system, she'd rather not have to look at it, thank you very much.

She moved forward.

The floor of the tunnel began to level somewhat. Years of

rust and rot mixing with the natural soil and whatever animal—maybe even human—waste had turned hard and sunk back into the ground. The thought crossed her mind that perhaps some of what she was now walking on might—note that word—*might* be composed of human remains never discovered. God knew there were enough street people who disappeared or died unnoticed. Was it so farfetched to think that some of them might have died not only underground, but here? Aren't we all future fossils, anyway, when you get right down to it? People walked or drove across the remains of fossils every day—what the hell did they think asphalt was made from? Or vinyl, for that matter?

Or maybe even some of the surface of this floor. She could be walking across the decayed remains of someone's grandmother, or father . . . or children.

She shuddered involuntarily.

Don't go there, honey, she thought. Just . . . don't.

It didn't so much matter what she was walking on now, only that it was solid and flat and gave her some balance.

The remaining candles flickered and spat, creating crazy shadow patterns on the tunnel walls and exposing areas where the bedrock beneath the city had begun to force its way through the metal.

She stopped for a moment and studied one of the rusted, rotted areas where a small outcropping of stone was exposed. She leaned closer, holding the menorah as close to her as she felt safe.

There was moss growing on the rocks. Not only that, but it had begun to spread out onto the walls of the tunnel. She wondered just what this tunnel was or to where it was leading her.

She touched the mossy stones.

Looking at her fingertips, she saw the moss mixed in with the rust.

She sniffed the air once again. The stench of flames, yes; the smell of old waste, of course; the damp, rich, moldy odor of soil both moist and solid, but still, there was something more there. It wasn't the ghost of exhaust fumes from the subway trains that had begun to filter in from any one of a million places where such vapors could enter before latching onto something and becoming the grey smell of soot. It wasn't even the smell of the rusted metal itself—though for Jeane there was something oddly comforting in that smell, reminding her of her father's old workshop/storage shed that had sat toward the back of their property. She recalled the times she'd gone out there to bring him in for supper and found him puttering around, fixing things or just taking them apart to see how they worked (a habit that eventually infected Jeane, as well) and she'd step inside and there'd be that wonderful, weird, creepy, comforting, sharp metallic smell that seemed to tell her, Hey, c'mon in, we're doing cool and secret stuff out here, wanna help?

Keep your focus, she told herself.

And that's when it came to her.

The other smell, the underlying stench that she hadn't quite been able to place.

Death.

She was smelling the fumes from dead bodies—the rotting flesh and the hideous gases that began to hiss out when the corpse could no longer expand without some kind of release of internal pressure.

Oh, Jesus, she thought, I *am* walking on human remains. Some of those people probably wandered in here and died and rotted and now I'm up to my ankles in what's left!

The smell seemed so much stronger now than it had before, as if she had suddenly come across an unmarked mass grave or—

—was that a sound somewhere behind her?

Don't start getting paranoid now, she thought. Not on top of everything else.

Workable enough in theory, that, but at the moment, in practice, it left a little to be desired.

The men in black had taken her by surprise from behind when she'd been in another tunnel—another *structure*, at least—like this. She'd paid no attention then to the sounds she'd heard behind her, and look where that had gotten her.

She decided the best thing to do was meet her anxiety somewhere in the middle. From here on, every five yards she'd turn around and shine the light behind her.

It was either that or try walking backward through the rest of the tunnel, in which case the creature she knew for a fact was in here would be behind her, so she'd have to turn around anyway to make sure she wasn't about to run head-on into it and—

—stop it!

She took a breath, then another, then steadied her hands and nerves before deciding to return her attention to the condition of the tunnel itself.

The rusted-out areas and the rocks and the spreading moss.

Whatever this tunnel was part of, it had to have been down here for decades—maybe even centuries.

She remembered looking into the eyes of the creature and feeling the eons of loneliness behind its gaze.

She thought about all she'd seen and learned over the past thirty hours. Aliens and ships and Men in Black, oh my.

She stared ahead into the dark mouth of the tunnel.

Was it possible?

Was this tunnel perhaps the entrance to some alien craft that had been buried under the city of Washington, D.C., for centuries? If that were the case, then maybe the creature she saw wasn't the only one of its kind down here and—

—no. Scratch that.

She had looked into its ancient eyes. She had felt its isolation and impatience, its pain and confusion. Never before had she ever been in the presence of something that had been so alone. It was not just the only one of its kind down here. It very well might be the last of its kind anywhere.

So what did it want? What did it do with the blood and all the offerings the congregation had been supplying it with?

She paused.

She'd thought of that in the active tense: *supplying.*

During her brief but intense contact with the creature, it had let her know—perhaps on purpose, perhaps unintentionally—that the ceremony she'd witnessed was just one of many that had taken place before and would continue to take place until . . .

Until what? What larger purpose was being served here?

And where do I live? In cardboard boxes under the L . . .

Perhaps this creature—like the homeless and their underground congregation, like the child she'd been before the operations—was itself an outsider.

Yes. Something in that thought felt very right to her.

She began to move forward again, but this time the light seemed to reach even less far than it had before. It was as if the darkness before her was absorbing the light, swallowing it whole.

A shadow—and with it the stench of rotting death returned to her in a nearly overpowering wave. She froze, feeling something cold slither a slow path down her spine.

The darkness wasn't swallowing the light. The shadow was growing along the wall.

It couldn't be the creature she'd followed. It had been running forward, and there hadn't been any branches in the tunnel—she'd been keeping an eye out for that.

Whatever this was, it was big, and it smelled like a mass grave on legs—and it had followed her in here.

She took a deep breath, trying not to choke on the stink of a hundred open graves, counted three as she slipped her hand under her coat and gripped her firearm, then whirled around with weapon drawn.

Nothing could have prepared her for the sight of the thing that now stood less than ten yards away.

chapter

As he drove with McCain through the cold and rainy D.C. night, Ngan found himself musing about Shambhala.

Shambhala, the "Hidden Kingdom," is thought of in Tibet as a community where perfect and semiperfect beings live and are guiding the evolution of humankind. Shambhala is considered to be the source of the Kalacakra, which is the highest and most esoteric branch of Tibetan mysticism. The Buddha preached the teachings of the Kalacakra to an assembly of holy men in southern India. Afterward, the teachings remained hidden for a thousand years until an Indian yogi-scholar went in search of Shambhala and was initiated into the teachings by a holy man he met along the way. The Kalacakra then remained in India until it made its way to Tibet in 1026. Since then the concept of Shambhala has been widely known in Tibet, and Tibetans have been studying the Kalacakra for the last nine hundred years, learning its science, practicing its meditation, and using its system of astrology to guide their lives. As one Tibetan lama put it, how could Shambhala be the source of something that has affected so many areas of Tibetan life for so long and yet not exist?

Ngan smiled—somewhat sadly—as he considered the answer to that question, an answer known solely to those who, like himself, lived or had lived within the walls of the Monastery of Inner Light.

How that truth would change the world, he thought, if the world would believe.

He thought of how the Tibetan religious texts described the physical makeup of the hidden land in detail. It was thought to look like and eight-petaled lotus blossom because it was made up of eight regions, each surrounded by a ring of mountains. In the center of the innermost ring lies Kalapa, the capital, and the king's palace, which is composed of gold, diamonds, coral, and precious gems. The capital is surrounded by mountains made of ice, which shine with a crystalline light. The technology of Shambhala is supposed to be highly advanced. The palace contains special skylights made of lenses that serve as high-powered telescopes to study extraterrestrial life, and for hundreds of years Shambhala's inhabitants have been using aircraft and cars that shuttle through a network of underground tunnels. On the way to enlightenment, Shambhalans acquire such powers as clairvoyance, the ability to move at great speeds, and the ability to materialize and disappear at will.

Ngan knew it was not so much that the mystics acquired these skills as they were taught them.

The prophecy of Shambhala states that each of its kings will rule for one hundred years. There will be thirty-two in all, and as their reigns pass, conditions in the outside world will deteriorate. Men will become more warlike and pursue power for its own sake, and an ideology of materialism will spread over the earth. When the "barbarians" who follow this ideology are united under an evil king and think there is nothing left to conquer, the mists will lift to reveal the icy mountains of Shambhala. The barbarians will attack Shambhala with a huge army equipped with terrible weapons. The thirty-second king of Shambhala, Rudra Cakrin, will lead a mighty host against the invaders. In a last great battle, the evil king and his followers will be destroyed.

Ngan wondered if the child Leah was the incarnation, at long last, of Rudra Cakrin.

And a little child shall lead them, he thought.

By definition Shambhala is hidden. It is thought to exist somewhere between the Gobi Desert and the Himalayas, but it is protected by a psychic barrier so that no one can find the kingdom who is not meant to. Tibetan lamas spend a great deal of their lives in spiritual development before attempting the journey to Shambhala. Those who try to get there who are not wanted are swallowed by crevasses or caught in avalanches. People and animals tremble at its borders as if bombarded by invisible rays. There are guidebooks to Shambhala, but they describe the route in terms so vague that only those already initiated into the teachings of the Kalacakra can understand them.

Strange sightings in the area where Shambhala is thought to be seem to provide evidence of its existence. Tibetans believe that the land is guarded by beings with superhuman powers. In the early twentieth century an article in an Indian newspaper, the *Statesman*, told of a British major who, camping in the Himalayas, saw a very tall, lightly clad man with long hair. Apparently, noticing that he was being watched, the man leaped down the vertical slope and disappeared. The major stated that this "snowman" was carrying something that could have been a human child. To the major's astonishment, the Tibetans with whom he was camping showed no surprise at his story. They calmly explained that he had seen one of the snowmen who guard the sacred land.

Ngan often wondered who that British major was, for it was quite possible that he had seen the yeti who had taken Ngan himself when he was a very small boy.

In the years after his return to the monastery, the Ascended

179

Masters taught him much about the so-called "snowmen," and the true nature of Shambhala.

A more detailed account of these "snowmen" guardians—and the one that provoked Ngan's memory when he finally encountered it—was given by Alexandra David-Neel, an explorer who spent fourteen years in Tibet. While traveling through the Himalayas she saw a man moving with extraordinary speed and described him as follows:

"I could clearly see his perfectly calm, impassive face and wide-open eyes with their gaze fixed on some invisible distant object situated somewhere high up in space. The man did not run. He seemed to lift himself from the ground, proceeding by leaps. It looked as if he had been endowed with the elasticity of a ball, and rebounded each time his feet touched the ground. His steps had the regularity of a pendulum. Upon his shoulders, clad in the wooly coat of some long-dead mountain animal, there rode what appeared to my eyes to be a child. It was laughing. But whether this child was human or not, I cannot say for certain, and the thought that had I been more adept or brave I might have saved this human child from a terrible fate will haunt me until my death."

While people—especially Tibetan lamas—have been searching for Shambhala for centuries, those who seek the kingdom often never return, either because they have found the hidden country and have remained there or because they have been destroyed in the attempt. Tibetan texts containing what appear to be historical facts about Shambhala, such as the names and dates of its kings and records of corresponding events occurring in the outside world, give Tibetans additional reason for believing that the kingdom exists.

Recent events that seem to correspond to the predictions of the mythic kingdom add strength to their belief. The disintegration of Buddhism in Tibet and the growth of materialism throughout the world, coupled with the wars and turmoil of the twentieth century, all fit in with the prophecy of Shambhala.

But Ngan knew the truth. Shambhala, though hidden by a

psychic scrim from easy detection by the outside world, was, in reality, one of the largest Grey station-ships currently moored on Earth. The monks of the Monastery of Inner Light knew the way to the ship's hiding place, but they rarely shared that information with outsiders. When the Red Army invaded Tibet, it was to find this particular ship. Though they were unable to locate it—and many Ascended Masters and their pupils were tortured and executed as the Chinese attempted to extract this information—the Red Army nonetheless was able to locate and recover a much smaller scout ship near the village of Lungdo.

Chairman Mao's inner circle oversaw the recovery of the ship, as well as the capture and interrogation of its crew. Communist China quickly laid claim to a victory (in covert circles, at least) for the march of world socialism on par with America's retrieval of the saucers at Roswell.

Whatever became of those Grey scouts taken by the Chinese, no one ever knew. Ngan prayed every night that they were safe or had somehow managed to escape and find their way back to Shambhala.

Ngan often shuddered at the thought of what mass slaughters might have resulted if the Chinese had not discovered the Lungdo craft.

He wondered silently—as he always did whenever he allowed his mind to ponder such things—whether or not the yetis who had taken him as a child had somehow instilled secret knowledge deep within his subconscious, thus preventing him from maintaining any clear memory of his time with them. There were days when he thought this way of thinking was simply a remnant of childhood fancy, but at other times, like now, it seemed less fantastic. After all, the yetis had been taught many things by the monks of the Monastery of Inner Light—whom they saw as their friends and of whom they felt very protective. They were taught the art of mindwalking by the Ascended Masters who, in turn, were shown how to perfect the art of mindwalking by the Greys of Shambhala.

Had the Greys of Shambhala somehow known that he

would one day come into direct contact with the being they believed was their creator? Had they instructed the yetis to take him when he was a child and, using the perfected mind-walking techniques, instill within him their sacred questions?

So what could those questions be?

Jimmy Nighteagle was always referring to the street people as "hollow houses," vessels with more emptiness than life within them. It was Jimmy's belief that these empty places in the soul were very open to receiving knowledge and enlightenment, for the soul was always struggling toward a state of transcendence wherein it would achieve a state of unity with the Great Spirit.

Was it so difficult to believe that this creature, this Ylem, could reveal to Ngan the empty places in his own spirit?

Or perhaps it was through Leah that these mysteries would be solved. For perhaps she truly was the incarnation of Rudra Cakrin, and they were in the first days of the Final Battle, evidenced by the rising Dark Tide.

If so, they had to emerge triumphant, lest the entire world fall to ruin and evil.

"So where exactly did this thing come from?" asked McCain.

He was riding shotgun in a black van that Ngan was driving. They were heading toward the place where Parcel Street dead-ended into Riverside Avenue, an area notorious for its crime and homeless population. McCain wasn't crazy about the idea of going into that neighborhood at night, but Ngan seemed to know exactly why they needed to be there, and that was good enough.

Startled from his reverie, Ngan said, "If you were aboard a vessel at sea, old sailors would call it the Point of No Return."

"That's very colorful—not to mention cryptic—but in case you haven't noticed, we're not at sea, this van couldn't pass as a vessel even to a blind horse, and there aren't any old sailors around from whom I could solicit an opinion, so why don't you pretend I'm, say, a doorknob salesman from Hoboken and explain it to me in less metaphoric terms?"

Ngan looked over at him for a moment. "You're being unpleasant with me, Michael. Are you certain you're not in any kind of pain?"

McCain started to fiddle with his leg brace, then stopped himself, started once again, then pulled back his hands and pressed them into his lap, creating one ten-fingered, white-knuckled fist. "No, I'm not certain that I'm not in any kind of pain—excuse the double negative—but if you're trying to distract me from your answering my question, it won't work. What do you mean that it came from the 'point of no return'?"

"There is now less of the universe before us than behind us, Michael. Somewhere beyond where we are at this moment, the universe has stopped its expansion and has begun to contract, to implode. I believe that this creature's—this being's—home world existed there, at the point of contraction."

"So it came here from the end of the universe?"

"A bit simplified, my friend, but close enough to the truth."

"What's all that got to do with what's happening?"

Ngan took a deep breath and spoke in a rapid, deadly cadence. "Do you know the old legend about the City of Atlantis? That it saw its own destruction and so sent out various chosen ones to the corners of the Earth to keep its culture alive? The poet, the physician, the artist, the singer, the philosopher, etc. This creature, this being, was—is—all of those things. It is a poet, a mathematician, an artist. It is the last of its kind. It has been in contact with races we never knew existed. Perhaps it is named Ylem because it was here before the known universe came into existence, I don't know, but something came along and destroyed its home."

"The point of contraction?"

"I believe so, yes. A world cannot very well continue if the space that it occupies no longer exists."

McCain considered all of that. "Then what happened to the others?"

Ngan shrugged sadly. "Their world was physically destroyed in one cataclysmic sweep. So, too, were their physical forms. Make no mistake about the powers this race possessed, Michael—their bodies were merely vessels to contain a consciousness so far advanced that even the likes of Einstein, Hawking, Sri Chinmoy Ghose, and even the Dali Lama would tremble at the truth of it."

"So what happened to them?" McCain asked.

"Maybe they are now nothing more than pure consciousness. Finding the answer to that question is for another time, and for greater minds than ours. Ylem has no home to go back to. For eons it's been hiding here, withering in pain and loneliness for the weight of the knowledge it carries."

"And what exactly is that knowledge?"

Ngan glanced at his friend. "Only she can tell us that."

"She? You mean the little girl, Leah?"

"Yes."

McCain shifted in his seat and pressed his hands deeper into his lap. "God, this feels so strange. I have never been so aware of my internal parts as I am now."

"It makes you uncomfortable?"

"Hell, yes."

Ngan nodded. "Then perhaps you would not mind if I provided you with a little distraction from your . . . *awareness*?"

"Anything."

"Very well. You know, of course, about the Greys."

"Yes."

"And your connection to them?"

"Yes."

Ngan turned a corner and pulled to a stop. The rain was coming down much harder. A red traffic light scattered rubies across the van's windshield.

"Would you like to know how I discovered the truth about Leah?" asked Ngan.

"It might be helpful at this point."

Ngan began to tell the tale.

It was 4:09 in the morning.

By the time the president sat down to breakfast at 7:30, it would all be over.

chapter
7TEEN

The thing that stood before Jeane took her breath away in a near crippling and oddly elating rush of awestruck fear.

It stood at least eight feet tall and a yard wide, filling the tunnel behind it and blocking any means of escape. Its skin was almost completely transparent, only there were no internal organs that she could see. Instead, its interior was filled with a grotesque, roiling form of primordial soup. There were bits of bone and skull, wet and shredded tissue, large pieces of lungs and intestines, free-floating hands and eyes, and rags of flesh that were once the skin of a face before its owner had been opened up to die then be absorbed. The cloudy liquid in which these pieces floated glowed like radioactive waste. Once, as the liquid flowed around, Jeane swore that one of the faces was trying to form the words "Help me."

The thing reeked of death and decay.

It moved forward, pulling itself slowly more erect, amoeba to fish to coelacanth to Cro-Magnon to Man to a Thing Beyond Man and, finally, to a Thing Beyond All Things. Its head was roughly diamond-shaped, a small forehead that widened at the jaws and mouth before angling back into its neck. It opened its mouth to reveal no teeth, only a black pit. Jeane saw the brief glittering of stars in that darkness.

It looks like a deformed glass ape, she thought, then decided she was wrong. An ape would not have claws like this creature did, long and thick and sharp, claws that, once attached to a victim, would not release their grip until either the victim or the creature itself was dead.

It moved with surprising grace and power.

Not an ape at all. It's more like a bear, Jeane thought.

She had no way of knowing that the creature she faced was a prototype of the Armodont, a creature created for the Greys' gene banks—and one they later perfected—whose sole purpose was to destroy enemies among the Greys' own kind.

Only this prototype—designed in haste by Ylem centuries before the first Grey stepped foot on Earth—was unable to distinguish between a Grey and almost all other life forms. To it, all things not Ylem were enemies . . . except for those few pale, hairless creatures whose minds had touched its own. It found some of these odd creatures—it sometimes associated the word "human" with many of them—to be objects of pity, or scorn, or fascination.

But mostly they were objects of fear and danger and not to be trusted.

Yet there was something about this human that confused the creature. It could not tell if the human meant harm or not.

Still, it readied itself to attack and absorb. That was its primary function, after all, and the creature was nothing if not loyal to its purpose.

It moved forward.
Slowly.

For her part, Jeane could easily think of 3,417 other places she'd rather be right now than facing this thing—including back in grade school where all the kids made fun of her because of her eye. At least back then she had the comfort of knowing that the bell would eventually ring and she could go home where everyone loved her and no one laughed at the way she looked.

Anything would be better than standing here.
Trapped.
With this thing moving slowly toward her.

Jimmy Nighteagle was agitated and unable to get back to sleep, so he climbed onto the small wagon that Merc had built for him and began to roll from one end of the room in the abandoned building to the other—his version of pacing.

"What's up with you tonight, Chief?" asked Merc, wiping the sleep from his eyes. "Feeling a disturbance in the Force, are you?"

Jimmy gave his friend a quick, irritated glance, then shook his head and continued to roll back and forth. Somewhere on one of the floors above them a junkie groaned in his sleep. The air stank of sweat, urine, feces, and rotting food. The sharp odor of burning trash can fires filtered in through one of the smashed windows.

Jimmy knew something was wrong. His dream had been very disturbing.

"Hey, Chief, slow it down a little, huh? I'm getting

a case of motion sickness watching you."

"Send a note to the complaint department."

Merc pulled himself up into a sitting position and dug a cigarette out of his pocket.

"Those things'll kill you," snapped Jimmy.

"Maybe, but at least they're quiet."

Jimmy continued his "pacing."

"You gonna tell me what's on your mind," said Merc, "or should I wait for the book to come out?"

Jimmy slowed his movements but did not stop. "Did I ever tell you about the Dualities?"

Merc sighed. "Is this like another verse to the Sachem Cha-Cha-Cha?"

"I suppose so, yes."

Merc studied his friend's face for a moment. "You dreamed about Ylem again, didn't you?"

"Yes."

Merc exhaled a long stream of smoke, rubbed his eyes, then gave a quick nod of his head. "So you're thinking that this thing is trying to tell you something?"

"I'm not sure. I only know that its presence in my dreams is the closest I've ever come to having an actual vision."

"So you still believe that this thing is real?"

"I *know* it's real. So does Leah. She's actually spoken to it."

"So what's with all this 'dualities' stuff?"

Jimmy rolled up to Merc and stared at him. At first when he spoke, it was in slow, measured rhythms. By the time he finished, his speech had fallen into a rapid, deadly cadence that chilled Merc to the core.

"All natural phenomena on this plane of existence," said Jimmy, "are produced by two primordial forces: gravitation and electromagnetism. Those are white physicist's terms for the cosmic Dualities as they are perceived in the physical universe. These are cited in the *Walum Olem* as the principal irreconcilable elements; gravity being the manifestation of the *chindi*, electromagnetism the manifestation of the *kisi*. As electrons swirl in the electromagnetic field of the atomic nucleus and planets spin in the gravitational field of the sun, so does the individual journey down the Road of Life with the *chindi* and *kisi* forever struggling to control consciousness and actions."

He softly sang:

> *I have passed you on the Road,*
> *My Divine Creator's life-giving breath in which*
> *the Dualities struggle.*
> *I have felt touching me their breath of hatred . . .*
> *. . . their breath of euphoria . . .*
> *. . . their breath of loneliness . . .*
> *. . . their breath of fecundity . . .*
> *. . . their breath of terrible barrenness . . .*
> *The breath of all Irreconcilables swirling*
> *without and within*
> *adding weight to my journey*
> *and my lungs.*

Merc shook his head. "Not sure I'm following you, Chief."

"Before coming into existence the individual is a *N'alungu'mâk*—a Reconciled Being. They possess nothing so small as either the *chindi* or *kisi*, but, rather, the *GansXewulo'kwân*— the *chindi-kisi*-Transcendent. The memory of this state-of-perfect-consciousness being is hidden in the *alunsin'utai*, the subconscious, and it is the desire to be returned to this state that compels every word, thought, and act.

"Before birth *Kitanito'wet*, the Great Spirit, secretly gives every *GansXewulon'kwân* a purpose, points them toward the Road of Life, and the journey of birth begins.

"On the biological plane, the *GansXewulon'kwân* enters the egg or womb. Then, in the issue of a new birth, as the child screams and life enters its body, the *chindi* and *kisi* are separated, incapable of coming together again until the moment of death. The transformation of cosmic matter into energy and the transfiguration of instinctual forces into creative power depend upon the separation and eventual reconciliation of these primal dual forces. By the end of a physical lifetime an individual must have amassed enough secondary life forces— be it through knowledge, meditation, love, experience, or empathy in its purest, most unselfish form, to create the impetus necessary for the reconciliation to take place. Only then can the *GansXewulon'kwân* return to the Seventh Dimension and become one with *Kitanito'wet*."

"Thanks for clearing that up," said Merc.

"So you understand?"

"Hell, no, I don't understand. Look, pretend I'm a potato chip vendor from Iowa and put it in words I can understand."

"True Transcendence, a genuine reconciliation of the Dualities, can only be accomplished when one understands that the world is an illusion—a mental construct. This knowledge, plus a willingness to understand that the self is likewise an illusion, liberates one to merge with the Universal Mind in a state of True Enlightenment."

Part of an ancient prayer flashed through his mind then.

They who are born are destined to die; and the dead to be brought to life again; and the living to be judged, to know, to make known, and to be made conscious that He is the Great Spirit, the Maker, the Creator, the Discerner, the Judge, the Witness, the Complainant; He who will in future judge, blessed be He, with whom there is no unrighteousness, nor forgetfulness, nor hatred of persons. Know that everything is according to reckoning; and let not your imagination give you hope that the grave will be a place of refuge for you. For perforce you were formed, and perforce you shall be One with the Great Spirit upon the moment of physical death.

"Inside every living being," said Jimmy, "is an empty space that longs for some sense of purpose to fill it. Only then can it be truly whole."

"*That* I understand."

Jimmy waved a hand, silencing Merc. "For several days now, since my dreams of Ylem have become more vivid, I awaken with a sense that, even though it means Leah no harm, it nonetheless sees her as a missing piece of its own reconciliation."

Merc thought about that for a moment. "So you're saying that it wants to . . . make her a part of it?"

"Not exactly."

Merc crushed out his smoke and immediately lit another one. "I'm in no mood to play Twenty Questions with you about this, Chief. Just tell me what you think the problem is."

"I think this creature, this Ylem, is readying Leah and itself for transference."

"Come again?"

"I think it may be preparing her to accept its essence."

"You mean like . . . possession or some kind of *Exorcist* number?"

Jimmy nodded. "Quite possibly. That act of merging is, I think, its way of bringing the *chindi* and *kisi* together again. Not only two minds but two souls combining to create one. A forced spiritual evolution."

"Will it hurt her?"

Jimmy shrugged. "I'm certain that it doesn't *want* to hurt her, but . . ."

"The road to Hell is paved with good intentions," said Merc, rising to his feet. "Look, Chief, I'm still not sure I fully understand the . . . whatchamacallit . . . metaphysical details of what you're talking about, but if you think Leah might be in trouble we'd better haul ass and get over there. Anything tries to screw with her, it'll have to go through us first."

Jimmy nodded. "Sounds like a plan."

chapter

9TEEN

Jeane was all set to shoot at the thing when a huge shadow spread across the wall.

Something was behind her.

She turned, weapon still at the ready, and saw the creature named Ylem. It was crouched down, legs bent, because it was far too tall and wide to travel through the tunnel upright.

Its dark, almond-shaped eyes sparkled with the reflected flames of the candles. It looked first at her—she could still sense the profound loneliness behind those incredible eyes—then it focused its attention on the other creature in the tunnel.

For several moments, the three of them stood frozen, then Ylem reached into its pouch and removed a bright silver disc that reminded Jeane of a CD.

Ylem pushed out its arm, holding the disc in the palm of its massive hand. There was a sound like a great rush of wind, and Jeane backed away, pressing herself against one of the tunnel walls.

The thing that looked like a glass bear made a soft, whimpering sound, and the disc in Ylem's hand began to glow. It came on slowly, at first, the inverted reflection of a candle flame in a polished silver spoon, then it began to grow, to swirl outward until the bluish-red light filled the disc with a whirlpool of light.

The light began to spin faster, far beyond the surface of the disc, growing wider and brighter, assuming three dimensions as it began to spill forward, toward the creature of glass.

The sound of rushing wind became the scream of a freight train barreling down on top of them. Jeane pressed her hands against her ears, trying to block out as much of the noise as she possibly could but it did no good whatsoever. She was aware of every exquisite moment as the sound waves impinged on her tympanic membrane, setting it in motion and carrying the vibration through the hammer of the malleus, the anvil of the incus, and the stirrups of the strapes into the cochlea. Received by the basilar membrane and transferred to the endolymph liquid, the sound disturbed the sensitive filaments of the organ of Corti and generated electrical impulses that soared up nerve pathways into her brain, encountering its complex electrochemical network—

—and the sound registered—

—as a massive but muted ocean roar—

—then the sound of waves scattering on a beach—

—then one wave breaking apart—

—becoming a small pool into which a pebble was dropped—

—and the ripples expanded outward in concentric circles, becoming a rhythm—

—then rhythms.

Rhythms.

Rhythms and pulsing.

Rhythms and pulsing and tones.

The rhythms and the pulsing and the tones of the universe. The rhythms and the pulsing and the tones of insects and heartbeats, of whisperings and thunder and bodies locked in sex; the pulsing runs of birdsong and tolling bells and whistling breaths; tones of infant birth cries, canticle moans of graveside mourners; cicada arpeggios; descants from whales breaking the surface and the trilling of single cells in division and in death; the thunderous tympani of gorillas in Africa beating their chests; the chirping of crickets; the growl of cancer cells devouring delicate tissues; modulated vibrations of a million locusts in migration; the primeval groans from shifting tectonic plates; the *gloriae* of melting polar ice caps; madrigal dawn; *andante* night; and the brassy, sassy blues from the light of a long dead star as it staggered like a drunkard toward the Earth.

As the sound grew, so did the light, spiraling farther outward toward the creature of glass.

The onslaught of sounds became a physical weight in Jeane's brain, and she sank slowly to her knees. The spiraling light shot over her head and began to wrap itself around the creature of glass, gaining momentum.

She stared at the sight, knowing full well that she was witnessing something no human being had ever seen before.

The light was absorbing the creature of glass.

Bit by bit, in flecks and particles, the creature was breaking apart and dissolving into the light, becoming one with it as it continued to envelope the creature's physical form and return in sharp bursts to the center of the silver disc, matter into energy into a state of entropy.

She could not look away.

The world proceeded backward, forward, downward, sideways, becoming another world looking into another world that shifted and changed and faded into shadows to be replaced by another, firmer possible world. There were children laughing, playing, growing old, dying, turning to ashes, blowing away with the snow. There were trees growing, toppling, rotting, turning to ashes, blowing away. Mountains rose and crumbled before her eyes, and with them races of people and creatures so fantastic she nearly wept at the sight. She was back home, an old and bitter woman, broken by grief. She also stood across from this old woman, young and alive and bright-eyed at the Possibilities. The two of them met each other in the middle of the room, whispered, "And where do I live?" then became one, grew even younger. They became shrunken and pink-cheeked, an infant vanishing back into the womb of its mother who spun back into time and vanished.

She thought she would be lost there forever, shifting, turning, rising, falling, becoming old and young at once, a babe and an invalid, longing for a touch, a kind voice, laughter, forever unbound, being broken down into mere particles, each of which contained a part of her essence—

—the last of the spiraling light zipped around what little remained of the creature of glass, absorbed it, then returned to the center of the silver disc where it swirled backward, growing smaller and smaller until, at the last, it was the smallest pinpoint of light in the center of the disc. It blinked brightly once, very quickly, then was gone.

In the center of the disc there was now a strange symbol where one had not been before.

It looked just like a coin.

The creature called Ylem slipped the disc back into its pouch and stared for a moment at Jeane. She opened her mouth to speak then realized she had no idea what to say— assuming that this creature understood human speech.

What did you have in mind, hon? she thought. *"Live long and prosper?" "May the Force be with you?"* or just a quick *"Klaatu barada nikto"* to cover all the bases?

Ylem never gave her the chance to speak. With a quick sideways jerk of its head—*Follow me*—it turned from her and began its trip back into the tunnel toward its ship.

Jeane found the three candles that were still burning, slipped them into the menorah, and fell in step behind the creature.

"For several days," said Ngan as he and McCain continued driving, "my meditation had become uneasy, fragile, unfocused. I kept seeing this image of a little girl, a waif in rags. All around her there was a bright cosmic light too strong to be a mere aura. When I asked her name, she told me 'Leah.' Then she made the Gesture of Turning the Wheel of Dharma— one of several sacred hand gestures passed down from the Ascended Masters."

Ngan approximated the gesture as best he could while keeping one hand on the steering wheel.

"The thumb and index finger of the right hand stand for wisdom and method combined. The other three raised fingers symbolize the teaching of the Buddhist doctrine, which leads us to the paths of the beings of three capacities. The position of the left hand symbolizes the beings of the three capacities, who follow the combined path of method and wisdom.

"The next time I met her during my meditation, she followed the Gesture of Turning the Wheel of Dharma with the Gesture of Pressing the Earth."

Again, he approximated the gesture.

"The right hand gestures pressing the earth. The position of the left hand symbolizes meditation. Together, they stand for the Buddha's overcoming of hindrances while meditating on emptiness.

"The third time, the Turning and Pressing gestures by her were followed by the Gesture of Supreme Accomplishment and Meditation. The nerve channel associated with the mind of enlightenment, *Bodhichitta* passes through the thumbs. Thus, joining of the two thumbs in this gesture is of auspicious significance for the future development of the mind of enlightenment." Ngan demonstrated.

"I wish you'd stop that," said McCain.

"This is vital to the matter at hand."

"No—I wish you'd stop taking both hands off the wheel to show me how the gestures are made."

"I only remove them for a second, and we are not driving all that fast."

"Still, it makes me nervous."

"Very well, then."

Ngan pulled over to the curb and parked. He demonstrated precisely how the third gesture was made and said, "The gesture of the right hand symbolizes bestowal of supreme accomplishment. That of the left hand symbolizes meditation. Together, they stand for the Buddha's power to bestow supreme and general accomplishments on his disciples, while he meditates on emptiness. Are you beginning to see a connection among the gestures?"

"Reminds me of sign language."

"Very good, yes. The origins of modern sign language are contained within these sacred gestures."

"So the Ascended Masters created sign language?"

"Its basis, yes. These three gestures—" Ngan repeated

them in quick succession. "—were the first ones taught to the Masters, who then passed them along to students such as myself. Those three gestures, in the order in which I showed them to you, are a sign of friendship and respect.

"The Masters suspected that as man's technology grew more advanced and his methods of communication multiplied, these three sacred gestures might be discovered and learned by those who meant them harm. A fourth gesture was added to the sequence in response. This final gesture was never written down, never illustrated in the sacred texts, and was known only to those of us who came from the Monastery of Inner Light.

"I cannot show you how this gesture is made. It is called the Gesture of Turning the Wheel of Dharma and Meditation. The gesture of the right hand stands for turning the wheel of Dharma, while that of the left hand symbolizes meditation. The two conjoined symbolize teaching the Dharma while in meditation on emptiness."

By now Ngan had once again started the van and was driving away from the curb.

"I knew that in order to enter my meditations, this Leah had to either possess great psionic power or was being used as a conduit by someone or something with that kind of ability. Either way, I knew that she had to be somewhere close by—her image was far too clear and strong."

McCain thought for a moment, then said: "So the farther away a person is physically . . ."

"The less substantial their presence while in the meditative state, yes."

"So how did you find her?"

"Process of elimination. Since she was dressed in old and dirty clothes, I knew she was poor. Since her own personal dreamscape was littered with garbage, I knew she was homeless, and since she always carried the thought of her friends with her, I knew she would show those friends to me if I asked."

"Did she?"

"Yes. One of them was an old shaman who had no legs and played the saxophone on street corners, hoping that people would toss money into his cup."

McCain's eyes grew wide. "Chief Wetbrain?"

Ngan nodded. "That is a nickname given to him by some of the more unfeeling members of the human race, but, unfortunately, it stuck."

"Everyone—well, maybe not everyone, but a lot of people who work in downtown D.C. know the Chief. I've heard him play his sax. He's great."

"Yes, that he is," said Ngan. "His real name is Jimmy Nighteagle, though I did not know this at the time. I knew that—"

"Even in a city with a population the size of D.C.'s, there couldn't be that many homeless shaman who had no legs and played the saxophone on street corners."

Ngan nodded. "Process of elimination."

"So what happened when you found the Chie—uh, Jimmy?"

"Leah was with him. She recognized me at once and made—"

"The three sacred gestures?" McCain interrupted.

Ngan looked at McCain. "I would appreciate it, Michael, if you would stop interrupting me. I find it irksome."

"*Irksome*? When did you start using words out of Sinclair Lewis novels? Okay, okay, don't look at me like that, I'm sorry. I won't interrupt anymore—but I was right about the three sacred gestures, wasn't I?"

"No."

"No?"

"She knew the fourth gesture, as well. Which meant—"

"—she'd either been in contact with someone else from the Monastery of Inner Light, or—"

"Or that the sacred gestures . . ." Ngan swallowed—this next part was very difficult for him to say: ". . . were *taught* to the Masters by other beings, beings with whom she had been in contact."

McCain reached over and placed a hand on Ngan's shoulder. He thought perhaps he understood his friend's confusion. If what Ngan suspected was true, then the basis of his entire life came into question, and with it, his own personal identity.

McCain thought he might understand about suddenly being forced to question one's identity.

Ngan smiled at him, then pointed out the window and said, "Look."

On both sides of the street, the homeless were emerging from alleyways and condemned buildings. Some crawled out from sidewalk grates or pulled themselves from the back seats of stripped and abandoned cars.

McCain and Ngan turned to look out the back windows and saw that several more homeless—dozens, in fact—were trailing behind them.

"I noticed it a few minutes ago," said McCain. "Right after we pulled away from the curb."

"I don't think they are following us, Michael."

"Neither do I."

Their numbers began to grow, all of them seeming to head in the same direction.

"I remember when I was a kid," said McCain as he watched the massing homeless, "there was this old guy in our neighborhood who used to come around twice a week and go through everyone's trash cans looking for bottles he could return for the deposit money. I used to make it a point to set my alarm clock so I'd be able to get up in time to watch him. My bedroom window looked down on the place where the street veered off and became the alley where all our neighbors kept their trash cans. I remember this old guy. He never looked like he was sneaking around, never seemed to be worried about getting caught. He wore a long coat and a wool cap that he kept pulled down over his ears even in warm weather. He rode an old bicycle with two metal mesh baskets hanging over the back. He always put the bottles he found in those baskets. The thing I remember best, though, is that even if he had to dig all the way to the bottom of the trash can, he'd always put the trash back inside the cans after he was done. I liked watching the way he'd tidy up after himself when he was done. As a kid I thought, 'That's the way I want to live when I grow up.' He was so free, you know? Like something out of a Steinbeck or Hemingway novel. Mysterious and romantic."

McCain shook his head. "Christ, what a stupid child I was." He looked out again at the homeless parade. "There's nothing romantic about the reality of 'being free' like this. It's tragic and sick-making and sad. Look at them. We live in a country that can cough up ten billion dollars to manufacture Mars probes that don't work, yet somehow when it comes to using money to build shelters or fund assistance programs for the homeless, there never seems to be any cash on hand for that—oh, no."

"Careful, Michael. You're coming dangerously close to talking about politics."

McCain snorted a short, derisive laugh. "The older I get, the more I come to believe that so-called political issues are just a smokescreen to keep the general population cowed and too confused to see the truth. I mean, if you stop to think about it, all problems confronting the human race are and always will be, at their core, moral ones—matters of conscience, human decency, and compassion. They only become 'political' when someone or a large group of someones can gain wealth, power, fame, or real estate—preferably all four—by exploiting them."

"Would it surprise you to learn that I agree with you, Michael?"

"Yes, actually, it would." McCain watched the people outside for another moment. "It's like they're falling in step for a parade. Lemmings to the sea."

Ngan stared at them. "Look at their eyes, Michael. They appear to be in a kind of trance."

"Mass hypnosis?"

"Quite possibly."

The two men looked at one another.

"Ylem?" asked McCain.

"Yes," replied Ngan, driving a bit faster now.

"But why?"

"Because they are the hollow houses. They are the worthy ones."

McCain decided to let the "hollow houses" reference go for the moment, but asked, "What do you mean, 'the worthy ones'?"

Ngan studied the rain-soaked, shambling parade of hopelessness as they drove past. A few quickly became a dozen, then two dozen, three, four . . . until it became impossible to count. Men, women, and children marched through the freezing rain with great purpose and even greater determination.

"I mean that they are the poets," whispered Ngan, "magicians, artists, philosophers, and mathematicians of a New Atlantis, citizens of a discarded world that sank deep into our own long ago. They've known humanity at its best and worst and yet still choose to be a part of it. Most if not all of them would save the world—themselves included—if given the chance. The empty space within their hearts has been filled with the hope of redemption that Ylem has offered them. Ylem is calling them, and to Ylem they will go."

"Why is he calling them?"

Ngan pressed down on the accelerator. "To protect Leah."

"She's in danger?"

"She's always been in danger, Michael, but I think now that that danger must be very, very close."

"So Agent Meara will have to wait?"

"Yes. We have to get to Leah as soon as possible."

Ngan jerked the wheel to the left and tore around a corner at sixty miles per hour.

chapter
TWENTY-1NE

When Jeane Meara was a little girl her father, an avid hunter, shot a deer and split it open from its neck down to its hind legs, then hung it upside down in the basement to drain. Jeane didn't know it was down there. She went down to get something for her mother—she'd long ago forgotten what. It was dark, and she didn't like to go down there because the light switch was all the way over on the other wall, which meant that she had to walk across the basement in order to turn it on. It always seemed like a twenty-mile hike through the darkest woods to her, that walk across the basement to the light switch.

She got to the bottom of the stairs, took a deep breath, and started hiking through the forest, then she slipped in a puddle of something and fell on her stomach. Jeane cried out. She was having trouble getting up, so her mother came down and walked over and turned on the light.

There was so much blood everywhere. Jeane was so frightened she couldn't even scream. The deer was hanging there, its eyes wide, staring at her while the rest of it gushed blood and pieces of guts. Jeane didn't know if the deer was bleeding on her or if she was bleeding on it—she wasn't even sure if the thing was dead. Jeane reached out to her mother and tried to speak, but she couldn't. She panicked and reached out and grabbed one of the deer's legs to pull herself up, but the line snapped and the gutted thing fell on top of her, choking her with the stench of the cold death in its hollow belly, covering her in gore and thick viscera.

The fear she felt then paled in comparison to what she was feeling under the streets of D.C.

The tunnel was changing the farther into it she walked, slowly transforming into something that was a nightmarish fusion between the mechanical and the flesh.

The floor of the tunnel was awash with a thick, almost-dried brown fluid that rose to the top of her shoes like some great molasses spill. The walls were covered in a thin layer of pinkish, nearly translucent material that reminded her of the naked, quivering flesh of the newborn rats she'd encountered when first entering the tunnel. The organic-looking stuff dripped from the ceiling or hung in massive strands, like cobwebs that grew thicker and stronger the farther she moved into the tunnel.

The creature she'd followed had long ago released a pain-filled scream and run ahead into the darkness, leaving her alone. For a few seconds she considered turning back but decided that might not be such a good idea. Besides having veered off twice to take different branches of the tunnel—all but guaranteeing she'd never be able to find her way back without the creature guiding her—there was the threat that the men in black would be waiting for her somewhere along the platform of the subway station. They might have already discovered the abandoned area where the homeless church had conducted its surreal mass.

She'd reached the point of no return, so she continued forward.

The organic strands began to throb and glow the closer she got to the end of the tunnel, where a bright spill of harsh white light beckoned, its glow making the candles superfluous. Jeane dropped the menorah and gripped the wrist of the hand she was holding the pistol with to steady herself and her aim.

She moved on.

Several of the organic strands had been torn apart by the creature's bulk and flailed around like downed electrical wires, only instead of sparks these strands spewed forth ribbons of a milky red substance that looked like a cross between blood and phlegm, like severed arteries gushing.

She quickly maneuvered her way through and past the strands, holding her breath so as not to breathe in the stench emanating from them.

She at last reached the end of the tunnel and stepped into a much larger, brightly lit chamber.

If what she'd encountered inside the tunnel was sickening, what she saw now was nearly obscene.

The chamber was massive, easily a hundred feet wide and nearly as tall. Every inch of it was covered in grey and pink strands, the filaments growing thicker and more substantial as they rose from the floor toward the dome in the center of the ceiling, arcing and crisscrossing the lighted spaces like flesh-colored buttresses in a cathedral designed by a lunatic. Stalactites and stalagmites of greying epoxy were everywhere, dripping, rising, hanging across the great central space of the chamber like clotheslines made of ribbed cartilage.

Hanging from these thicker strands was a foul wash of what appeared to membranous sacs. Jeane stared at them, and—aided by the bright light, the source of which she could not discern—she saw dark shadows moving inside the sacs.

They were wriggling, pulsing, and throbbing like a row of human hearts dangling from bloody threads.

Her eyes then focused on the dome in the center of the

ceiling, which she now saw was not a dome at all but something that resembled a gigantic model of the human brain. Thick, fleshy web tendrils surrounded it. It glowed red in its center.

From the middle of this "brain" hung one long, smooth, thick strand that reminded her of a straw or an IV tube. It was open at the end, one heavy, iridescent globule of liquid balancing on the edge.

There was a huge indentation in the floor directly beneath it, a sort of reverse *bas-relief* sculpture that seemed to perfectly form the shape of the grey creature's body. She could easily picture it laying down inside this depression and taking nourishment from the "straw."

She stood very still, and soon became aware that there were vibrations—soft, gentle, almost imperceptible—rippling through the floor in precise rhythm with the pulsing of the sacs and the huge, hideous brain-thing in the center of the ceiling.

A slight breeze blew around her with each ripple.

It's breathing, she thought.

The ship was alive.

She moved slowly through the center of the chamber until she reached an angled platform, the only thing in the chamber not covered in organic filaments. She pulled herself onto the platform and nearly shrieked when it began to rise, triggered by the weight of her body.

It rose so fast Jeane thought she might pass out from the sudden pressure, but as soon as that fear revealed itself the platform stopped.

She was now standing in a doorway, staring into a square white room with a window on the far wall and a black, glass-like floor. The only object in the room was a large metal structure that looked like an oversized autopsy table.

She stepped into the room.

The creature had been here recently, she could still sense its essence in the atmosphere.

Crossing slowly to the table, she noted that the other three

walls were composed of square drawers, not unlike the drawers of a morgue. The comparison did little to settle her nerves.

She crossed to the window and looked at what lay on the
other side. There were frozen figures, dozens, maybe even
hundreds of them, all encased in something that looked like
dried lava. Some were vaguely human in shape and concept,
but most were the bodies of creatures and beings she'd never
encountered, not in movies, storybooks, fairy tales or even
nightmares.

She remembered the rat she'd found at the explosion site,
how it too had been in a state like this.

Her gaze shifted to the words written on the wall near the
window.

> *and where do i live?*
>
> *in the alleys behind the*
> *cans*
> *abandonment my blanket*
> *no way to slough the fever*
>
> *and where do i live?*
> *in songs unheard*
> *in the flutter of bound wings that*
> *don't know they're bound*
> *where?*
> *somewhere else*
> *not here*
>
> *within the cell, life is long, life is hard,*
> *within the cell, life is hard*
>
> *who will take me?*

A chill snaked down her back. She didn't bother reading
the rest of it. Even if she wanted to read the rest of it she

wouldn't have been able to. The wall to her right split sharply down the center and began to open.

She ran across the room and through the doorway. The platform that had lifted her was now gone. She thought about jumping for a moment, took a coin from her pocket, and dropped it down the darkened shaft.

Five seconds.

Six.

Eight.

Twelve seconds, and still no sound of the coin striking the metal surface of the platform. No way she could make the jump and survive.

She spun around.

The wall continued opening.

A huge shadow began to bleed downward into the white room.

She looked around for somewhere to hide but there was no place.

She took a deep breath, then gripped the wrist of her gun hand and steadied her weapon. The shadow began to shrink as the thing that cast it closed the space.

Voices.

Human voices.

Male.

An image of the men in black flashed through her memory, and she knew they'd found her. Somehow they had found her, and here she was, trapped.

She wondered if the creature would use her blood for testing, because she knew there was no way the men in black would let her live.

Fine, but she was going to make damn sure she took as many of them with her as she could.

Jeane closed her eyes for only a second, just long enough to utter a silent prayer, then aimed her weapon and held her breath.

chapter
2WENTY-2WO

Leah felt chilly and sick and scared as she heard the voices above her.

"The bitch! I'll kill her, I swear to God!" Merc, screaming.

"Not if I get my hands on her first, you won't." Jimmy, crying.

Leah tried to move, tried to say something, but her body was stiff, cold, and rigid. She couldn't even blink her eyes.

Am I dead? she wondered, then figured she must be or else Merc and Jimmy wouldn't be acting this way.

Merc pulled out a gun. "I'll bet you anything that old whore went over to Jewel's to get herself a little more candy before she takes off."

Some things do not seem to die at all.

"Jesus—Merc!" screamed Jimmy. "Get back here!"

"What is it?"

"She's . . . God almighty, *she's still alive!* Here, feel her pulse—no, you idiot, in her neck."

"Oh, God . . ."

"Christ, Merc, I don't know what to do."

"I thought you were a medicine man."

"*Sachem!* I was a *sachem* in training. A *spiritual* healer."

Jimmy lifted Leah's body into his arms and said, "C'mon, Merc, pull me out of here. We gotta find a cab and get her to the hospi—"

"Oh, *God!*"

"What? Merc, you're scaring me, what're you looking—"

"Over there—*in the light!* Oh, *God!*"

A breeze, old and tired.

A touch, warm and safe.

Fingers, long and willowy.

Light.

So much almond-eyes light . . .

And Ylem moved toward them, taking Leah from Jimmy's arms and touching the tip of one finger to her forehead and meeting her on the banks of her Secret Spring . . .

. . . *while above them the stars began to fade like guttering candles in Leah's mind, snuffed out one by one. Out in the depths of space the great celestial cities, the galaxies, cluttered with the memorabilia of ages, were dying. Tens of billions of years passed in the growing darkness. Occasional flickers of light pierced the fall of cosmic night, and only spurts of activity delayed the sentence of a universe condemned from the beginning to become a galactic graveyard. Light flowed inward, and the sky snowed a blizzard of galaxies as the lens of night burned brighter than the sun, than all the stars in supernova, and the human race fell on its knees, blinded forever by the white-hot darkness in its eyes.*

The air crackled with rage.

"I will do this for you, if you want me to," said Ylem/Buddy. "They deserve nothing better, yet they deserve so much more."

"Buddy?"

"Shhh. Just tell me what to do."

"Be here in the morning when I wake up."

"If that's what you want."

"Can't you ever go back?"

"This is home now. It has to be. My real home doesn't exist anymore."

"I'm sorry."

"I know. Thank you."

"For what?"

"For teaching me about worthiness. And love."

"Am I dead, Buddy?"

"No, but the time is upon us to fly."

Leah smiled. "Like Jimmy's song."

"Yes, like Jimmy's song."

Leah felt herself freed from her body, everywhere and nowhere at the same time, becoming light in its truest meaning, becoming light in its purest intention, including the darkness, and for a moment she was aware of a coldness that transcended temperature, a chilling sense of timelessness that touched her mind rather than her flesh, and within that coldness she heard an echo— distant but strong—of utter loneliness, and she recognized this sound because she'd been hearing it in the back of her own mind for all her life, only now it was fading away, away, away as the empty space left in its wake was filled with a blossoming awareness of all the knowledge left behind by the descendants who had simply been the first cell living over and over again, and though she didn't yet understand everything revealed to her, she smiled deep within herself, knowing she would understand, in time. . . .

chapter
2WENTY-THR3E

The man known to McCain and Ngan as "The Shop-keeper" sat in his van waiting at a stop light, impa-tiently drumming his fingers on the steering wheel.

Behind him, the mobile computer terminal/commu-nications center blinked and buzzed and whirred con-tentedly as it tracked the physical location of the Hoffman Institute's two field agents.

Dr. Nakami had called him at home thirty minutes ago and instructed him to get back to the antique store. Whatever was going to happen would happen in the next few hours, and McCain and Ngan, following estab-lished Institute protocol for field agents, would return to or contact the store when the situation was contained.

The Shopkeeper sighed, thought about lighting a cigarette, remembered that he'd quit six months ago, and laughed softly to himself.

He did not see the car pull alongside him or its window roll slowly down.

He saw neither the barrel nor the long, shiny bore of the Enfield EMI Semiautomatic .280 as it pushed out, then righted its position.

He looked up when the light changed from red to green, then slightly shifted his sitting position and stretched his neck to the right. As a result, the bullet did not enter his left temple as the assassin had intended but instead blew his jaw to pieces and spun him out of his seat.

The Shopkeeper landed on his chest, head pointing toward the rear of the van. No pain had yet registered but blood, tissue, and bone fragments were already clogging his throat.

He heard a car door open, then slam closed. He pushed forward and grabbed the leg of the computer terminal, pulling himself into a kneeling position.

A voice outside said something.

A hand reached through the shattered driver's side window and unlocked the door. The Shopkeeper reached forward and pressed a dark green button on the computer keyboard.

A man dressed in a long black coat, wide-brimmed fedora, and dark glasses climbed into the front of the van.

The Shopkeeper entered a quick command into the computer.

The man in black pulled a Colt Python from under his coat and took aim.

The Shopkeeper had just enough time to press the "Enter" key, then something behind him exploded. His chest opened up like a blossoming flower. He fell to the floor and lay there, gasping for breath, and watched his blood dribble off the terminal.

On the computer monitor, a command began to scroll.

```
*** WARNING *** WARNING *** WARNING *** WARNING ***
ans=1: kbin=split(/./unpack('R*' pack ('D+D*, keyword (initi-
ate)))
Packet Type: Terminal Key Packet
Keyword: Dead-Bang
Program Name: Playtime
Algorithm: 3 (RSA)
```

N:

    Mark:

0x556A4A67   76A4A655x0   00:00:57

   H M S

—30— —30— —30— —30— —30— —30—

  « » i¥

Read Command: None

Pause Command: None

Stop Command: None

DSR Sequence Initiated.

Reason: Unknown connection made from within system *R*

Playtime initiated at: 23:59:09 8 November 2000

Estimated time of completion: 23:58:08 8 November 2000

Last Command: Say Bye-Bye

*** WARNING *** WARNING *** WARNING *** WARNING ***

A voice shouted, "He did something to the computer!" and
the Shopkeeper would have smiled if he'd still had the proper
equipment to do so. He hadn't done anything *to* the computer, he
had done something *with* it. There was a difference. As the business end of the Python pressed against his forehead he wondered if Dr. Nakami would be proud of him when he found out,
or if he'd be angry, or if he'd mourn for him. Something bright
happened, and he felt part of his skull implode, then it was dark
and quiet and cool and he wasn't feeling anything at all.

As the command scrolled down the screen, a tiny red light
snapped on and glowed fiercely.

The light was attached to a device that had been welded to
the underside of the van, directly under the gas tank.

On the front of the device was a counter, on which glowed
quartz-green numerals.

00:00:50.

00:00:49.

00:00:48.
00:00:47.

When the counter reached 00:00:30, something within the device made a soft *click!*

The man in black stared at the command on the screen.

Outside the van, his partner shouted, "What's going on? I got the old man on the horn outside and he wants to know."

Not taking his eyes from the screen, the other man in black called out, "I'm not sure."

Under his feet, on the underside of the van, the counter reached the thirty-second mark and made a clicking noise.

The monitor screen went blank.

The second man in black climbed inside the van. "We have to try to retrieve the coordinates from the damn thing."

He joined his partner in front of the monitor.

They exchanged confused glances, then looked back at the screen.

Below them, the counter reached the fifteen-second mark, then the following words crawled slowly across the screen:

Time. To. Say. Bye. Bye.

By the time they realized what was happening, the two men in black had just one second in which to scream, and scream they did.

But there was no one there to hear them, aside from the "old man"—who Jeane had thought of as "Middle Man." He sat in a car on the other side of the city, listening to the night silence that was being broadcast back to him through his cell phone.

He bit down on his lower lip and gingerly touched the bandage on the side of his head, growing ever more impatient for one of the operatives to return to the car and give him an update.

He heard the two operatives scream.

The counter clinked down: 3 . . . 2 . . . 1 . . .

And that's when the van exploded.

Where there had once been silence, there was now rumbling, merciless thunder.

Where there had once sat metal and rubber and safety glass, there were now rolling yellow flames and curling, snarling grey smoke.

Glass shattered.

Flaming metal blew upward and out, slamming against the buildings on either side of the street, then clattered down onto the roof of the men in black's long, dark sedan.

The gas tank of their car added a second explosion a few seconds later. The flaming gas spread outward like lava from an erupting volcano, pooling under cars parked on both sides of the street.

And they, too, began to explode.

Within eleven seconds of the initial blast, every vehicle with twenty yards of the van was blown apart.

The man Jeane had thought of as "Middle Man" closed his eyes and gritted his teeth, then pulled the cell phone away from his ear and broke the connection.

The driver of the car waited nearly thirty seconds before turning around and saying, "Are you all right, sir?"

"Middle Man" made no reply.

"Mr. Blackmore, sir?"

"Yes?"

"Are you all right, sir?"

Blackmore—formerly known as "Middle Man"—slowly raised his gaze to meet that of his driver's.

He thought for a moment of the little girl, Leah, then the screams returned to his memory.

He stared at the driver who, like himself, wore the wounds of the confrontation with Agent Meara. In the driver's case, his eye was covered with a large, thick bandage now being held in place with an eye patch.

"There's a tribe in Africa—" said Blackmore, "—well,

what's left of the tribe, anyway—called the Masai, and every so often they choose one of their elders, or a cripple, or some other useless member of the village, and they give them a huge party, then take them out into the jungle and leave them there for the hyenas to eat alive. It's their way of not only controlling the population but of thinning out those elements that might taint the purity of their tribal genetics.

"That is why we will not fail to capture this being and its ship. Genetic superiority is on our side. For you see, this world, my friend, from pole to pole, is a jungle. Whether that jungle is composed of vines and swamps or boardrooms and contractual pen-strokes, it's all the same, no different from the one where the Masai feed the hyenas. Its inhabited by various species of beasts, some that rut in caves and devour their young, others that wear tailored suits and dine on their business rivals' broken stock speculations. All of these beasts have only one honest-to-God function, and that is to survive. There is no morality, no law, no imposed man-made dogma that will stand in the path of that survival. That humankind survives is the only morality there is. For us to survive as a race, we must be superior, we must dominate all lesser creatures, and in order to ensure that, it is not only vital but necessary to destroy, to eliminate, to thin out and expunge any undesirable element that threatens to stop the march of progress.

"People like this Agent Meara or those buffoons from the Hoffman Institute, they may have money and technology and friends in high places, but they're operating in a vacuum. All they can see is the foliage and vines. *We*, you and I, we can see the jungle. We know how to move through it. We know where the hyenas hide."

He fell silent again for a few moments, then—releasing a hard breath—looked at the driver and said, "I think it's time to bring in backup."

"Another team?"

"As many as we can get," said Blackmore. He punched a speed-dial number.

Sitting in his private office on the topmost floor of the Hoffman Institute's San Francisco branch, Dr. Itohiro Nakami stared down at the report that had been handed to him less than three minutes before.

Across from Nakami stood a grey-haired African-American gentleman whose kind face seemed perpetually at odds with the cold, steely determination behind his gaze. His name was Samuel Layacona, head of the Hoffman Institute's Intelligence Division. He had been the one to receive the initial signal from the Shopkeeper informing the Institute that an SDR (Self-Destruct Response) had been initiated.

Everyone who was part of the upper-echelon of the Institute knew what that meant. A field agent had been put in a position where the only option was to kill himself and as many of the enemy as he could take with him.

The Shopkeeper had been smart, though. Layacona

had to give him that much. He'd zipped all of his crucial files and programs so they could be sent intact within ten seconds of his activating the SDR.

The Shopkeeper had given his life in the line of duty and had possessed enough foresight to protect his data.

None of the information in his computer had been lost.

Layacona pulled himself from his reverie and looked at Nakami. "Sir?"

"You needn't worry yourself, Samuel, my mind hasn't drifted elsewhere." He put down the report. "I suppose we should be grateful for the data retrieval."

"That's what I was thinking, sir. Plus he managed to out two of their operatives."

Nakami rose from his chair. "Forgive me if I seem suddenly sentimental about this, but I fail to see where the unnecessary deaths of three people is cause for celebration."

Layacona cleared his throat and looked down at his shoes. "I didn't mean to imply that their deaths were a good thing, I only meant—"

Nakami silenced him with a wave of his hand, then walked over to the far wall where a large, intricate quilt was hanging. Nakami folded his hands behind his back and examined the quilt closely.

"During World War Two, my parents were taken from their home and put in a camp built to hold Japanese-Americans. It didn't matter that they had both been born here, had been American citizens their entire lives. No, they were 'Japs,' and all 'Japs' were potential spies. My father used to take these walks around the camp at night, and soon he became acquainted with an American soldier named Gene who guarded the gate at the south end of the camp. It was a very large camp, triangle-shaped, it was, with watchtowers and searchlights and electrified barbed wire. There was an old Japanese tailor being held there with his family and this tailor, he started talking to Gene and my father every night. The tailor was working on a quilt, you see, and since a needle was considered a weapon he could only work on the quilt while a guard watched him, and when he was done for the night he'd have to give the needle back. When my father would tell this story to me, he often referred to it as the 'Needle Patrol Fable.'

"The tailor was working on a 'memory quilt' that he was making from all the pieces of his family's history. He had been working on it section by section for most of his life. According to what he told Gene and my father, the quilt had been started by his great-great-great-great-grandfather. The tailor had added to it part of the blanket his own mother had used to wrap him in when he was born, plus he had his son's first sleeping gown, the tea-dress his daughter had worn when she was four, a piece of a velvet slipper worn by his wife the night she gave birth to their son. . . .

"The tailor would cut the material into a certain shape then use paint or other pieces of cloth stuffed with cotton to make pictures or symbols on each of the patches. The way my father described it, the tailor would start at one corner of the quilt with the first patch and tell them who it had belonged to, what they'd done for a living, where they'd lived, what they'd looked like, how many children they'd had, the names of their children and their children's children, describe the house they had lived in, the countryside where the house had been. . . .

"My father said it made him feel good, listening to the old tailor's stories, because it meant the tailor trusted him enough to tell him these things. Even though he was a prisoner of war and Gene was his guard, the tailor told him these things. Father said it also made him feel kind of sad, because he'd think of how many people—of all races, not merely the Japanese—didn't even know their great-grandmother's maiden name, let alone the story of her whole life. But this old tailor knew the history of every last member of his family. He'd finish talking about the first patch, then he'd keep going, talking about what all the paintings and symbols and shapes meant, and by the time he came around to the last completed patch on the quilt, he had recited something like six hundred years of his family's history. 'Every patch have hundred-hundred stories.' That's what the old tailor said.

"The idea was that the quilt represented all the memories of your life—not just your own, but the ones that were passed down to you from your ancestors, as well. The tradition was, at the end of your life, you were supposed to give the quilt to a younger member of your family and it would be up to them to continue adding to it. That way, the spirit of your family never really died because there would always be someone and something to remember that you had existed, that your life had meant something. This old tailor was really concerned about that. He said that a man dies twice when others forget that he had lived.

"About six months after Gene and my father started the Needle Patrol, the old tailor came down with a severe case of hepatitis and had to be isolated from everyone else. While he was in the infirmary the camp received orders to transfer a hundred or so prisoners, and the tailor's family was part of the transfer group. Gene tried to stop it but nobody would lift a finger to help—one sergeant even threatened to have Gene brought up on charges if he didn't let it drop. In the meantime, the tailor developed a legion of secondary infections and kept getting worse. Feverish and hallucinating, trying to get out of bed and babbling in his sleep, he lingered for about a week, then he died. Both Gene and my father wept when they heard the news.

"The day after the tailor died Gene was typing up all the guards' weekly reports when he realized that all three watchtower guards—and these towers were quite a distance apart from one another—reported seeing the old tailor at the same time, at exactly 3:47 in the morning. And all three of them said he was carrying his quilt. Gene said he read that and got cold all over, so he called the infirmary to check on what time the tailor had died. He died at 3:47 in the morning, of course, but he died the night *after* the guards reported seeing him. Until then, he'd been in a coma for most of the week.

"Gene enlisted my father's help and together the two of them tried to track down the tailor's family, but they had no luck. It wouldn't have mattered, anyway, because the quilt came up missing.

"My father didn't tell me about any of this until my twenty-first birthday. He'd taken our family to New York City so I could see a real Broadway show. On our last day there we started wandering around Manhattan, stopping at all the little shops that lined both sides of the street. We came across an antique store that sold so-called 'Early Pioneer' furniture. There was a rather tacky display in its window, and my parents always found amusement in store window displays, so we stopped to take a look. One of the pieces was a large ottoman. I remember my mother asking my father if he thought there were people foolish enough to pay six hundred dollars for a footstool. He did not answer her right away, so I asked him the same question. When he didn't answer this time I turned around and saw how intensely blanched his features had suddenly become. He ran into the shop, climbed over some tables to get into the window, and tore what looked like a dusty old blanket off a rocking chair.

"It was the quilt that Japanese tailor had been working on in the camp. They only wanted a hundred dollars for it so my father bought it. We took it back to the hotel room and spread it out on the bed."

Nakami gestured at the quilt on the wall.

"Isn't it beautiful, Samuel? All the colors and pictures, the craftsmanship . . . I remember getting teary-eyed when Father told the story. Come closer, Samuel, look down here—in the lower right-hand corner—this patch with these four figures stitched onto it. Do you see how three of them are positioned high above the fourth one? See how they form a triangle?"

Layacona nodded. The fourth figure was down below, walking kind of all stooped over and carrying what at first looked like a bunch of clothes, but on closer inspection Layacona saw it for what it really was.

"It's a picture of someone carrying a quilt," he whispered.

Nakami nodded. "Or, rather, the tailor's *spirit* carrying the quilt, wandering the camp for the last time, looking for someone to pass his memories on to because he couldn't find his family. Please remember, the tailor wasn't yet dead when the three tower guards reported seeing him, he was only in a coma."

The two of them stood in silence for a few moments, admiring the craftsmanship.

"This is why I decided to pursue paranormal interests, Samuel. This quilt proved to me that there *is* a supernatural world—how else do you explain the tailor being spotted by the guards? What other explanation is there for his being able to stitch together this last patch while he was in a coma?"

"There isn't any other way to explain it, sir."

"No, there isn't." Nakami turned around and crossed to his desk. Layacona admired the quilt for a few seconds more before joining the Institute Director.

"In my mind," said Nakami, "is a memory quilt of my own making. It holds pictures of every person I've ever known who has died senselessly or whose death served no greater purpose. I now have to add a new patch to this quilt in my mind, Samuel, and I find it no less distasteful now than I did when I began it. Ian was a good man, a fine man, and a trustworthy friend.

"I do not wish to add any more patches to this quilt. Do you understand me, Samuel?"

"I think so, yes."

Nakami stared at him, unblinking. "Very well, then. I want you to contact the D.C. branch at once. Tell them that I want two helicopters fueled and running within the next thirty minutes, one for carrying personnel, one for carrying scientific equipment. I want them warmed up and running, understand? They must be able to take off the *second* Ngan or Michael sends the signal."

"I'll see that it's done, sir."

"I also want a full medical team in a mobile unit ready to go as soon as the helicopters take off."

"Yes, sir."

"And Samuel?"

"Yes?"

"I want the helicopters armed—but make certain that everyone knows that no extreme force is to be used unless absolutely necessary."

"You're hoping that the mere presence of the weapons will diffuse any potential conflict?"

"I've already got too damned many patches on my quilt."

"Understood, Dr. Nakami."

"One more thing, Samuel."

"Yes, sir?"

"Don't call me 'Dr. Nakami' anymore. It makes me feel like I'm some old, fusty professor boring the life out of his students."

"Yes, sir."

"Now please go and do what I've instructed. We'll work on that 'sir' thing another time."

"What about the explosion?" asked McCain.

Ngan said nothing.

McCain waited a few more seconds, then asked the question again.

This time, Ngan said, "My contact with Ylem has left a lot of . . . fragments in my memory. There was the information that he intended to convey to me, but there was also . . ." Ngan sighed and shook his head.

"Secondary impressions, maybe?" asked McCain. "Stray thoughts. Extraneous bits of information that were floating around in the background of its mind?"

Ngan nodded. "Yes. I can't be certain what much of it means, not without Leah to act as interpreter between Ylem and myself, but . . . I think the explosion was the first stage of Ylem's ship's self-destruct program."

"What do you mean, the *first* stage?"

Ngan turned a corner. Here, too, were dozens of homeless people moving in the same direction.

"Ngan? You okay?"

Ngan sighed and shook his head. "I don't know, Michael. The contact with Ylem was . . ." Again, he shook his head. "We've been so busy and this . . . this is the first time I've been still enough for my mind to settle somewhat and . . . and it's a mosaic inside me right now. Bits and pieces of information, impressions, knowledge, words in a language I don't understand, mathematical equations that I can't comprehend . . ." He looked at McCain. "And I am scared, Michael. One of the great disciplines taught to me by the Ascended Masters was the discipline of thought, the ability to compress one's knowledge into the smallest of flower buds and to water that bud with one's private thoughts, so that at any given time knowledge may be obtained by simply allowing the bud to blossom fully. But the petals have begun to . . . to come off since my contact with Ylem. Does this make any sense to you?"

McCain nodded. "Yes. Your mind has come into contact with something it wasn't prepared to deal with—at least, not *as* prepared as you thought." He leaned closer. "It's something more than that, isn't it?"

"Yes."

"Tell me, then, old friend."

Ngan closed his eyes for a moment, took a deep breath, and turned toward McCain. "There is a stray thought," he said, opening his eyes, "whose message is still somewhat . . . garbled . . . but each time it crosses my mind, it leaves me with a sense of time passing too quickly away."

McCain started to speak, then thought better of it.

"I know how that must sound to you," whispered Ngan. "So please allow me, just this once, the luxury of oversimplifying. The first time this thought came to me, there was something hidden within it that concerned nine hours. The next time, six-and-a-half. Most recently . . . five."

"Five hours?"

"Yes."

"Do you think that's how long we've got left before Ylem's ship destroys itself?"

"Quite possibly."

"Does the institute have anyone who knows how to cancel the program?"

Ngan smiled. "If it does, it's kept it a secret from me."

"Yeah," muttered McCain. "I'm starting to find out they're very good at keeping secrets."

"You have a talent, Michael," Ngan said, only his tone making it clear he intended to change the subject. "You accept what people think, you listen, and you draw conclusions from emotional responses. You would make a good . . . therapist?"

McCain smiled slightly but didn't know what to say.

They pulled up to the curb, and Ngan killed the engine. "In the back, Michael, is a large wooden box. Here is the key to the lock. Go open it and take as many weapons as you can carry."

McCain opened the box and removed a Mossholder handle-grip pump-action shotgun, a .44 Magnum auto-mag, a Tec-9, and a snub-nose .22. The Tec-9 and shotgun came with shoulder straps that allowed him to conceal them underneath his coat. The Magnum went into his left coat pocket, the .22 into his right.

"Ngan?"

"No."

McCain was surprised by the response. "I didn't even ask you—"

"You were going to ask me if I wanted any weapons from the box. The answer is no."

"But—"

"You're armed enough for the both of us. I would, however, suggest you reach into that little compartment on the side and remove a couple of the grenades."

McCain did as Ngan suggested. "These don't look like standard-issue grenades."

"They're tear-gas grenades."

McCain patted himself down quickly, made sure he had everything he could comfortably carry, including extra clips and rounds, then climbed out the back of the van where Ngan waited for him.

"I see you're doing better without the crutch." Ngan observed.

McCain realized then that his leg felt fine, despite its hideous appearance. "Yeah, it's okay."

Ngan handed him a small electronic device about the size of a pager.

"What's this?" asked McCain.

"In the event that we are separated and you need to get away, press the blue button. It will send a signal to the rescue team that is waiting for us."

"Ngan?"

"Yes?"

"Are you going to be okay? I mean—and don't take this the wrong way—but are you going to be able to focus?"

"I think so, yes. Now please stop worrying about me."

"Fine. Can I ask another question?"

"Could I stop you?"

"If it comes down to an either/or situation, who do we rescue—Ylem or Leah?"

Ngan was silent for a moment.

"I hated to ask," said McCain, "but we have to have a backup plan."

Ngan took a deep breath, then placed a hand on McCain's shoulder. "There *is* no either/or as far as the two of them are concerned. They—and the coins—"

"The freeze-dried monsters?"

"Yes. Ylem, Leah, and the coins are not expendable, but *we* are."

McCain stared at Ngan in stunned silence for several seconds, then said, very softly, "Shit."

"My sentiments exactly."

They quickly noted the groups of homeless people that were massing up and down both sides of the street, but they did not see the four men in black who crouched on one of the rooftops in the shadows and rain.

McCain followed Ngan into the abandoned warehouse.

Jeane held her pistol in front of her as Ylem entered the chamber carrying Leah in its arms.

Behind the creature were two men. One appeared to be in his late thirties, the other—the one who had no legs and who was being carried by the first man—was obviously a Native American whose age Jeane could not determine.

As soon as the four of them were in the chamber, Jeane pulled out her ATF identification and shouted, "No one move!"

Merc looked at her and shook his head, chuckling. "Now I've seen everything. You might as well put your gun down, lady, 'cause I don't think it'll do any good against our friend here."

As if to emphasize Merc's point, Ylem gently placed Leah's unconscious form on the metal table, turned toward Jeane, and stared at the gun she held.

For a moment, the center of Ylem's black eyes

glowed with red pinpoints.

The gun in Jeane's hand quickly became so hot she couldn't hold it. Dropping the gun and cursing, waving her hand up and down, back and forth, in an effort to cool the slightly singed flesh, she looked at Merc and Jimmy and said, "What *is* this thing?"

"This 'thing,' " said Jimmy, "is a friend. It means none of us any harm—in fact, it's trying to save Leah's life."

Merc snaked a hand down under his coat and pulled out his gun, pointing it at Jeane. "And if you try to stop it from helping her, I swear to Christ, lady, I'll dust your ass right here and now."

Ylem made no attempt to disarm Merc.

Returning its attention to Leah, Ylem gently brushed the hair away from her face, then removed two small silver discs from its pouch. One, it placed in the center of Leah's forehead. The second, it placed in the center of its own.

"What's going on?" asked Merc.

Jimmy stared at the tableau in a curious mixture of awe, relief, and terror. "I'm not sure."

"Jeez, Chief, you don't suppose that it's trying to . . . to move into her like you dreamed?"

"I don't know."

Jeane moved to pick up her gun but was suddenly struck immobile, as were Merc and Jimmy.

She looked across at them and said, "Can you guys move at all?"

"Do I *look* like I'm moving?" replied Merc.

"No, miss," said Jimmy in a gentle voice. "I can't move, either."

"Why are you doing this to us?" Jeane shouted at Ylem.

Because you must not interfere, came the voice in her skull.

Dizzy, Jeane looked at Merc and Jimmy and knew that they had heard the response, as well.

The disc on Leah's forehead began to glow a soft, bright blue.

The disc on Ylem's forehead began to glow an equally soft

and equally bright yellow.

Then—just as Jeane had seen in the tunnel—the glows began to spiral past the borders of the discs, growing wider and more substantial, until both Ylem and Leah were hidden within a swirling funnel of bright green light.

Ngan saw that the barrels had been knocked away as if by a small explosion.

"What is it?" said McCain as he came up behind Ngan.

Ngan held up his hand, silencing McCain, and put himself into a light meditation trance.

He sensed the energy all around them.

Within them.

He could even feel the echo of Ylem's physical presence, as well as Leah's, but something was wrong.

Terribly wrong.

And in his trance he saw Leah's mother and the man with her, saw what they'd done to Leah, how they'd left her to die.

Rage.

Deep, snarling, howling rage.

Ngan was trembling at first, then shuddering, and finally shaking with such force that he was wrenched from his trance.

The world he saw now was not the same one he'd seen a moment ago. The world in front of him was now only blackness and stars and the deep country of empty space, as if he were looking through the observation portal of a space shuttle. The view from here told him that he was light-centuries from Earth so don't bother trying to deny it. He couldn't even find any of the familiar constellations that from the beginning of history had been friends and compasses to humankind. He sensed for a terrifying moment that the stars that blazed around him had never before be seen by the unaided human eye. Most of them were concentrated in a glowing belt, broken here and there by ebony bands of obscuring cosmic dust. He wondered if he weren't being given a glimpse of the center of someone's interior galaxy—perhaps even his own—whose true form lay only in the prehistoric depths of the unconscious, but that couldn't be because everything within and without told him that he was *physically* disconnected, so inconceivably removed from reality that it mattered not a tinker's damn if he were exploring his own interior cosmos or one that had never been glimpsed by even the most powerful of radio telescopes—

—*Come. Quickly,* the voice beckoned to him, and Ngan realized that he was picking up one of the stray bits of thought that Ylem had left behind for him to find.

The fragmented thoughts and images in his mind began to coalesce. The beating of his heart began to slow, as did his breathing. The bud was blossoming. The flowers of knowledge were visible to him again.

It took a moment for him to get his bearings, and once he did he knew what had to be done.

"Michael?"

"Are you all right?"

"I'm not sure—but that doesn't really matter at the moment. Activate the rescue signal."

"But we don't—"

"Do it. Now."

McCain removed the transmitter from his pocket and pressed the button.

"Leave it right here," said Ngan. "Put it on top of one of the barrels."

McCain did so. "How long until they arrive?"

"Perhaps as long as twenty minutes. Come on."

Ngan slipped down into the semi-squared shaft that had until now been hidden by the barrels. McCain quickly followed him. There was a ladder attached to one wall of the shaft. Both men climbed down it as quickly as they could.

Light.

From where they now stood, they could see a brilliant green light emanating from an arched doorway perhaps a hundred yards down the corridor.

Without saying a word, the two men looked at each other, then started toward the light.

Outside, the crowd of homeless people continued to grow larger. From their vantage point on the roof of the building across the street, the four men in black looked in both directions.

"There must be a thousand of them," said one.

"At the very least," said another.

"Ready the stun rifles, then," said the third as he rose to his feet. Each of them carried a stun rifle and an Uzi that hung from a shoulder strap under his coat, a knife, a grenade, and one hypodermic syringe filled with Sodium Pentothal.

They started toward the rooftop doorway.

The fourth man in black, who until now had remained studiously silent, said, "I'm going to call the old man and let him know we're probably going to need more help."

"Where is he?" asked the second man.

"Waiting with the chopper crew."

They opened the door and began running down the stairs, stun rifles warmed up and ready.

The first man said, "Remember—if it moves, shoot it."

The rest acknowledged the order as they continued down the steps then, finally, through the downstairs doors and out into the street.

They fired at random, clearing a path for themselves to the warehouse.

chapter
2WENTY-7EVEN

Leah awoke on the table in the Rusty Room and rolled over to see Jimmy and Merc standing beside her.

"How're you feeling?" asked Jimmy, reaching out to touch her, then pulling his hand back at the last moment.

"I feel okay," said Leah. "You don't gotta worry about touching me."

"I know," said Jimmy, "it's just that . . . well, the last time I touched you . . ." He took a step backward, and only then did Leah realize that Jimmy was . . . standing.

"Oh, Jimmy . . ."

"You did this," he said. "You gave my legs back to me. We were . . . we were all frozen after Ylem placed you on the table, then there was all this light . . . this radiant green light, then . . ." He couldn't finish.

"Then," said Merc, "the light just"—he snapped his

fingers—"stopped. As soon as the light stopped we could move again, so I carried Jimmy over here and he took your hand, then . . ."

"Then . . ." said Jimmy, smiling through his tears and pointing at his new legs.

Leah rose up on the table and looked at Merc. "Can I do anything for you, Merc?" she asked.

"You two're gonna have to . . . to give me a little while to get my mind around all of this." He leaned over and brushed some of Leah's hair out of her eyes. "You sure you're feeling all right?"

"Uh-huh. Did you guys meet Buddy?"

Merc looked at Jimmy. "Well, I guess you could say that. Dude made himself quite an entrance."

Leah giggled. "I'll bet you were scared, huh?"

"No," said Merc. "I been scared. This was *way* past that."

"I damn near fainted," said Jimmy. Looking around, he added, "I'm sorry about him."

"Sorry?" asked Leah.

No one said anything more to her for a moment, until Jeane decided to speak up. "Leah?"

The child faced her and smiled. "You're Jeane, aren't you?"

Jeane was stunned. She hadn't told anyone her name. "Y-yes. Yes, I am."

"You saw the ceremony, didn't you?"

"Yes."

Leah climbed down from the table, crossed to Jeane, and took hold of her hand. "They're all Buddy's friends, like me. He helped make them all feel better, like when they got sick or sad or something. They wanted to thank him, so they were helping him to understand."

Jeane cocked her head to one side. "What do you mean, understand?"

"About human beings and how they were made, how their bodies and minds worked."

"But what about all the machines they gave him?"

Leah smiled. "Buddy was trying to find a way to repair the ship with whatever machine parts he could find on Earth."

"I see," whispered Jeane. "I'm truly sorry about Buddy."

She gestured over to the metal table. Leah turned to look.

Ylem lay on the floor, his skin a hideous pallor of grey and white. Gone were the muscles and mass. Gone, also, was the smoothness of his skin. What lay on the floor by the table was old and desiccated and no bigger than a two-year-old child.

It was the corpse of an ancient, drained thing.

"That's not Buddy," said Leah, no trace of sadness in her voice. "That's just something he walked around in."

"Where is he now?" asked Jeane.

Leah smiled. "He went to his new home. Sort of." She walked over and gave Jimmy a hug. It felt *great* to hug him standing up!

Jimmy kissed the top of her head, then stroked her hair. "What do you want to do now?"

"I want to go get Denise."

Merc smiled. "Do we have to be nice about it to Jewel?"

Leah's smile grew wider. "No. Jewel isn't Worthy."

Jimmy and Merc looked at each other.

"Then we're gonna find Randi," said Leah. "And all the others just like us.

"And the dark-coat man. I want my brothers and my little sister back."

"You sure you're up to this?" said Jimmy.

"Uh-huh. I will take care of you. I will help us all make a home."

Jimmy tilted her head back with his hands and looked into her eyes. "*Peye'wik?*"

"No," said Leah. "It Is *Here.*"

"Well, what're we waiting for?" said Merc, jacking back the slide on his 9mm. "Let's get this invasion started."

"Not so fast," came a voice from the doorway.

Everyone turned to see Ngan and McCain enter the chamber. Ngan's gaze met Jeane's. "Agent Jeane Meara?"

"Yes . . . ?"

"Congratulations. You've just been recruited as a field agent for the Hoffman Institute."

"What makes you think I—"

McCain interrupted, "Because from what I understand, right now half the federal government is out to kill you once you go back up top."

Jeane stared at him for a moment. "Have we met?"

"No."

She shook her head. "Odd. Something about you seems familiar. Did you always have a beard?"

"Hey, folks," said Merc. "Not that I'm against people gettin' better acquainted, but could we maybe continue the 'Getting-To-Know-You' chit-chat somewhere a little safer?"

Leah crossed to McCain and gently placed a hand against his chest. "I know you," she whispered. "In here—" She thumped his chest "—is the truth."

McCain remembered what he'd been told about the Greys: *They can recognize you on a cellular level.*

"Take my hand," said Leah.

"Do you know who I am?" asked McCain

Leah smiled. "Take my hand."

McCain did so—

—and was suddenly overwhelmed by the tidal wave of sensations that engulfed him. He heard thoughts and sensed dreams and absorbed myriad impressions as they were passed from psyche to psyche with compulsive speed and more sensory layers than his brain, anyone's brain, *anything's* brain could possibly absorb. The atmosphere was packed with millions upon millions-squared of swirling, drifting, reeling bits of consciousness. At that moment he was attuned to the majestic cacophony to such a degree that he heard, as plaintive and delicately strained as any rhapsody, the murmur of every cell, the percussive sounds of termites banging their heads against the floors of their dark resonating nests, the drumming feet of mice, the synchronic rustling made by flowing blood as it brushed against arterial walls, the clicking of synapses, the introverted cries of a million lonely people shrieking their anguish into the cold, empty, uncaring night. McCain realized that somewhere, underlying all life, there was a continual music that had been playing since life began, and that its sounds, its rhythms and pulsing and tones, were the refrain of something more, the distant memory of the chorus from an earlier song, a sub-organic score for transposing the inanimate, random matter of chaos into the enigmatic, lavish, magnificent, improbable, ordered dance of living forms, rearranging matter and consciousness into miraculous symmetry, away from probability, against entropy, lifting everything toward a sublime awareness so acute, so incandescent and encompassing he thought everything within him would burst into flames for the blinding *want* underneath it all—

—and in this communion he was given the answer to several secrets about the universe, about all Dark Matter, about the worlds within worlds that humanity passed through every day without even realizing it, and though much of this knowledge was hidden away in his mind, not to be remembered for many years, it nonetheless gave him comfort and strength and courage.

Leah pulled her hand away. "Do you understand now?"

"I . . . I think so, yes."

Then you'll understand that I can't come with you, whispered the voice in his head.

The words were forgotten almost as quickly as they were spoken, but he would remember them later.

He would remember much.

Later.

Leah turned next to Ngan, reaching out her hand. "You've been missed," she said to him. "Please, come to me. I've got a message for you."

Ngan crossed to her, then took hold of her hand.

As soon as they were holding hands, many of the small and—until now, unseen—spheres in the walls began to glow—not any single color, but all colors, one bleeding into the next until it was impossible to tell the difference between gold and red, red and grey, grey and blue, and with each burst of color and combinations of colors there came musical notes. The first was a lone, soft, sustained cry that floated above them on the wings of a dove, a mournful call that sang of foundered dreams and sorrowful partings and dusty, forgotten myths from ages long gone by. The song progressively rose in pitch to strengthen this extraordinary melancholy with tinges of joy, wonder, and hope as the songs of the other spheres and colors joined it, becoming the sound of a million choral voices raised in worship to the gods, becoming music's fullest dimension, richest intention, whispering rest to Ngan's weary heart as the light moved outward in waves and ripples, altering his inner landscape with every exalted refrain, voices a hundred times fuller than any human being's should ever be, pulsing, swirling, rising, then cascading over his body like pure crystal rain, and suddenly the rain, the music, was *inside* of him, assuming physical dimensions, forcing him to become more than he was, than he'd been, than he'd ever *dreamed* of becoming. Ngan dropped down to one knee, the sound growing without and within him, and he was aware not only of the music and the colors and whirling spheres of glass but of every living thing that surrounded him—every weed, every insect, every glistening drop of dew on every blade of grass and every animal in the deepest forest, and as the song continued rising in his soul, lavish, magnificent and improbable, Ngan heard thoughts and sensed dreams and absorbed myriad impressions as they danced in the air, passing from spirit to mind to memory with compulsive speed and more sensory layers than he was able to comprehend, lifting everything toward a sublime awareness so acute, so alive, so incandescent and all-encompassing that he thought he might burst into flames for the blinding *want* underneath it all.

It was the closest thing to splendor he'd ever known.

Leah, still holding his hand, gently coaxed him onto his

feet and led him across the Rusty Room, all the while delivering messages and information.

Ngan stood before one of the drawers that composed the far wall and—illuminated by the ever-glowing spheres—began to press on the various sculpted protuberances that as a whole formed the pattern of a frozen fractal.

A whir, a buzz, a deep thrumming, and the drawer slid open to reveal a panel of lights and switches and keys behind.

Leah let go of Ngan's hand.

He needed both hands to do what needed to be done.

Jeane retrieved her weapon from the chamber floor.

Merc double checked to make sure the safety was off on his 9mm.

McCain pulled the Mossholder from under his coat and jacked a round into the chamber.

"Who are you?" asked Jeane.

"Michael McCain." A sad sort of smile, then, "My friends call me Fitz."

"Are you a Hoffman agent, as well?"

"Yes. Listen up, folks. There's a chopper on its way to pick us up. It's important that we all stay together."

"No arguments from me," said Merc.

Jimmy echoed his sentiments.

Ngan finished entering the sequence of codes into the panel—

—which immediately went dark.

"Were you able to cancel it?" asked McCain.

Ngan blinked, then shuddered, then slumped against the wall. "Yes."

Jeane looked at McCain. "Cancel what?"

"You don't want to know."

"But—"

"Trust me on this one."

Ngan took hold of Leah's hand and showed her the "coin" she had given him. "Do you remember this?" he asked.

"Uh-huh."

"How many people have you given one of these to?"

"Just you and Merc and Jimmy."

"You're certain about that?"

"Uh-huh."

Ngan, looking renewed and exalted, kissed the top of her head, then stood up and said, "Gentlemen, please tell me that you have those 'coins' in your possession."

"Damn straight," replied Merc, digging his "coin" from his pocket. "Think I'd be dumb enough to lose a present from Leah?"

Jimmy brought out his "coin," as well.

Ngan took them, then faced Leah again. "Where are the rest of them?"

"I got some here," she said, reaching into the pocket of her tattered skirt. She handed them over to Ngan. "The rest are in Buddy's ice bank."

"Will you show me where that is, please?"

Leah giggled.

"What's so funny?" asked Ngan.

"You're standing on it."

Ngan arched an eyebrow, then looked down at the floor.

There was a sliding panel of frosted glass under his feet. So much black ice had formed on the glass that it looked like any of the tiles that formed the floor.

Ngan stepped back, knelt down, and asked Leah if she would open the ice bank for him.

She did.

Ngan reached down and removed the typewriter-sized black case. His body sagged slightly from the relief.

Rising to his feet, he smiled and said, "Let's go."

McCain picked up Ylem's desiccated body—which couldn't have weighed more than twenty pounds—and slung it over his shoulder. "I'm sorry I have to carry you like this," he whispered to it. "You deserve a lot better."

Everyone began heading toward the corridor where, waiting at the end, was the ladder.

Before she left, Leah crossed over to the hole to say good-bye to the River of Ash People, then read the last words Buddy had left for her on the wall.

someone come
give this body no limits
slough the fevers
with your cool hand

make the flesh home

within the skin, life is long, life is hard
within the skin, life is hard

but not for much longer.

where do I live?
someone come

who will take me?

Leah looked down at the black glass floor and saw her reflection. For just an instant, long enough for her to know for sure, she saw her face become two, one superimposed on top of the other, and smiled as she looked into the black-almond eyes that watched the world from behind her own.

Buddy was inside her now, sharing her body, sharing his mind and knowledge.

And giving her his power.

So now he'd never be alone again.

She pressed her finger into the rust and wrote:

I am here
someone's come
I will take you.

"No more living in hollow houses," she whispered. "We'll make ourselves Worthy again. I promise."

She thought she heard the Ash People singing thanks.

chapter
2WENTY-8IGHT

The four men in black were waiting for them when they emerged from the chasm once hidden by the barrels.

Each man had positioned himself at a different location around this section of the warehouse to ensure that Agent Meara and the others would be surrounded.

They waited until they were certain no one else was coming out of the hole, then opened fire.

Merc threw himself on top of Leah and took five rounds in his back and left side. He was dead before he hit the ground.

Jimmy caught a round in the shoulder and dropped into a pile of trash and discarded pieces of wood.

Jeane and McCain threw themselves down on the floor and rolled until each was behind a barrel, then began returning fire.

Ngan spun quickly around in a full circle, noting the location of each muzzle flash, then set down the case next to McCain, hunkered down and ran in a half-squat toward an opening between two of the shooters.

McCain pulled the case closer to his body and yanked the Tec-9 from under his coat, hosing the area with covering fire for Ngan.

Jeane took a deep breath, readied herself, then rolled from behind her barrel while continuing to return fire.

One of the men in black was using an automatic and plowed a path directly behind Jeane as she rolled, all the while firing her pistol in the direction of the shots. She finally stopped behind a pile composed of lumber and barrels, and reloaded her weapon.

She watched as her shooter moved closer in a squatting run, ejecting the empty clip from his Uzi and inserting a fresh one.

She looked behind him and saw other figures moving, running, some rolling, others crawling. There was so much movement it was impossible to tell how many of those figures might be the enemy, and she suddenly felt trapped and angry because she'd let herself think that it was all over, she was safe, but it didn't look like that was going to be and that made her even angrier—

—but not so angry that she lost her focus.

She watched her shooter—stared at him, unblinking. He seemed to be moving in slow motion, coming toward her, raising his weapon, activating the laser tracker, its red beam slicing from side to side like the cane of a blind man.

Pick your moment, she thought.

Jeane saw that several of the other figures both behind and in front of the shooter were children.

No.

Absolutely not.

At least McCain was firing in the other direction, drawing the others' attention to him—or maybe causing them to lay low until he had to reload—so she had maybe five seconds to make a decision.

She holstered her weapon.

Her shooter hadn't started firing yet, and though she'd never been much of a gambler, she decided to chance it. Maybe he wouldn't shoot unless she shot first.

She looked around on the floor for something she could use, something easy to handle, something she could be fast with, something light enough to allow for speed and power but heavy enough to do the job—broken bottles, sections of jagged pipe, shards of shattered glass.

If this were *The A-Team* or *McGyver* she'd be able to pull a piece of string from her pocket and turn all of this debris into a small but functional nuclear device. That was stuff she used to love watching on TV, but this wasn't television and she sure as hell wasn't a little girl anymore, she was a grown woman in one hell of a spot, and she remembered how she and her father used to laugh at all the villains on those TV cop shows, the way they'd always get themselves into a corner and fire until they were out of bullets then *throw* their damned gun like it was going to do any—

—hold the phone there, Jeane.

She peered over the side of the barrel and saw that the shooter was moving slowly, turning in circles, the laser beam slicing round and round.

She pulled in a deep breath, looked up at the ceiling, exhaled, then said, "I don't believe what I'm about to do."

In a series of movements so quick and smooth they seemed part of a well-choreographed dance, Jeane pulled her gun from its holster, ejected the clip, rose to her feet and spun around, put two fingers in her mouth and whistled loudly, then shouted, "Hey, killer!" and by the time her shooter spun toward her the gun was already airborne, snarling through the air, flipping end-over-end like a hatchet tossed in a lumberjack competition, and before he could squeeze the trigger Jeane's pistol slammed right in the center of his forehead and that was it for his evening.

Jeane dropped back down behind the barrels, laughing despite herself. "God bless television."

When McCain was satisfied that Ngan had reached the shadows unharmed, he took one of the tear-gas grenades from his pocket, pulled the pin, and tossed it toward the nearest muzzle flash.

The grenade exploded with a loud *fwumph!* and tendrils of heavy, low-lying smoke began to spread out like webbing from the guts of a spider.

Within seconds, the gas cloud had formed a barrier between them and two of the shooters. People coughed and cried out.

McCain tore away a section of his shirt and tied it around his face to block out as much of the gas as possible, but there were no windows inside the warehouse that were intact. The wet, cold breeze came whistling through soon enough, shoving the gas cloud back and up, up, up—

—to reveal the throng of homeless people who'd come in from the rain.

McCain saw that, right smack in the middle of all the chaos, a little girl no older than two and dressed in rags, had fallen down and was paralyzed with fear. She could do little more than lay there and cry, looking around for someone to help her, to come get her and take her away to someplace warm and safe and—

—and suddenly McCain became angry as hell—angry because his whole life had been revealed to be a sleight-of-hand trick, angry because all of these homeless people were being used as shields or for target practice by the men in black—and at that moment it was no longer about him or his life or the institute and its secrets—

"Mommy!" screamed the little girl.

—it was about the fear in the heart of this little girl lying facedown on a filthy warehouse floor while gunfire erupted around her. It was about the pain and loneliness that was in this child's heart and would in some measure remain with her for the rest of her life, creeping into her sleep then into her daydreams until there was nothing in which she could take joy, and that was the worst thing of all, to take something as fragile as a childhood and toss it out into the streets where it was tainted and beaten and starved and humiliated and—

—and McCain leaped to his feet, bullets buzzing by his ears like insects, and ran toward the little girl. She was all he could see, she was the only thing he cared about, for him there was nothing else in the world, nothing else in the universe, only her, only her pain and fear, hang on, honey, hang on, I'm coming, just stay right like you are, that's it, don't move, I'm almost there. . . .

He swooped down and grabbed her from the floor, holding her tight against his chest, protecting her, whispering, "It's all right, it's okay, you're safe now," and the gas was snarling around them and the guns were flashing and the bullets were whistling—

—and he didn't even feel the round he took in the back of his right shoulder.

McCain threw himself to the right, careful to use his body to protect the child—the child, only this child, this moment—and holding her tight he hit the ground in a roll, coming up behind a pile of old lumber and barrels where a figure whirled around to face him.

"Don't sneak up on me like this," said Jeane.

The little girl in McCain's arms rubbed her eyes, cowering at the sound of gunfire, and held her arms out toward Jeane, crying, "Mommy?"

It was only then that McCain realized that the little girl was blind.

He bent down his head and kissed her cheek, feeling a tear slip from his eye.

Jeane moved next to him and took the little girl into her own arms.

The men in black had managed to shoot and stun roughly thirty people before entering the warehouse and were confident enough that they'd frightened the rest away.

They were wrong.

Surrounding the chasm were now at least two hundred homeless people, all of them looking down on Ylem's sad corpse.

Two of the men in black emerged from the shadows, shooting directly into the crowd. Many of the people were hit and dropped like sacks of wet cement, but many more were not hit by the gunfire.

"Who did this?" screamed one man.

"They did—the ones in the dark coats," McCain screamed from behind the barrels, "The god-damned men in black!"

The homeless man nodded once, then turned toward the others.

With a unified scream of fury, the crowd of homeless people split into two groups and fell upon the men in black, disarming, then beating, and killing them.

"He was our savior!" someone cried.

"Who will take us now?" screamed someone else.

McCain and Jeane could do nothing more than watch.

Jimmy Nighteagle could do little more than weep for his fallen friend. "Who's gonna tell everyone the story of the Chief Mobile?" he croaked, holding one of Merc's hands in his own.

In the shadows beyond all of this, Ngan was searching for the fourth and final shooter, his body ready for combat. He had just begun to pivot when he saw a thin leather strap come flying down across his field of vision. He managed to get his hand up in time to prevent the strip from constricting around his throat.

Ngan spun around, his would-be strangler holding tight, and saw that this was, indeed, one of the shooters and not some poor homeless derelict who was frightened for his life. This one had a pistol and was trying to aim at Ngan's head but there was too much movement right now for the guy to get off a good shot. Any hit right now would just be lucky, even though the guy could take Ngan with it if he was quick enough, which he wasn't, but that was all right with Ngan because right now he was dominated by pain both from within and without, and pain changed his world, put a cloud around him that he couldn't see through, preventing him from acting in accordance with logic and experience and training.

For a moment, as the thin leather strap cut into the flesh of his hand, Ngan was feeble and clouded and clumsy and ripe for death.

Ngan's brain began to clear as he remembered part of an ancient Prayer for Strength.

> *I AM, I AM, I AM the power of light*
> *I LIVE, I LIVE, I LIVE in the power of light*
> *I AM light's fullest dimension*
> *I AM light's purest intention*
> *I AM light's power, power, power*
> *Flooding the world of the Self everywhere I move,*
> *Blessing, strengthening, conveying*
> *The power of light that I AM!*

He hit those words hard in his mind because the fourth shooter emerged from the shadows and was moving around, trying to get a decent shot, and so what if his mind was clearing up, a bullet could crush clear tissue as well as cloudy, and the strangler behind him was strong, almost as strong as Ngan, and he had to use that to advantage somehow, had to do something extraordinary, something remarkable, unique and awe-inspiring, that was all, nothing to it, and he had to do it in the next five seconds.

Go.

I AM light's fullest dimension.

The Strangler was strong but the Strangler was taller than Ngan—

—and the man with the gun was getting closer—

—and the Strangler was quick but the Strangler was now stationary—

—and the fourth shooter raised his gun into the firing position, supporting his firing arm with his free hand, a classic shooting-range stance—

—so if you can budge the Strangler, if you can unsettle his balance, if you can do that—

—Ngan faked going right—

—and went right.

The shooter whirled left and fired into empty air, and the surprise on his face was all that Ngan needed. He put everything he had into completing the next move, and behind him he could feel the Strangler's strip loosen slightly as the man's balance momentarily deserted him—

—and with all the power in his body, Ngan hunched forward, pulling the Strangler with him, and when he had his balance, Ngan put all of his strength into a shoulder throw, sailing the Strangler helplessly over him and into the too-slow shooter.

The two of them went down hard, and the shooter was stunned as he hit, losing his grip on his weapon, and the gun skidded across the floor. Ngan saw it but so did the Strangler, and the Strangler went for it, scrabbling and sliding along the rain-soaked floor like a desperate roach.

Ngan let him.

His right hand was next to useless, bruised and bleeding from the leather strap, so he merely watched as the Strangler got closer to the gun—

—then Ngan kicked the Strangler's head off—

—or tried to.

The Strangler was ready and grabbed Ngan's foot and

snapped it around, tripping him—but not before Ngan got off one good spiked kick into the Strangler's shoulder, then followed it up with a blow from his left hand that only grazed the Strangler's head. Even on his knees, even still dazed from the throw, even bleeding from the deep gashes left by the shattered glass on the floor and Ngan's vicious kick, the Strangler could still move, and Ngan went for another left-hand blow, and again the Strangler spun free. Another left hand barely connected as the Strangler writhed and twisted, and he really was like a roach, a water bug that you could see and chase but somehow never catch, and both of them went for the gun then, but it was clumsy going for both of them, pained going, skidding-on-the-soaked-floor going, and when Ngan saw that he might not get to the gun first he kicked at it and sent it spinning toward the exit hole and smiled as it teetered on the edge then fell in with a soft *plop!* as the Strangler chopped him on the neck, but Ngan faked sideways enough so that the Strangler missed the kill—but that didn't mean it didn't hurt like hell, didn't make his nerves shriek, didn't start clouding his brain again, which served to slow him momentarily. Ngan would not allow that to happen—not for long, anyway—If I cloud, I'm gone, it's that simple—so he wriggled away from the Strangler's grip and connected with a spiked kick to the side of the Strangler's head, ground-zero on a death spot, and when his foot hit there was a double cry of pain, and who was to say whose was the greater agony, his or the Strangler's. All he could be sure of was that the Strangler's was over a lot sooner.

Ngan never liked killing, could never get used to the idea that his training could take another human being's life, even if it was in self-defense, and he knew that he'd pay for this later with lost sleep and much prayer but at least the danger to Leah was lessened now, at least he could find some comfort in that—

—then the fourth shooter came at him.

Ngan drew back and turned his hand into a fist and his arm

into a club and ran toward the fourth shooter—which the guy wasn't expecting, judging from the look on his face—ran up a slanted board half-stacked on a pile of trash, then leaped off the edge and went sailing through the air.

At the last second, Ngan flipped his body around, somer-saulting, and slammed a hard chop into the side of the shooter's neck before flipping once again to land on his feet.

The shooter, though not dead, was nonetheless out cold. Ngan felt an odd sort of satisfaction.

A blindingly bright light swept across the area beyond the window, and Ngan heard the unmistakable sound of the heli-copter's blades. He ran over to the others.

He didn't hear the shooter's painful moan, nor did he see the man try to lift himself from the ground and fail miserably.

He did not see the shooter's hand slip into his pocket and press the button on the small transmitter he carried with him.

Only then—the signal sent to the old man to move in—did the shooter fully lose consciousness.

Ngan saw none of this.

He ran over, helped McCain to his feet, and Jeane soon joined them. All three were coughing from the remnants of the tear gas.

"One of Leah's friends was killed," coughed McCain, ges-turing toward Merc's body. "He threw himself on top of her to protect her from the gunfire."

Jeane wiped her eyes, let fly with a series of racking coughs, then said hoarsely, "The Indian's missing."

At the same time, Ngan rolled Merc's body over.

Leah was gone.

chapter

Like a great body of water composed of faces, the crowd of homeless people outside the warehouse parted for the survivors as they walked toward the waiting helicopter.

Ngan was first, carrying the black case, which he loaded into the helicopter, then turned to the commander of the Tech Retrieval Unit. "The self-destruct program has been canceled," he said to the man in the Hazmat suit. "Go through the doors over there"—he pointed to the exit he'd just come from—"and you will see a large pile of barrels. There is a wide hole in the ground near the barrels. That is the entrance to the ship." He gripped the man's arm. "But first, take care of the bodies. In particular, the body nearest the entrance to the ship. His name was Merc, and he was my friend, and you will treat his body with respect. Do you understand?"

The TRU commander nodded his understanding, then set about organizing his team.

261

Ngan leaned against the side of the helicopter and watched as Jeane and McCain approached him through the parted crowd.

For his part, McCain had never felt the presence of so much grief in his life.

Cradling Ylem's body in his arms, he made slow progress through the crowd of homeless people, but not out of choice.

The blind girl's mother had found her, safe with Jeane and McCain, and had hugged both of them in her thanks. McCain thought of how happy they had looked as they walked away into the night, after they said good-bye to Ylem, their friend, their savior.

Like all the people surrounding him.

If McCain had had his way, he would have run to the helicopter, but the crowd wouldn't let him.

They wanted to say good-bye to their god.

Shaking, palsied hands reached out to touch Ylem's face, shoulder, legs, hands. Children wept. Old men shook their heads and turned away, overcome.

But all of them scrambled to touch their god of the alleyways, their messiah of cardboard-box shelters, their savior of Will Work For Food.

"Someone come," a few of them whispered.

"Who will take us now?" asked others.

"Within the cell life is hard, life is long," they chanted as one. "Within the cell, life is hard."

Then, much more quietly, "And where do we live?"

"Under the tracks of the L," came the reply, "in a cardboard box that's falling apart."

"And where do we live?" sang a child.

"In the alleys behind the cans," they replied. "Abandonment our blanket, no way to slough the fever. No friends to live in our hollow houses."

Hands reaching, touching, then left hanging in the rainy, cold night air.

McCain started to shake. The crowd's grief was fast becoming an actual physical weight on his shoulders and inside his chest.

He found himself starting to weep, as well.

Ngan and the helicopter looked five miles away.

"I'm not gonna make it," he whispered.

"Yes, you will," said Jeane, pressing a hand into the small of McCain's back and pushing him forward.

"That hurts."

"I don't care," said Jeane.

Finally, they reached the helicopter, and Ngan helped McCain load Ylem's corpse into the black body bag, then secure it on one of the two long seats that sat facing one another in the cabin area.

Jeane was the last to climb inside. She slid the heavy door closed behind her, and the crowd outside fell silent.

Ngan was shaking.

"What is it?" asked McCain.

"I . . . I'm afraid. . . ."

"So am I, old friend. I think we've been shown too much tonight to *not* be afraid."

Ngan laughed.

McCain was surprised. "What is it?"

"I wasn't talking about what's happened," said Ngan. "I'm talking about *this*." He gestured outward at the interior of the helicopter.

It took a moment for McCain to realize what Ngan was trying to admit to him. "Oh, my God—you're afraid to fly?"

"Yes."

McCain's eyes met Ngan's, then the two of them looked at Jeane, and all three of them—compelled by the need to release some of the tension roiling inside them—laughed.

The pilot did a quick system check, made sure everyone was securely in their seats, and took off.

McCain looked out the window as the helicopter rose into the cold night air. Even though it was just a few minutes past seven in the morning, it was still dark outside. The sea of pale, sad, lonely, confused faces looked up at him, it seemed, and continued to watch as they grew farther and farther away, at last becoming mere pinpoints of light, stars a hundred-billion miles away, nothing left of their existence except a brief ghost-light that was quickly and coldly swallowed by the darkness.

No one said anything.

Their quiet laughter quickly spent itself, and the strain of the last few hours began to settle on them.

Not surprisingly, it was Ngan who was the first to close his eyes, pulling himself into a light trance.

It wasn't just to make himself not think about flying. He wanted to visit Leah's Secret Spring one last time.

Gone were the pipes and rusted metal and broken bottles and filth. The stairway leading down to the spring was lined with lush green foliage. The bank below was covered in colorful sea shells.

Leah was sitting there, tossing pebbles into the center of the stream, giggling at the wide ripples.

"Hi, Cain," she said, not turning around.

"Hello, Leah."

"You don't gotta worry about me, you know."

"I know, but I'll still miss you."

She tossed another pebble into the spring. "I'll miss you, too, but we're gonna be okay."

Ngan became aware of a presence behind him, and turned to see Ylem standing there, his hands filled with sea shells and pieces of driftwood.

"Did you do this by yourself?" Ngan asked Leah.

"You mean let him out? Sure did." She leaned back on her

elbows and cocked her head to the side. There was something so mature about her sitting that way. Ngan felt as if he were watching her grow up right before his eyes.

"I remember what you told me about this place," said Leah. "About how I can control what happens here. About how it will always be here waiting for me. I wanted to show Buddy. I knew he'd like it." She shrugged. "Besides, here I can let him out, and we can play Hide-and-Go-Seek. It isn't much fun to play by yourself."

"I see," whispered Ngan. And he did.

Ylem moved past Ngan and laid the sea shells and driftwood next to Leah.

"Where's Jimmy?" asked Ngan.

"He's hiding. We're playing a game right now, only since Jimmy's new—I mean, since this is his first time here—he needs some time to get used to the place."

Ngan knelt next to her and gently took hold of her hand. "Where are your bodies right now?"

He knew it was impossible for them to be there while their physical bodies were conscious and mobile, so that meant that, somewhere in the finite world, the two of them were lying still.

Leah giggled. "That would be telling."

Ngan smiled. "Yes, I suppose that it would be."

"It's not that I don't want to tell you, Cain," she said. "It's just that . . . I'm having fun, y'know? I get to do all the kid things Mommy'd never let me do. And Jimmy, he watches over me real good, you don't gotta worry about that. And if anything really bad happens, Buddy takes over."

Ngan looked at Ylem. The creature stared back at him, then slowly gave a nod of his massive head.

I am Protector of the Hollow House, said his voice in Ngan's mind.

"Good," he replied, then rose to his feet. "I have to go now, Leah."

"I know."

"May I come back?"

"Sure, you can. We'd like that. Maybe next time you can be 'It.' "

"I'd like that."

Ngan started up the steps.

"Cain?" she called after him.

"Yes?"

She blew him a sweet, little girl kiss. "I met a yeti on my way here," she said. "It said to tell you hi and that you're right. You have been trained for a greater purpose. It wouldn't tell me more than that, only to say that you'd know what that purpose was when it was the right time." She smiled. "Maybe next time I'll tell you where we are in your world. Or maybe the time after that."

Ngan caught her kiss in his hand and pressed it against his cheek, then continued ascending the stairs, slowly bringing himself up and out of the trance—

—just in time to hear the pilot shout: "What's that crazy son-of-a-bitch *doing?*"

The helicopter banked hard to the right, arcing out over the Potomac.

Ngan looked out the window on his side.

They were being pursued by a sleek, black, and deathly quiet helicopter.

"Goddamn thing never showed on the radar!" screamed the copilot.

The large side door on the black helicopter slid open to reveal a man with a semiautomatic rifle. He was seated on the floor of the helicopter, his legs thrust outside, feet locked against the inside of the landing brace.

He wore a bulletproof vest that was attached to a harness. The harness was attached to a steel cable that was pulled tight above his head and ran the length of the helicopter's interior. This way, he could shift and slide his position however necessary in order to get a good shot.

Ngan saw the muzzle-flash from the rifle

There was a loud *ding!* against the outside of the door, and the steel popped inward, creating something that looked like a human thumb dipped in hot metal.

"What the *hell?*" shouted the pilot.

"Teflon-coated hollow-points," yelled Jeane.

"*What?*" screamed the co-pilot.

"Cop Killers!" McCain explained.

The black helicopter suddenly dipped and banked left, passing underneath them. Both McCain and Jeane removed their seat belts and found the harnesses on their respective sides. Ngan reached under the seat and found the assault rifles that had been placed there in case of an emergency. McCain slipped on his bulletproof vest and attached himself to the harness. Jeane followed suit.

Ngan checked both rifles to make sure each had a full clip, then—trying very hard not to pass out from fear and motion sickness—handed one to McCain, and one to Jeane.

The black helicopter rose up on the other side like a dark beast from Greek mythology, the Kraaken incarnate.

The pilot shouted, "You two ready?"

"Go!" Jeane said for both of them.

"Hang on."

They went into a shallow nosedive, dropping from the black helicopter's path of fire. Ngan unlocked both side doors and slammed them open.

McCain and Jeane quickly sat on the floor, locking their ankles and legs behind the landing bars on the outside of the helicopter.

"Go!" shouted Ngan.

The pilot pulled back on the controls.

They righted their position, then began to rise toward the black helicopter.

Both of the helicopters were having trouble. On a cold and rainy November morning like this, the pilots were encountering heavy headwinds. Neither helicopter could achieve a speed exceeding a hundred knots.

Even at this speed, the machines were getting knocked around pretty hard.

At least we're over the water, thought Ngan. At least we don't have to worry about innocent people below getting killed.

The next few shots from the black helicopter missed them completely, giving the pilot the opportunity to put a little more distance between them and their pursuers.

Below them, as they streaked down the sky, the Potomac looked wide, dark, and choppy, like a grinder whose sharp-toothed gears were made of water. If they were to be shot down . . .

Ngan wouldn't think about that. It was too frightening.

McCain plowed off three shots. Only one struck its target, and even then all he'd managed to do was blow out one of the passenger windows.

The pilot tipped the helicopter to the left and downward, and the black helicopter followed. For a minute, the two machines simply kept crisscrossing one another, then the pilot of the black helicopter decided it was time to play a game of Chicken.

He brought his machine up roughly a hundred yards in front of the helicopter carrying Ngan and the others, moved it around so he was facing the pilot of the other machine, and shot forward.

Seventy yards between them now.

Sixty.

Forty-five and closing.

"*Move!*" screamed McCain.

"Wait for it," shouted the pilot.

Thirty yards.

Twenty-five.

Another ten yards and there wouldn't be time to move out of the way.

Twenty yards.

Nineteen.

Eighteen.

Ngan closed his eyes and waited for the impact.

It never came.

With a margin of less than two yards before it would have been too late, the black helicopter suddenly wrenched upward, shooting over the top of the other machine.

McCain leaned out and shot straight into the air.

The black helicopter banked right, dipped, and swung around behind them before moving over and pacing them from the side.

Now it was Jeane's turn.

She took her position, leaning half-in, half-out of the helicopter, the harness straps stretched nearly to the max. Jeane—who was actually afraid of heights—told herself to not look down at the dark, turbulent dark waters beneath her.

She took careful aim and said a short but fervent prayer— the kind of prayer whispered by the accused right before the jury renders its verdict.

She squeezed off six shots.

Not a single round did the slightest damage to the black helicopter.

The next two passes went the same way—except that the shooter from the black helicopter managed to hit Ylem's bagged corpse in the midsection. The wide hole began to release a thin, phosphorescent white liquid that pooled on the floor of the helicopter, then began to hiss as it slowly burned through the steel.

McCain and the others had no time to deal with it.

Another pass, and McCain tried once more to hit either the shooter or the pilot—but that was damn difficult if not out-right impossible when the machines were moving this fast and bucking up and down in headwinds this strong.

The machines crisscrossed again.

The black helicopter came up on Jeane's side.

This time she decided to try for the tail rotor.

She shouted for the pilot to get as close to the other machine as possible then bank hard to the right.

The pilot nodded and gave the machine as much power as he dared.

Jeane readied herself.

One more little prayer wouldn't hurt, she decided.

The pilot started banking to the right.

Jeane hit the tail rotor with her third squeeze of the trigger.

The other machine flew on for a few more seconds, started pitching left and right, then simply dropped from the sky.

There was no other way to describe it.

One moment it was right next to them, the shooter readying himself to blow Jeane's head off her shoulders, then it dropped right out of the sky, straight down into the dark water below.

Jeane could hear people screaming. She could see the mask of frenzied panic that replaced the pilot's face as he struggled to keep the machine under control. She looked down and watched the cockpit vanish into the water.

The feathery fluttering of the tail rotor vanished soon after.

Guess a little prayer every once in a while never hurts, thought Jeane.

Their helicopter leveled out and righted its direction.

"Not bad," shouted McCain.

"Damn straight 'not bad,' " she replied.

"I think you might want to see this," said Ngan, pointing down toward the Potomac.

McCain and Jeane looked.

A large, fast, dark boat was racing toward the sinking helicopter. The men in black had evidently planned for every possibility, including being shot down and falling into the river.

The two pilots and the shooter swam away from the black helicopter and scrambled onto the boat. A few seconds later, someone on the deck fired up at them with a rocket launcher.

The missile missed by a good fifteen yards.

The rocket shot up and past the helicopter, rising and arcing until the laws of gravity stepped in, then began to fall back toward the water.

"I think," shouted Ngan to the pilot, "that it might best serve our interests if we were to leave before they try another one."

"Or the first one comes back down," added McCain. "Might fall down and go 'boom.' "

The pilot swung the machine back on course and gave it as much power as he could.

They were well gone by the time the first rocket crashed into the Potomac and exploded on impact. The explosion sent waves of water and pieces of discarded garbage slamming onto the deck of the boat.

Blackmore threw the rocket launcher aside, wiped off his face, then turned toward the two pilots and the sharpshooter, who had also been drenched from the explosion.

"You no doubt have an explanation," he said to the three men.

"Yes, sir," said the sharpshooter, not daring to meet Blackmore's gaze.

"This explanation," said Blackmore. "Is it going to upset me?"

"I think it's safe to say that, yes, sir."

"Ah."

Blackmore turned away from the men and watched as the helicopter carrying Jeane Meara and the others grew smaller and smaller, then vanished from his line of sight.

"Some day soon," he whispered through clenched teeth, "dear Agent Meara, that I promise you. Some day soon."

Inside the helicopter, Jeane and McCain had removed their bulletproof vests and were now safely buckled into their seats.

Jeane's exhaustion was now replaced by the enormity of everything that had happened to her in the last twenty-four hours.

Her career with the ATF was over, she knew that.

She also knew that her career with the Hoffman Institute was only beginning.

A new start.

A clean slate.

Endless possibilities.

So why did she feel so lousy?

Despite herself, she began to cry. Not much, mind you, no deep, body-wracking sobs, but there were tears nonetheless. They were tears of exhaustion, of relief, of confusion.

She looked over at the bag that held Ylem's corpse.

She wondered if the world would ever know the wonder that had once walked among its people.

She felt a hand on her shoulder and turned to see Ngan's kind eyes and face.

"What is it, Agent Meara?"

She pointed to Ylem's bagged corpse. "I was . . . I was just wondering . . ."

"Wondering what?"

She pulled in a deep breath to steady herself, then said, very softly, "Where do I live now?"

99% BEcoming 98

cCain, Jeane, and Ngan stood among the dozens of passengers waiting to board the flight to Chicago that was scheduled to take off in forty minutes.

Ngan was visibly anxious.

"Sure you don't want some of my motion sickness medicine?" asked Jeane.

"No, thank you."

McCain reached into his pocket and removed a small bottle of pills. "I've got some Ativan the doc gave me."

"No, thank you."

"Something with codeine, maybe?" McCain persisted. "Pain killer . . . make you good and drowsy."

"No, thank you."

"Sleeping pills?" asked Jeane.

"No. Nothing."

"Antihistamines?" asked McCain.

"No."

"Wanna run to the airport bar and get a couple of drinks before—"

"No."

McCain exhaled, irritated. "Then how about I pick up a chair and break it over your head? Jeane and I could claim you as our carry-on luggage."

Ngan stared at him. "You're enjoying this, aren't you?"

"Finding out that the Mighty UncleAgain has a weak spot—you'd better believe it."

"I never imagined you'd grow up to have such an evil streak in you, Michael."

"I may be evil, but at least I don't do a William-Shatner-on-That-Plane-Episode-of-*Twilight-Zone* every time I have to fly."

"You're standing very close to me right now, Michael."

"Yes."

"I could hurt you very badly."

"But you won't."

A beat, then, "No, of course not, but I thought I sounded nearly threatening there for a moment, didn't you?"

When McCain did not respond, Ngan looked at Jeane, who shook her head and smiled.

The loudspeaker announced that the flight to Chicago was now boarding.

The three of them looked at each other, then picked up their luggage and fell into line.

Ngan looked like a man being walked to the electric chair.

"Offer's still good on any drugs either of us have on our person," said Jeane.

Ngan swallowed. Once. Very loudly. "Ask me again once we're in our seats."

"Will do."

The line did not move for several moments, then moved a few feet, then came to a stop again.

McCain busied himself with looking out the window at the people wandering by.

The debriefing had lasted four days and had taken a

noticeable toll on all three of them. Several sections of Ylem's ship had been dismantled and were being examined. The ship was of such a size, though, that it would necessitate digging up nearly half of downtown D.C to get at all of it, so the institute would settle for what it could get. The rest would be kept in place, Top Secret, and would be occupied round the clock with scientists and technical experts for many months—more likely years—to come.

Explaining how they lost Leah had been the worst part.

A lot of people were very, very angry about that.

Which, McCain supposed, was why the three of them were being transferred to the Chicago office, in effect becoming the institute's entire Chicago Branch.

From what McCain had heard about the Chicago office, this wasn't exactly an honor being bestowed them. It was more like a commuted sentence. He looked at Ngan and Jeane.

The three of them were a team now. How well it was going to work out, he had no idea, but it felt kind of good to no longer be alone.

His gaze was drawn to the sight of a homeless woman outside the airport, pushing a shopping cart. Sitting inside the cart, looking happy and loved, was a little boy of perhaps three. He clutched a broken robot toy to his chest. He and his mother looked as if they were singing.

The woman stopped her cart and proceeded to dig through one of the many trash receptacles that lined the front of the airport entrance.

After a few moments, McCain became aware that Ngan and Jeane were watching the scene, as well.

Jeane was the first to say something. "Do you guys suppose she's okay?"

"I hope so," said McCain.

"Leah will be fine," whispered Ngan. "She is much more than she was before. She was deemed Worthy, after all. She is on her way to becoming what, perhaps, we once were before we fell from grace."

Outside, the woman wiped her hands on her coat and, having found nothing in the first can, moved to the next.

Ngan stared at her, then said, very, very softly, "There's an ancient Zoroastrian legend about the first parents of the human race. They were two reeds so closely joined together that you couldn't tell them apart. They knew that nothing would get accomplished as long as they remained like that so, reluctantly, they separated, as was decreed by God. In time they united as a husband and wife were meant to unite, and there were born to them two children whom they loved so tenderly, so irresistibly and totally, that they ate them up. After that, God—to protect the human race—reduced the force of man's capacity to love by ninety-nine percent. Later, those same parents gave birth to seven more pairs of children, all of whom lived and went on to procreate so you could walk the Earth today."

McCain turned toward him. "*Huh?*"

Ngan pointed at the woman outside. "Look at the way she smiles at the boy. Look at how happy the boy is, despite their circumstances. That is something holy, Michael, what we're seeing."

"Holy?" said Jeane.

"Yes," replied Ngan. "That woman is fighting to claim back some of that ninety-nine percent God took away from the human race. I think that fable is actually a warning to us in disguise."

The woman shook her head and moved on to a third trash can. The little boy was looking worried.

And maybe a bit hungry, as well.

"I'm going to go give her some money," said McCain.

Jeane grabbed his arm. "Oh, no you don't—you're not going to run off and leave me with Fly Boy here. Besides, the line's moving again."

Outside, one of the airport security guards stared at the woman, then spoke into his walkie-talkie.

"Shit," said McCain. "I think he's going to have her and the kid hauled off."

"Not your problem," said Jeane.

McCain shot her an angry glance. "And it's attitudes like that that have helped keep things the way they are."

"You going to lecture me about society's responsibility to the homeless?"

"Someone ought to."

Neither of them said anything for a couple of minutes. The line moved, stopped, moved, stopped.

"Did you hear that?" said McCain.

"What?" asked Jeane.

"That was the sound of my death getting three minutes closer."

"God, you're no fun."

"Look who's talking."

"Hey, I can—"

"Shh," said Ngan, then, "Look."

A worker from one of the fast food restaurants in the airport came walking toward the front entrance doors a few seconds later. He was carrying three bags of what appeared to be boxed fried chicken and biscuits. He walked outside and the security guard waved him over. The guard counted out some bills into the kid's hand, then took the bags of food, walked over to the homeless woman, smiled, and handed them to her and her son.

The boy started clapping his hands and laughing.

"Did you hear that?" asked Ngan.

"What?" asked McCain.

"That was the sound of ninety-nine percent becoming ninety-eight."

The woman and her little boy strolled away, happy and smiling, and with food.

And, perhaps, a little more hope.

McCain smiled after them.

It was almost enough to make a person feel Worthy.

eNd of 1

DARK·MATTER™

(Two)

If Whispers Call

Don Bassingthwaite

A pale blue glow illuminated the mist back in among the trees, moving slowly but steadily. Jeane couldn't make out the source of the glow, but she could guess at where it stood. Something was moving in Bachelor's Grove Cemetery.

It wasn't the only light in the mist, though. Back down the turnpike, two more lights had appeared, the same color, height, and size as those that had vanished moments before. The only difference was that these were moving a lot faster. Jeane could already sense the beginnings of the same horrible roar beating against her.

"Back into the car!" she shouted.

McCain didn't need any additional urging. He ran back, trench coat flapping, and threw himself into the driver's seat. He pushed the car into drive almost before jeane had her door closed. She wrapped the seatbelt tight around herself and held on. The car's acceleration was smoother this time, but it still sent the engine howling through rapid gear shifts. McCain kept the gas pedal pressed to the floor, pushing them faster and faster through the mist. Jeane glanced behind them.

Somehow the lights in the mist were still gaining on them.

"Fitz. . . ."

December 2000

DARK☀MATTER™

(Three)
In Fluid Silence
G.W. Tirpa

Fitz blinked again but the syrupy liquid still coated his eyes, giving everything a dull golden sheen.

"You live," a heavily-accented voice asked.

"*Ich wollte heimgehen*," Fitz answered in German. He didn't remember ever learning how to speak German. "*Ich friere*."

"That will pass," the voice said. "And when it does, you will have arisen."

March 2001

(Four)
Of Aged Angels
Monte Cook

The fire flickered. Cendrine could see that it was dying. "Father Sauniere certainly has many secrets."

"Even God has secrets, my dear." Marie replied.

At that moment, the door to Sauniere's sickroom opened, the thick stench of medicine and poultices issuing forth toward the young girl. Cendrine's uncle followed quickly behind the odor. Father Riviere's face hung, a pale yellow mask, as though he had lost blood. No strength—no conscious command—remained in his muscles. A rosary dangled from a grip so weak that Cendrine waited for it to drop to the ground. It did not.

Marie seemed unaffected by his appearance. "Did you administer the last rites, Father?"

"After what I heard . . . what he confessed . . . I could not. Of course I could not."

July 2001

DARK●MATTER ™

(Five)
By Dust Consumed
Don Bassingthwaite

McCain caught the motion out of the corner of his eye: a streak of white thrusting itself from the shadows, lunging directly at Ngan. It was a worm, a fat worm, corpse pale, as long and as thick as his forearm, but moving with the speed of striking snake—and growing. By the midpoint of its lunge it was as large as a big dog. By the time it was descending, it was as tall as a man and just as broad. Just as McCain grasped that impossibility, the worm's belly split open along almost its entire length, exposing a gigantic mouth ringed with teeth. He heard Calamity let out a gasp. It was the only reaction any of them could manage.

December 2001

STAR✶DRIVE®

Adventure beyond the stars with Diane Duane

The Harbinger Trilogy

Starrise at Corrivale
Volume One

Gabriel Connor is up against it. Expelled from the Concord Marines and exiled in disgrace, he's offered one last chance by the Concord to redeem himself. All it involves is gambling his life in a vicious game of death.

Storm at Eldala
Volume Two

Gabriel and his fraal companion are scratching out a living among the dangerous stars of the Verge when they stumble onto new, unknown forces. Only their deaths seem likely to avert disaster. But an astonishing revelation from the depths of time makes the prospect of survival even more terrible than a clean death.

Nightfall at Algemron
Volume Three

Gabriel Connor's quest to save the Verge and clear his name leads him to a system ravaged by war and to the ruins of a long-dead alien civilization. Along the way, he discovers that to save himself and all he holds dear, his one salvation may also be his ultimate destruction.

Available April 2000

STAR✦DRIVE®

*To the edge of the galaxy
and back!*

Two of Minds
William H. Keith, Jr.

In the urban underground hell of Tribon
on the planet Oberon, life in a street gang
doesn't offer many possibilities. That is,
until one day Kai St. Kyr robs the wrong
man and finds himself in the middle
of a power struggle that stretches
beyond the stars.

Available July 2000

Gridrunner
Thomas M. Reid

When a black market courier journeys to the Verge, she must
enter the virtual world of the mysterious Grid. Together with an
undercover agent, she finds herself embroiled in a desperate
conflict between a crime syndicate, terrorists, and her
own boss. The solution lies in the Grid.

Available September 2000

Zero Point
Richard Baker

Peter Sokolov is a bounty hunter and killer for hire. Geille Monashi,
a brilliant data engineer, is his quarry. After Sokolov and Monashi
encounter an alien derelict in the farthest reaches of space, they
have only one chance to survive. They've got to trust each other.

On the Verge
Roland J. Green

War erupts on Arist, a frozen world on the borders of known space.
The Concord Marines charge in to prevent the conflict from escalat-
ing, but soon discover that an even darker threat awaits them.